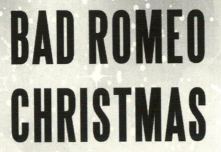

BAD ROMEO CHRISTMAS

A STARCROSSED ANTHOLOGY

LEISA RAYVEN

This is a work of fiction. All of the characters, organizations, and events that are portrayed in this novel are either products of the author's imagination or are used fictitiously.

WWW. LEISARAYVEN.COM

First edition: November 2016
Cover design: Regina Wamba, Mae I Designs
Formatting: CP Smith
Cover photograph: Deposit Photos
ISBN 978-0-9953847-1-2

AUTHOR'S NOTE

Hello, my darling readers! Thank you so much for joining me in this collection of novellas. I hope you have as much fun reading these vignettes as I had writing them.

Before we get started, let me explain a little about the timeline of these novellas: Because I had a ton of people screaming they wanted to see Ethan and Cassie's lives after the end of *Broken Juliet*, our first novella, *Have Yourself a Sexy Little Christmas*, takes place a couple of months after the post-coital proposal. (Note, it therefore takes place BEFORE their wedding. In other words, prior to the *Wicked Heart* epilogue.)

The other two novellas (*The Naughty List* and *Happy Horny New Year,*) take place the following year.

Clear? Good.

Now that's out of the road, please read on.

(Don't mind me hanging around so I can snuggle you. Just pretend I'm not even here.)

Leisa x

This book is dedicated to all those amazing fans who have taken these characters into their hearts and minds, and loved them like long-lost friends. I adore you guys more than anything. (Except guacamole. Guac rules.)

BAD ROMEO
CHRISTMAS

Part One:

Have Yourself a Sexy Little Christmas

ONE

ETHAN

December, a year ago
The Apartment of Ethan Holt
New York City, New York

Bing Crosby wafts through my apartment as snow flutters outside the window. Usually, this is my favorite time of year, but right now, I wish I were anywhere but here.

She's looking at me. My Cassie. The love of my life I fought so hard to win back after too many years apart. The same incredible woman I begged to marry me a few months ago and who miraculously said, yes.

Right now, she's gazing at me with nervousness and hope, and me being the asshole I am, I'm about to lie to her.

I don't feel good about it, but it has to happen.

When she took me back, I promised to never keep anything from her, but I also said I'd never hurt her again, and if I tell her the truth right now, it will cause her pain. I figure I've done enough of that during our time together.

"Well?" she asks as she fixes me with those beautiful goddamn eyes that can melt me with a single glance.

I make a vaguely positive noise and smile. "Hmmmm."

"Ethan, come on. Be honest."

Nope. Not gonna happen.

My stomach's churning and my palms are wet, and as usual when I'm around Cassie, my dick is more hard than soft. Hardly ideal conditions to give the performance of my life.

I summon the fortitude of Prometheus and smile as I stand and walk over to her. Then I realize I need a distraction, so I reach over my shoulder and pull off my T-shirt. Her eyes immediately widen as she rakes her gaze over my torso.

Yep. Distraction achieved.

It sounds egotistical, but I love seeing her react to my body. I could live to be a hundred and never tire of how her expression turns dark and sultry. Or how she subconsciously licks her lips when she reaches out to me.

I grab her and pin her against the wall, hands above her head. "If you want me to be honest," I say, "then believe me when I say I'd *honestly* like to take off your panties and feast on you. Right ... the hell ... now." I graze my hand up her thigh, but before I can touch anything interesting, she pushes it away.

"Does that mean you liked it or not?"

I make that vague positive sound again and press my face into her neck. "Hmmmm. Delicious." And she is. As I kiss and lick, I can feel her caring less about what I have to say and more about the other things I can do with my mouth.

Excellent.

The point where her neck meets her shoulder is her sweet spot. If I suck on it in just the right way, I predict she'll be putty in my hands, in three, two, one...

"Ethan." She puts both hands on my chest and pushes. *Shit.* "Stop trying to distract me and tell me what you think about what I cooked for dinner."

I drop my head and sigh. A long time ago I'd have had no problem lying to her. These days I'm out of practice. I look her in the eye and do my best. "I think you're fucking amazing. That's what I think." *Totally true.*

"You liked it?"

"'*Liked* doesn't even come close to describing how I feel."

Also, true. I hated it with the fiery passion of a thousand suns. She told me it was chicken pot pie, but really, there was no discernible taste in there except horror and misery. While I was chewing, I swear my stomach tried to crawl up my throat and strangle me. Even now, it squirms and turns, threatening to vacate the building in the messiest way possible. Swallowing it and not spitting it into my napkin is a testament to our love.

And, God, I do love her. That's why I want to protect her from the harsh truth that her 'food' is beyond terrible. I mean, I'm incredibly proud that my Cassie is amazing in a lot of ways, but cooking isn't one of her talents.

Thankfully, my semi-truth seems to have worked. She beams at me and backs up so her butt is grazing my crotch as she does the world's sexiest victory dance.

"Hell yes! I cooked you deenah. And you lahved eet. I am a genius. And you are sexay." Her out-of-tune singing is made even more silly when she puts her hands against the wall and starts twerking. She makes me belly laugh. Fucking glorious woman.

See? Sometimes lying is necessary. I love how happy she is. How her eyes sparkle with pride over what she's achieved. She should always feel that way.

"Okay, then," she says, as she bounces on her toes and pushes me back toward my spot at the dining-room table. "Finish it off, then. I'll get started on desert."

Oh, fuck. "Uh ... but—"

"You said you were starving, right? But you've only had one mouthful. Eat, babe. You're a growing boy." She stretches up on her toes and nuzzles my cheek. "And when you're done, I'll have a feast of my own." She runs her fingers through my hair and pulls my head down so she can whisper in my ear. "In case you didn't get it, I'm talking about your award-winning penis. I'm going to feast on that gorgeous cock of yours until you explode. Would you like that?"

I close my eyes and try to keep breathing. Usually she could talk me into committing murder with the promise of one of her spectacular blowjobs. But convincing me to eat the rest of her meal? Wow. Tough call.

I duck and weave.

"You think I have nothing better to do tonight than wait for you to put your mouth on me?" I scowl at her. "Fuck that. Let's skip over everything except orally pleasing your man."

She kisses my chest. "Stop it. You know how much snarky, asshole Ethan turns me on. Now, eat, before we both forget all about dinner."

Yes, wouldn't that be tragic?

She pushes me down into my chair and perches on the edge of the table. Then she gives me a generous glimpse of her cleavage as she loads up my fork and brings it toward my mouth.

In my head, the theme from Jaws starts up.

As the *Forkful from the Black Lagoon* approaches, I clench my jaw and beg my stomach to behave itself. I want to marry this woman, and if I projectile-vomit on her, she may never talk to me again.

When the fork reaches my mouth, I call on every goddamn ounce of acting experience I've ever had and force myself to smile as I wrap my lips around its heinous payload.

Oh. Fuck me. It's like pure, undiluted evil. I blink and try not to let my disgust show.

"So good," I mutter around the toxic substance. "Really. I can't believe you cooked this." Bred it from genetic waste matter? Yes. Cooked it? No.

Cassie leans over and kisses my neck. "I'm so glad you like it." She trails one hand down to my crotch and strokes what she finds there. "Hmmm. You're *really* enjoying it, aren't you? Wow. Giant food boner."

Wrong.   Cassie-sitting-in-front-of-me-dressed-in-lingerie-and-an-apron boner. I could be eating rocks right now and still be hard as a ... well ... you know.

She looks down at my crotch and sighs. "As much as I want to play, I have to finish making dessert. You keep eating. I'll be done in five minutes."

She gives me a quick kiss and disappears into the kitchen. I look around, frantically searching for some way to dispose of what's on my plate without breaking her heart. For a start, I spit out what's left in my mouth. It distresses me that it looks better going out than going in.

I glance around and assess my options:

1) Throw it off the balcony. Hmmm ... tempting but risky. If it hits anyone I could be arrested for engaging in chemical warfare.

2) Bury it in the potted plant near the door. Nope. She'd smell it. Hell, people in the apartment next door would smell it. Also, I really like that plant and don't want it to die.

3) Shove it down the garbage disposal. Never going to work. Even if I walk into the kitchen naked and sporting the world's largest hard on, she's still going to notice the full plate of her food being dumped into the sink.

4) "Nuke it from space. It's the only way to be sure." Not a real option, but I just like using that quote from *Aliens* as often as possible.

"How're you doing?" she calls from the kitchen. "Dessert will be ready in two minutes. Almost done?"

"Yep," I say. "All gone. I was trying to savor every bite, but my mouth had other ideas. Just need to pee. then I'll come help you, okay?"

"Sure!"

I grab the plate and stride into the bathroom before quickly shutting the door. With a final shudder of disgust, I scrape the food into the bowl and hesitate before flushing. "Leonardo, Michelangelo, Raphael, Donatello ... if you boys are down there, I apologize for what I'm about to do. Forgive me." I press the lever and hope like hell the nearest sewage treatment plant is equipped to handle what's headed its way.

I quickly wash my hands, and then act nonchalant as I take the empty plate back into the kitchen.

"All done. Didn't even touch the sides."

Cassie gives me a dazzling smile. It seems out of place in the disaster area that used to be my kitchen. There are bits of mangled food, vegetable peelings, and globs of flour on nearly every surface. In the midst of everything, Cassie is blithely stirring something in a saucepan on the stove. The slight haze of smoke that lingers in the air doesn't seem to bother her. As a precaution, I flick on the overhead fan.

She watches me with appraising eyes as I rinse my plate and

stack it in the dishwasher. When I straighten up and glance at her, she gives a frustrated sigh.

"What?" I ask.

Another sigh. "Just you. Half-naked."

"That annoys you?"

"Yes."

"Because?"

"I'm trying to concentrate. Your muscles are distracting."

I strike a pose and flex. "What? These old things?"

Her eyes glaze over as she gazes at my biceps. I've been working on them recently. They're kind of huge.

With another grunt, Cassie turns back to her saucepan. "Stop it. I have no time to grope you right now."

I stand next to her and take her hand before pressing her palm against my abs. Her eyelids flutter. "Sure, you do."

She inhales sharply and stares into my eyes as her fingers gently trace the ridges on my stomach. I used to work out because it helped alleviate my anxiety and pent-up aggression. These days, I do it to be healthy. Oh, and to see my woman look at me like she wants to fuck me until I can't stand. That's exactly how she's looking at me now.

She pulls her hand back and frowns. "You realize that you turn me on so much, it hurts, right? I'm talking actual, physical pain, Ethan."

"Good," I say and adjust my erection where it's pulsing uncomfortably against my fly. "That makes us even."

She gives my chest, abs, and shoulders one more look before shaking her head and turning back to the stove. "You're killing me, here. Good thing this is almost done. Ready for more?"

"So ready." She's talking about food, but I'm not. I stand behind her and wrap my arms around her waist. My intention is to get out of the way so she can work, but this position also allows me to rub myself against her ass, and that's a major win for me.

She moans and pushes back into me. "Evil, annoyingly attractive man."

I chuckle as she continues to stir and grind on me at the same time. "Not that I mind you turning my kitchen into a culinary war zone, but why the sudden urge to cook? I thought you hated it."

"I don't hate it. I'm just not good at it. You make it look easy."

"That's because mom taught me to cook from when I was five."

"Exactly. My mom never taught me. Well, to be honest, Judy isn't much of a chef, anyway. Everything she makes is clumpy, and grey, and gross."

"Then she passed along her skills beautifully," I think but have the good sense not to say.

"But why now?" I ask. "I'm happy to cook for us. I enjoy it. And you seem to enjoy eating it."

"I do. Your food is amazing. But ..." She switches off the burner under the saucepan and turns to face me. "You and Elissa bring all of these amazing dishes to your parents' place every Christmas Eve, and I want to be able to contribute. This will be our first holiday season as a couple. I'd like to make it special."

I cup her face and smile. "As long as you're there, it will be special. Trust me. You don't have to go to all this trouble." *Also, I love my family and want them to survive the holidays.*

"Actually," she says as she wipes her hands on her apron. "I've enjoyed it way more than I thought I would. As long as I follow the recipe, I figure I can't go wrong, right?"

"Right." *Wrong. So very, very wrong.*

The bell on the oven chimes, and she excitedly turns to pull out a tray and lay it on the counter.

I frown at what I see. "Ah, wow. That's an amazing looking ..."

"Apple strudel," she says proudly.

Jesus. It looks like a melanoma.

Her smile fades. "Although, to be honest, it's a little darker than I intended."

"Don't worry about it. For your first time, you did a great job."

"Aw, supportive fiancée ... I love you."

"Sexy chef woman ... I love you, too."

She stretches up to kiss me, and I grip her hips as I kiss her back. She is sexy, no matter what she's wearing or what she's doing. But I have to admit, the black lacy underwear under the frilly apron doesn't hurt. I've recently discovered I have a thing for underwear. Specifically, *Cassie* in underwear. I've spent so much time at Victoria's Secret in the past few months, I'm sure they think I'm running an escort service.

The truth is I get over-excited about *removing* sexy underwear from Cassie's body, and the flimsy fabric doesn't cope well with my clumsy, desperate hands. Nothing lasts longer than a week.

Still. Worth it.

Cassie pulls me close, and I close my hands over her lace-covered ass as she opens her mouth to me. Though her lips are incredible, it's her tongue that always drives me insane. Soft. Warm. Unbelievably delicious.

It doesn't take long for us to get a little too heated, and I'm contemplating shredding her underpants when she pushes on my chest and pulls back.

"Hold that thought," she says, breathing heavily. "I don't want to ruin the dessert."

I'm fairly sure that ship has sailed, but nevertheless I step back and exhale as she slices up the strudel and places a piece in a bowl. Just when I think it can't look any worse, she scoops up a generous serving of what she's advertising as 'custard' and dumps it on top.

"You're not having any?" I ask as she hands me the bowl and a spoon.

She shakes her head. "Still full from the buffet lunch I had with Elissa. I doubt I'll eat for days."

I look down at the bowl. *After this, I doubt I will, either.* The outside of the pastry is nearly black, while the inside seems completely raw, and whatever she's done to the apples has left them looking gooey and grey.

I plaster on a smile and scoop some into my mouth. It takes every ounce of self-control I possess not to gag.

After I force myself to swallow, I clear my throat. "Did you cook these apples in sugar?"

She nods and points to the canister of white powder near the stove. "Yeah, a heap. The recipe said to use a whole cup. Too sweet?"

"Not at all." The canister she'd pointed to was salt. It was labeled, but obviously not well enough, and now, my tongue has shriveled to the size of a raisin.

I move on to the custard. Yep. Salty as hell. Also, the milk must have been too hot when she combined the ingredients, and the result is lumpy scrambled eggs with random crunchy bits.

I'm aware she's watching for my reaction. I ignore the taste and texture of what's in my mouth and conjure up how it feels to be inside her. She must buy the resulting moan of pleasure, because without warning, she drops to her knees and rips open my jeans.

"Uh, Cassie?" I say, my mouth full.

She doesn't answer. I've barely had time to swallow the melanoma strudel with congealed egg before she's licking me in a way that makes it almost impossible to stand.

Oh, dear God.

As grateful as I am for oral attention at any time, Cassie's timing couldn't be better. If she's concentrating on me, she's given up forcing me to eat any more of her food.

Saved!

I throw the bowl in the sink and lean against the bench as she goes to work. I don't even care that I break the bowl. Pretty sure all of the dishes will be ruined anyway. Sauce pans, too. I hear plutonium has a half-life of fifty years. Cassie's food will still be toxic way after that.

Warm lips close around me, and I hiss out a breath as I watch her.

Okay, idiot, stop thinking about her food and look at what the hell she's doing to you.

Fuuuck, she drives me insane. Seeing her put her mouth on me is one of the greatest joys of my life. The sensation alone is knee-buckling, but witnessing the woman I love taking such care to please me? It blows my mind. No matter how often she does it, I'll never see it as anything but miraculous.

I pull her hair back from her face, so I can see better. Then I tug all the strands back into a ponytail at the base of her head, and wrap it around my hand. I know she enjoys some light hair pulling, but I mainly do it so I can concentrate on something other than how she's dragging me to orgasm way too fast. When she closes her fingers around me and adds firm, slow strokes to what she's doing with her lips and tongue, I look at the ceiling and clench my jaw.

No, not yet, Holt. You're not a teenager. Calm the fuck down.

I take long, measured breaths, in and out.

Damn her and her magical mouth.

For the three years we were apart, I thought I'd developed impotence. Turns out I just wasn't attracted to women who weren't her. On the few occasions I tried to be with someone else, my dick refused to cooperate. He knew what we wanted.

I glance down at her, cheeks hollowing and then filling, eyes closed, moans of satisfaction vibrating on her tongue.

That is what we wanted. What we still want. Just her. Forever and always.

I'm seized by the urgent need to please her, so I pull her to her feet, pick her up, and carry her out to the dining room. She'd set the table with a wreath thing that had tinsel and candles. It looks great, and I appreciated the effort, but right now it's just in the way. It crashes into the wall as I sweep it with my arm.

"That wasn't expensive, was it?" I ask, and perch her ass on the edge of the table.

She winds her fingers in my hair. "Yes, but who cares? Kiss me."

She wraps her legs around my waist as I kiss her deeply, and when I lower her back onto the table and lay my weight against her, she moans.

I pull her arms away from me and press them against the sides of the table. "Grab the edge." She does as she's told then stares at me with hooded eyes while I slide off her underwear and spread her knees. "Don't move. Time for the main course."

I sit on a chair in front of her and wrap my hands around her thighs. Then I lean in to taste her.

Jesus. This is what I should have had on my tongue since I arrived home. Always delicious. Always perfect. Very little preparation time necessary. She arches and moans as I lick and kiss, and when I close my mouth over her and suck in earnest, I hear the distinct sound of her nails scraping the underside of the table.

"Ohhhh, God ... Ethaaaan."

When she moans my name like that, I feel like a god.

I increase my pace while adding the extra stimulation of my fingers. That takes her to the edge so many times, she eventually lets go of the table and grips my hair, so I can't move away any more.

"Ethan, please ..."

I love it when she begs. Not sure what that says about me, but I can't help it. There's no denying my body's reaction. My dick is rock hard and aching, and I'm so turned on I almost trip over my own feet as I stand and yank off my jeans.

Cassie watches me and tugs on the ties of her apron to remove it. I pull her up and unclasp her bra before pulling it off and throwing it across the room.

"Ethan —"

"I know."

Whenever we're together, there comes a moment when we can't stand not being part of each other for one second longer. It's like we're racing against the clock, full of savage anticipation and grasping, desperate need.

That's where we are right now, both so full of tension and impatience, we're rough and animalistic. Everything that stands in the way of us being joined is automatically the enemy. Cassie scrapes her fingernails against my hip when she helps pull off my boxer-briefs. I feel fabric tear, but I don't slow down. As soon as we're both naked, I pull her to the edge of the table and look down as I guide myself inside her.

Fuck. Fucking fucking *fuck*.

I drop my head and sigh.

Sweet, throbbing relief.

I frown in concentration while pushing in further. What I said earlier about never getting tired of seeing Cassie take me in her mouth? It goes double for watching myself disappear inside her. Quadruple for the look she gets as I fill her. No matter how often we do it, or how long it lasts, making love to Cassie is always a revelation. It's like I'm a thousand percent more alive when I'm part of her.

Even when everything between us went wrong, this never

stopped being right.

I start with shallow thrusts. Barely moving. When I feel confident I'm not going to embarrass myself, I go deeper. Stronger. We moan in unison, both getting lost in each other.

Whenever I'm deep in inside her, I can't believe I used to think that soulmates and destiny were ridiculous concepts. We fit together so perfectly, there's no doubt in my mind this woman's body was made for me. Every time I push in, she gasps. When I retreat, she groans like the loss of me is painful.

I feel the same way. How I thought I could ever live without her, I'll never know. One day, when scientists finally discover the meaning of life, I have zero doubt it will include a picture of my Cassie.

"I love you," she whispers. I increase my pace and put my hand between us to rub my thumb against her. She reacts by throwing her head back and arching off the table. "Oh, God, Ethan. I love you so much."

As I thrust and slide, she feels so good I have trouble keeping my eyes open. But seeing her like this, with her head thrown back in ecstasy as she chases down her orgasm? It's too spectacular to miss.

It's not long before she's holding her breath and grasping at me. She starts chanting, "Oh, God," over and over again, each one faster and louder than the last, and I make sure my hips and circling thumb keep pace with her rhythm. Then, she gasps and lets out a long, loud moan, and dammit, I can't hold on a second longer, because she's coming around me, and powerful muscle spasms grip and release until it feels like there's a firestorm inside of me. I manage a few more erratic thrusts before I'm groaning her name, and dizzying waves of pleasure hit me so hard I see stars. Every muscle tenses as I come, and come, and come, and when I'm finished, my legs give out. I collapse onto Cassie, and through our heavy, labored breathing, I can still hear Bing Crosby crooning about silver bells and white Christmases.

"I'm sorry," Cassie says, panting. "I kind of jumped you there. But God, Ethan. Watching you eat something I cooked? Unbelievably sexy."

I nuzzle into her neck and press kisses against her hammering pulse. "Why do you think I cook for you all the time? Watching you eat my food is as sensual as hell." I kiss her mouth, deep and slow.

When she pulls back, she whispers, "Green bean casserole."

I'm instantly confused. "If that's some kind of commentary on my sexual prowess, I'm offended. I just orgasmed the hell out of you, and you hit me with 'green bean casserole'? That's cold, lady."

"Silly man," she says with a smile. "That's what I want to take to your parents' place on Christmas Eve."

I was hoping this sexual diversion would make her forget about that whole plan, but nope. I love that she's trying so hard to impress my family, but she doesn't have to. When we announced our engagement, my mother was so happy she ugly-cried for a full twenty minutes. Dad actually hugged me for a change instead of shaking my hand, and Elissa nearly deafened me with her scream of joy. There's no denying all of the Holts are huge Cassandra Taylor fans.

Of course, after they taste her green bean casserole, that might change.

"I'll help you cook it," I say. *Please, God, let me help. I can't deal with you going solo again. I won't survive.* "I make a great green bean casserole."

She shakes her head. "Thanks, but I have to do this by myself, otherwise I'll feel like a fraud."

I nod. "Okay. But maybe you should have a practice run before next week."

"Sure. You can be my quality control."

If all of her tasting sessions end up with us fucking like this, I'll deal with as much horrible food as she can throw at me. However, I do make a mental note to pick up a couple of bottles of Mylanta and a giant canister label that reads, *SALT!* in neon yellow.

"Anything you need," I say, "I'll be there. Just let me know."

"You're the best," she sighs. "And your dick is magic. Nothing like green bean casserole. More like cucumber salad."

I chuckle as I pick her up and carry her into the bedroom

for round two. When I throw her onto the bed and cover her body with mine, I briefly consider warning my family about her cooking before they experience it for themselves. But then I think how much funnier it's going to be to stay quiet and watch their reactions. The image makes me smile.

No matter what happens, I have no doubt that Christmas with Cassie will be an occasion none of us will ever forget.

TWO

CASSIE

Fifth Avenue
New York City, New York

I laugh as Ethan turns to me and does his best Robert-de-Niro-as-Santa impersonation.

"Are you talkin' to me?" he says, all furrowed brows and squinty eyes. "Are *you* talkin' to *me*? Where are your parents, kid? They know you're sitting on a strange man's lap? Get outta here. I'm sick of lookin' at ya."

He has the mouth and head tilt down, and considering I've never been much of a De Niro fan, I really shouldn't find it as attractive as I do.

I lean against him and smile as we walk up Fifth Avenue. I'm still getting used to how Manhattan streets look like a scene out of a Christmas card. The windows drip with tinsel, ornaments, and twinkling lights, while carols from Bing to Mariah spill from the doorways. What's more, the light dusting of snow falling around us makes even the dirtiest of alleys seem like pristine winter wonderlands. Throw into the mix the Christmas tree vendors dotted along the way, the smell of chestnuts roasting on every corner, and the movie-star-handsome man at my side, and I feel like I'm in a Hallmark Christmas Movie of the Week.

To counteract my natural clumsiness, I grip Ethan's bicep while he clutches a collection of bags in his other hand. We've pretty much wrapped up our Christmas shopping, but I still haven't found him a present.

Men are always difficult to buy for, and Ethan's no help, because he keeps saying that all he wants is me. Well, that's sweet, but I don't think his parents and sister are going to be too thrilled about him unwrapping lil' ol' Cassandra Taylor in front of them on Christmas Eve.

I need something that shows him, and them, that I love him, while still staying at the G-rated end of the spectrum.

I stumble when Ethan stops suddenly. I follow his gaze to the brightly lit store window beside us and know what's coming.

"Ethan, no."

"Cassie, yes. That one. The white one with the bows. No, wait. The blue. Screw it, get them both. It's not like they're going to survive being worn more than once anyway."

We're in front of the *La Perla* window, and Ethan is staring at all of the silky garments like he's imagining me in all of that hideously overpriced prettiness. Then he gets this intense, feral expression on his face that makes me think he's going tear off my clothes, press me up against the glass, and fuck me right here on the street.

He actually has pushed me up against the window a few times, but so far my clothing has stayed intact. I'm not sure if that has more to do with the cold weather than his self-control, but either way I'm grateful. Ethan's not known for his restraint these days, especially when he gets like this. The expression on his face right now signals we have twenty-minutes, max, to get somewhere private, or risk being arrested for gross public indecency.

I'd like to say I'm able to be the logical, level-headed one in this situation, but that would be a filthy lie. He turns me on so much, he could ask me to go down on him here and now, and I'd risk frostbitten knees to please him. There's nothing hotter than Ethan when he's hanging onto his control by his fingernails. My whole body is on high alert as he clenches his jaw and studies me.

"Pick one," he orders, his voice deep and determined. "Or I'll buy them both."

"Ethan, no. They're too expensive. If you're going to insist on ripping lingerie off me, then we have to buy something that doesn't cost the equivalent of a month's rent."

He's not even listening anymore. He's staring at me and imagining what he's going to do when we get back to my place. Judging from the look on his face, I'm going to be naked for hours.

Tough job, but someone has to do it.

I shift my weight and try to deal with being this aroused in public. "You have to stop looking at me like that," I say and put my hand on his chest. "We can't go home yet. I still have to buy your gift."

"Cassie, I told you —"

"I know, but I'm getting you something, so deal with it. And I really hope you've gotten me something that I can open in front your family without everyone feeling super awkward."

He looks contemplative. "Hmmm. Maybe I'll rethink the crotchless panties." When I slap his arm, he smiles. "Have some faith, woman. Do you think I want my mother knowing how depraved I am when I'm with you? She'd have a fucking stroke. Don't worry, I have a kick-ass parent-friendly present for you. I'll save the edible massage oil and anal beads until we get home."

I drag him away from the window. "Glad to hear it. I haven't even wrapped the giant strap-on I bought to use on you." When all the color drains from his face, I laugh. "Joking. I've totally wrapped it. That enormous box under our tree? That's the Anal Intruder 3000. Nothing but state-of-the-art sodomy for the man I love."

He growls and kisses me. "You're not funny. I hope you know that. And for the record, no strap-ons. *Ever.* Just the thought of it has my sphincter running for cover." He throws his arm around me. "Now, stop torturing me so we can eat. I'm starving."

"But you ate all that casserole I made for lunch."

He gives me a sideways glance. "Yeah, but that was hours ago. Now I need seventeen steaks and a gallon of beer. A man cannot live on green bean casserole alone, no matter how ..." He clears his throat. "... delicious it is."

He thinks he's fooling me, but he's not. I know my food is terrible, and certainly not up to his high standards, but at least I'm not giving up, no matter how much he wishes I would.

We walk and chat for a while about where we're going to eat. When we pass a bookstore window, a lightbulb goes off in my brain. It reminds me of an amazing book I'd seen in a magazine a while ago. At the time, I was still in my Ethan-Holt-is-the-Devil frame of mind, so I turned the page so violently I ripped the paper. But our situation has changed, and now, it would be the perfect present to give him.

I turn to him. "Why don't you go on ahead to the restaurant? I'll be there in a few minutes. I think I know what to get you."

He leans down and gives me a soft kiss. "Am I going to like it?"

"I think so."

"Is it a certificate for unlimited blow jobs?"

"No."

"Really? You said I'd like it. What I like more than anything is your beautiful mouth wrapped around my big, hard —"

I push him away and laugh. "You're ridiculous. Go. I'll be there soon."

He walks backward and shrugs. "Fine. But don't say I didn't give you any gift ideas. I'm a simple man, Cassie. Easily pleased. When in doubt, go for the BJ. It's an Ethan pleaser, every single time."

I chuckle as I head into the bookstore. Years ago, if someone had told me that Ethan Holt would make me smile until my face ached, I'd have dismissed them as nuts. But now? He's everything I could have ever wanted in a man. My best friend. My rock. My ridiculously hot sex god.

A bell rings above the door as I step inside. It's not one of those giant book/gift/toy superstores. It's small and cramped with shelves, but it's impeccably clean and organized.

There's a woman behind the counter who looks like Betty Grable. Her hair's carefully curled. Bright red lips. She's wearing blue cat-eye glasses and reading a book that's sitting on the counter. As I approach, she glances up. "Hi. May I help you?"

I smile. "I hope so. I saw a book a while ago in a magazine. It was Shakespeare's *Romeo and Juliet*, but it had a really cool cover. Dark with a heart in the middle."

She smiles and nods. "Oh, yeah. I know the one. The company who published it put out all of Willy's most popular works. Great cover art."

She comes out from behind the counter and gestures for me to follow. "I only have a couple left." We're almost at the back of the store when she stops to scan the shelves. "Ah, yeah. Here they are." She pulls out a stack of books and hands them to me.

"Oh, wow. These are amazing." The top book is *Hamlet*, and the cover is a man's face reflected in a shattering mirror.

"The publisher did a great job," the lady says. "Edgy stuff. Sold real well."

She goes quiet as I inspect the stack. The others are *Much Ado About Nothing* and *Macbeth*, but at the bottom of the pile is exactly what I'm after. *Romeo & Juliet* is scrawled in elegant handwriting at the top of the cover, and in the center is an incredible image of a shattering glass heart. It doesn't escape me how perfectly that image sums up Ethan and me. We've both spent time living like we were a collection of broken pieces. These days, we still may rattle when you shake us, but it's safe to say we're more whole together than we ever were apart.

I run my finger over the beautifully imperfect heart and smile. "I'll take it."

"Want that gift-wrapped, sweetie?"

"Yes, please."

I leave feeling smug about how perfect my gift is. I don't mean to be competitive, but there's no way Ethan will find a better present than this. He's going to love it.

By the time I make it to the restaurant, it's packed. I pull off my coat and gloves as the hostess comes over. "Hi. I'm meeting my fiancée." Yeah, never really getting used to saying that word in relation to Ethan. "He's tall. Dark hair. Probably said something inappropriate to you."

She smiles. "Oh, yeah. I know the one. We're slammed right now, so I told him to wait at the bar, and I'd call him as soon as I had a table ready."

"Thanks."

She directs me down the back, and I smile when I catch Ethan's tall frame leaning on the bar.

As I approach, I see he's talking to a woman. Not unusual. When I'm not around, he gets hit on more than a crash test dummy. It comes with the territory of looking like he does. What is unusual is that I kind of recognize the woman. I wrack my brain to figure out who she is. I'm terrible with names, and if I've met her before, I really don't remember.

I'm a few yards away when she steps closer to Ethan and puts her hand on his chest. It's an intimate move. Not something an acquaintance would do, or even a friend.

Who the hell is this chick?

I stand just behind Ethan's shoulder and clear my throat. "Hey."

They both turn to me, and the woman makes no attempt to hide the head-to-toe assessment she gives me.

"Hey, there you are." Ethan pulls me into his side, and I can feel the tension emanating from him. "Cassie, this is ... uh ... Vanessa."

Vanessa? As in the-skank-who-broke-teenage-Ethan's-heart-by-sleeping-with-his-best-friend? I try not to let my shock show, even though I have a crapload of bitterness with her name on it. She was patient zero for the trust issues that kept the two of us apart for so long.

I've seen her picture, but the woman in front of me is far more glamorous than her teenage self. She's dripping in designer clothing, and her hair and makeup are so perfect, she could go right out and shoot a Dior ad campaign. Meanwhile, I've been walking around in the snow for a few hours and no doubt look like I live out of a dumpster.

I force myself to smile. "Hi, Vanessa. Nice to meet you."

"Vanessa," Ethan says. "This is Cassie Taylor." For once, he doesn't qualify my name with 'my fiancée' or even 'my girlfriend'.

Dammit, Ethan, if there was ever a time for you to pull your macho possessive bullshit, this is it. Claim me in front of her, for God's sake.

But he doesn't, and so Vanessa gives me one of those sympathetic smiles some women get when they think their ex has traded down.

Screw her. I resist the urge to grab her perfectly coiffed head and slam it into the bar.

"Cassie, hi. So great to meet the woman who finally tamed this beast." She squeezes Ethan's bicep, and I grind my teeth so hard I think I crack the enamel. "He was just telling me you two are engaged. That's ... sweet."

She says it as if she's describing a colonic.

I clench my hand in the middle of Ethan's back and grip his sweater, because right now I'm having a moment of total clarity in which I know the precise point I'd need to punch her in the throat to drop her like the sack of shit she is.

"Dining alone, Vanessa?" I ask. "We can always see if they can fit you at our table."

Ethan tenses but doesn't say anything.

Vanessa laughs, like the concept of her being alone is ridiculous. I grip Ethan tighter.

"No, not alone," she says with a condescending smile. "Just came in for a drink before heading off to a party. But I should let you two lovebirds go. I'm sure you have to discuss cakes and flowers, and whatever else engaged people talk about."

She leans forward and kisses Ethan on the cheek. "So great to see you, Bear. It's been too long."

Bear? Gross. I know I'm going to ask Ethan about that, even though I'm certain I'm not going to like the answer.

She pulls a card out of her purse and hands it to him. "Give me a call if you ever want to reminisce. I work downtown."

Ethan takes the card without looking at it. "Thanks. Hope you have a good Christmas."

She raises a perfectly sculptured eyebrow. "You know I will."

Right on cue, the hostess comes to tell us our table is ready.

We only take a few steps before Ethan stops and turns back to Vanessa. "Don't suppose you've kept up with Matt over the years, have you?"

Matt was his best friend in high school. From what I understand, they haven't spoken since Ethan broke Matt's jaw the day after he found him and Vanessa in bed together. One more suitcase of crap in Ethan's collection of emotional baggage.

Vanessa shrugs. "I haven't seen him for years. But we're Facebook friends. He's married. Has twin girls. Seems pretty happy."

A shadow passes over Ethan's face. "Good. That's ... good. Do you have a number for him?"

"Sure. Call me sometime, and I'll give it to you."

Ethan nods, and we head over to our table. For a long time, we sit there, each pretending to read our menus. The quiet is deafening.

"You okay?" I ask.

He looks up, and for a second he looks exactly as he used to in drama school: guarded, defenses up. Then he smiles and shakes his head. "Yeah. Sorry. That was just ... weird." He looks back down at the menu. "Unexpected and weird. She took me by surprise."

"Do you want to tell me about 'Bear'?"

He swallows but doesn't look up. "Uh ... yeah. Sure. That's what Vanessa used to call me after she'd been ... teasing me"."

"Teasing? As in—?"

He looks at me, and even though it's clear he doesn't want to talk about this, because I asked, he will. "As in ... *sexually* teasing me. She used to love withholding until I got this certain look on my face. Sort of a wild, rabid expression, I guess."

I know the exact look. I'd seen it earlier outside La Perla. "Oh. Yeah, I get it." I become engrossed in my menu so he can't tell how sick that knowledge makes me. I thought that look was for me alone. Apparently not.

"Cassie —"

"So, do you want to share a pizza, or—?"

"I don't look at you the same way I used to look at her."

I nod, and scan the list of pasta. "Of course you don't. I didn't think that —"

"Yes, you did." He pulls my menu down, and his eyes scream concern. "I know meeting her is uncomfortable for you. I understand. God knows, I can't even pretend I'm okay thinking about you with another man. But don't let her get under your skin.

She'd love that. Why do you think she called me Bear in the first place? She knew you'd ask me about it."

I know he's right, but he's also aware that switching off one's insecurities is easier said than done. As much progress as I've made with Dr. Kate in the past few months, sometimes old habits resurface. Because of his past, Ethan is an expert in recognizing the symptoms. He watches to see if I want to discuss it. I don't, even though my mind is churning with a hundred questions about Vanessa. I know the answers won't make me feel better, so I force myself to smile instead.

"You're right," I say. "I'm sorry. Let's just have a nice night."

He takes my hand, and after he presses a reassuring kiss to my palm, we go back to perusing our menus.

"Do you think you'll call her?" I ask, keeping my tone casual.

He shrugs. "I'd like to get Matt's number. He's reached out a few times over the years, and I've always ignored him. Maybe I should make an effort to clear the air. I feel like I've grown enough to give him the apology I should have offered years ago."

"Did Vanessa apologize to you?"

He laughs. "God, no. She has a lot of items in her bag of tricks, but apologizing isn't one of them. It doesn't matter. I forgive her anyway."

I drop my menu. "You do?"

He gives me a self-satisfied look. "One hundred percent. I'm actually glad I saw her tonight."

Well, that's something I never expected him to say. I want to ask him more, but right now my anxiety is making my skin hot and my pulse race. He has this kind of wistful, nostalgic look on his face, and I've never seen that before when he's spoken about Vanessa.

Even when I hated Ethan, I still thought of him as my first love. That's why what happened with him hurt so much. He was my first and only. But seeing Vanessa tonight reminds me I wasn't his. *She* was. He loved her so much it ruined him when she betrayed him.

If she hadn't slept with Matt, would she and Ethan still be together? Would he be planning his wedding to her right now, instead of me?

A waitress comes over and pours our water. "Would you like to start with something to drink?"

Ethan opens his mouth to order wine for both of us as he usually does, but I cut him off. "Vodka and tonic, please. A double would be great."

It turns out to be the first of many.

• • •

The Apartment of Cassandra Taylor
New York City, New York

The next morning, I wake up to an empty bed. I squeeze the heel of my hand into my eye socket as a sharp pain fires behind my eyes. "Oh, ow."

Dumb vodka. Dumb me for drinking it. Dumb Ethan for letting me.

He'd asked me several times if I was okay during dinner, and each time I'd waved off his concerns. He knew I was lying, but he let me wallow. Pressing me to talk when I'm battling dark thoughts makes me a tad aggressive. He's been there, done that, and knows very well that sometimes when logic fails, alcohol triumphs.

Of course, he also knows that alcohol usually makes me horny, so his motives weren't all selfless. He'd given his stamp of approval when I'd slid my bare foot up his leg beneath the table and into his lap. After that, he'd had trouble speaking. Who knew my foot was so skillful?

I continued to tease him for the rest of the night. Did I really return from the bathroom and tell him I'd removed my panties? Yep. Did I swirl my tongue around my spoon in the most provocative way possible as I'd eaten dessert? Yep. Did I take his hand and kiss his knuckles, before coyly sliding his index finger into my mouth as we waited for our check? Yes, I did. All of the above, plus more.

I wanted to remind him of how good I could make him feel. That I was the one he wanted. Not her.

That's why I was thrilled when he practically dragged me home in record time. I wasn't surprised when he threw me over the back of the couch as soon as we'd gotten through the door and proceeded to rip off just enough clothing in order to fuck me roughly from behind. With his newfound sensitivity, doggy-style isn't a position he initiates because he prefers to be able to look into my eyes, but when I push him hard enough, he'll release his inner caveman and go there. And God, that side of him is intoxicating. Especially when I'm feeling unworthy and in need of punishment.

I'd tried to push Vanessa out of my thoughts while Ethan was inside me, but every time he grunted and growled as he thrust, all I could think of was *Bear*.

I sit up and rub my eyes again. There's a definite soreness between my legs this morning, but at least it distracts me from my hangover; both from the alcohol, and from bitchface Vanessa.

I cock my head and listen. I can hear Ethan's voice somewhere in my apartment. Ordinarily I'd think he was talking to Tristan, but it's Saturday, and Tris is already at the yoga studio, aligning people's downward dogs and beating inner peace into them, whether they like it or not.

I pull on one of Ethan's old T-shirts I use as a nightie and crack open the door. His voice is coming from the kitchen. I sneak down the hallway and see him sitting on a stool at the breakfast bar, naked except for the towel wrapped around his waist. By the look of his hair and the delicious smell emanating from him, I assume he's already showered. His back muscles flex as he leans on the counter, his phone up to his ear

"I just didn't think I'd feel like this," he says quietly. "I mean, after everything we went through in high school, for God's sake. All the anger and bitterness I carried around for goddamn *years*. I didn't think it was possible, you know?" He listens for a few moments then chuckles. "Yeah, well, you always seemed to know me better than I knew myself. Still, you could at least pretend to be surprised. I have a life-changing epiphany, and you're all, 'yeah, I figured that would happen.' It's not good for my ego."

Goosebumps crawl up my spine the same time a bout of nausea hits me. I'm dreaming right now. I have to be. This can't be happening. He said he *might* call Vanessa, but I didn't expect it to happen so soon.

He rubs the back of his neck. "Yeah, Cassie's still sleeping. I haven't said anything to her yet. I wanted to speak to you first." He pauses. "I don't know how I'm going to explain it. I guess I'll just be honest. After everything I've put her through, I owe her that." He picks an apple out of the fruit bowl and rolls it in his hand. "Yeah, I think it's a good thing, too. Can I see you this week?" He chuckles again. "So you suggest we meet then tell me you're too popular to see me? Fine. Sort out your schedule and text me when you're free. I've missed you." He signs off then takes a bite out of the apple.

He's missed her? *Missed her?!*

I struggle for a few seconds with the urge to confront him, but if I don't want my head to explode in jealousy, I'm going to need to be way less hungover when we discuss this.

Accepting my own cowardice, I creep back down the hallway and crawl back into bed. As if my head wasn't pounding enough this morning, now this. He's missed her, so he's going to see her.

Of course he is.

I never truly thought about what would happen if he saw Vanessa again, but I guess now I know. He's going to see her and realize he's still in love with her, and then, boom. That'll be it for us. Engagement, off. Wedding, canceled. It'll be time for me to buy a whole bunch of cats and be forever alone.

I rub my eyes and take deep breaths.

Calm down, Cassie. You're projecting. Ethan loves you. He'd never hurt you like that. Stop letting old wounds dictate your state of mind.

It's amazing how I always hear my affirmations in Dr. Kate's voice. Right now, she'd be disappointed I'm jumping to the worst possible conclusion. I've gotten better at not doing it, but I guess I'm not bullet-proof just yet.

I almost scream in surprise when warm hands close around my wrists, and I open my eyes to see Ethan pulling them away from my face. "Hey. You okay?" He's sitting on the edge of the bed, looking at me with concern. "God, sweetheart. You don't look well. Are you going to hurl? Should I get a bowl?"

I almost laugh. Hangover vomits are the least of my troubles right now.

"I'm fine," I say and take his hand. "Just feeling a bit woozy. Nothing more sleep won't fix."

He leans over and kisses me gently. "Do you want me to stay? I have some errands to run for Mom, but I can always do them later."

"No, that's okay. I know if you miss out on those limited-edition ornaments out in Brooklyn, Maggie's going to freak out. I'll be fine."

He kisses me again. "If you're sure."

He gives me a smile then proceeds to get dressed. I try to keep my breathing calm while trying to imagine him ever meaning as much to Vanessa as he does to me. I can't do it. There's just no way any other woman could possibly love him as much as I do.

"So," I say, trying to be casual. "You're going to see Vanessa?"

He sits on the edge of the bed as he tugs on his boots. "I don't know. I mean, we haven't made a time to meet or anything. Why? Would it bug you if I did?"

"A little." Okay, so that's a massive understatement, but any honesty right now is a step in the right direction.

Ethan gives me a sympathetic look. "Cassie, if clearing the air with Vanessa bothers you even a little, I won't do it. Just say the word. Nothing is as important to me as you."

Aaaand, now I feel like an idiot for even bringing it up. "No, it's fine. Really." The logical part of me knows it would be healthy for him to confront her about how she treated him in the past. If I denied him that, I'd never forgive myself. "You should do it. I mean, you never got closure with her, right? It would be good to finally put the whole betrayal thing behind you."

"Yeah?"

"Yes, absolutely." *Jesus, okay, idiot. Don't oversell it.*

He finishes lacing his boots and leans over to kiss me. "Okay, I'll organize it. But remember, you can abort the whole thing at any time. And if you want to come with me, I'm fine with it."

I shake my head. "That would be weird. You guys have stuff to hash out. I'd just be an awkward distraction."

"Well, you're always a distraction. Even when you're not with me." He gives me a lusty smile. "So, I'd better take off. I'll see you at the theater tonight?"

"Yep. I'll be there." I may be a raging jealous freak by then, but I'll be there.

"Love you."

"Love you, too."

You'd think that would be enough to reassure me I have nothing to fear from Vanessa, right?

If only.

If. Only.

THREE

ETHAN

The Home of Maggie and Charles Holt
New York City, New York

"Mom! Dad! We're here!" I pull my key out of the front door and close it behind me as Christmas carols echo down the hallway. Knowing mom, I'm willing to bet she's had her extensive Christmas playlist on repeat for weeks now. Whenever Dad complains, she says, "Charles, the song says to 'jingle all the way', so get on board. No one likes a half-assed jingler."

No matter how many times she says it, Dad tries not to laugh but always fails. I can't blame him. It still makes me laugh, too. Mom has a way of cracking me up that no one else can match. Well, except for Cassie.

Wait a minute...

Panic seizes me as I wonder if I fell in love with a woman just like my mom. I quickly come to the conclusion that based on culinary skill alone, they couldn't be more different.

Phew. Oedipus complex averted.

As Cassie and I remove our coats, Mom calls out to come see her in the kitchen. That's followed by the sound of my parents' hyperactive Pomeranian, Tribble, yapping excitedly. She goes berserk whenever she hears my voice, and within seconds the tiny fluff ball appears, scampering down the hall in a blur of tan fur and excited black eyes. I take the precaution of ushering Cassie behind me. The little dog has gotten better at tolerating the woman she believes has replaced her in my affections, but Tribble can still be a bitch when the mood takes her.

"Hey, baby," I say, and scoop her up with one hand. "How've you been, Trib? Did you miss me?"

Tribble's whole body shakes as she tries to lick my face. "Come on. Stop it. I can't kiss you in front of Cassie. You know how she gets. She'll fly into a jealous rage."

Cassie comes to my side and squeezes my bicep. "Damn straight. And if you think I'm too cool to throw down with a microscopic dog, welcome to being wrong forever. So watch it, Tribble, or it's you and me with pistols at dawn."

Tribble immediately closes her mouth and glares at Cassie, who narrows her eyes and glares back. If I wasn't worried about being slapped or nipped, I'd laugh.

"Girls, please," I say. "You're both pretty. Can't you accept there's enough Ethan to go around?"

Cassie rolls her eyes and picks up the insulated bag that contains our food. Well, my food, plus her green bean abomination.

"One day, Holt," Cassie says, as she fixes me with a sultry expression. "I'm going to make you choose between me and that little dog, and on that day, we'll see who you really love the most." She leans in and whispers, "Keep in mind that if you don't choose me, that lacy pink thing you bought yesterday will never see the light of day. No pressure."

I almost groan when she swings her hips and walks through the living room to the kitchen. Dammit, I have plans for that ass and the lacy pink thing. Dirty, horny, pleasuring-my-woman-like-it's-my-job plans.

I glance at Tribble. "Sorry, sweetheart. She's bribing me with her hotness. You can't compete with that. But we can still be friends, right?"

She blinks at me before lunging forward and swiping her candy-pink tongue across my cheek.

"I'm going to take that as a yes, but cool it on the tongue kisses, okay? You need a mint, big time."

I put her down and head into the living room, trying not to trip over her as she winds around my feet.

The back of Dad's head peeks over the top of his chair as he watches television, and I get a flash of my old irritation that he didn't bother coming to say hello when we arrived. But as I get closer, I notice he's wearing a giant set of headphones, and when I touch him on the shoulder, he jumps a little before standing and giving me a smile.

"Son! Sorry, didn't hear you arrive." He pulls off the headphones and gestures to them. "Bought myself an early Christmas present. These babies are the only things that will block out your mother's incessant Christmas carols. They also have Bluetooth, so I can watch television in peace."

I glance at the TV screen, and after a moment realize that the tall actor dressed in scrubs and a white coat is me.

"Dad, really? This episode again?" A couple of months ago I was a guest star on a popular medical drama. I played a brain surgeon. Dad just about passed out with happiness. If he couldn't have the satisfaction of his son being an actual doctor, then he was sure as hell going to revel in him being a fake one.

"It's just a great episode," he says with a shrug. "You rattle off that medical jargon like a pro, son. I still say you would have made one hell of a doctor."

"Yeah, apart from all that pesky throwing up at the sight of blood."

"Minor obstacle." He smiles and claps me on the shoulder. "Would you like a drink?"

"Is it likely a leomorphic xanthroastrocytoma will occur in the upper hemispherical leptomeninges of the brain?" My dad blinks at me. "The answer is 'yes', Dad. Obviously."

He smiles. "See? I totally bought you knowing that stuff."

As he heads over to the bar to pour us whiskey, I think about how far our relationship has come in recent years. Dad no longer criticizes me about my chosen profession, and I don't lash out like a defensive asshole every time he speaks to me. Sounds simple, but it took us a long time to get here, all adult and self-aware.

I think the turning point came when I had my motorbike accident in France a few years ago. The thought of losing his only son made Dad reassess how he treated me, and in turn I got therapy for all the crap that made me behave like an idiot. Now, we're closer than we've ever been, and I wish I hadn't wasted so much time pushing him away.

He hands me a generous tumbler of whiskey on the rocks and clinks my glass with his. "Merry Christmas, son."

"Merry Christmas, Dad."

As I'm swallowing my first mouthful, I hear the front door open.

"Hey, guys!" my sister calls down the hallway. "We're here."

I put my glass on the coffee table, and head to where Elissa and her best friend, Joshua Kane, are stamping slush off their shoes and shaking snowflakes out of their hair.

"It's really starting to come down out there," Elissa says with a smile. "Merry Christmas, big brother." She stands on her toes to hug me.

"Merry Christmas, Lissa." When I let her go, I turn and shake Josh's hand. "Hey, Josh. Mamma and Poppa Kane have fled Manhattan as usual?"

He squeezes my hand before taking off his glasses and wiping them dry on his t-shirt. "Yep. They're like clockwork. As soon as the first snow falls, my parents make the great Jewish pilgrimage to warmer climates. They've gone to Australia this year. I made sure they bumped up the value of their insurance policies before they left, of course, because we all know everything in Australia can kill you. Who knows? I may be an orphan before the new year."

"But a rich orphan?"

"Exactly."

I smile and shake my head. Josh has been Elissa's best friend since she was fifteen, so having him at our place for Christmas is as expected as Mom's Christmas carol binge. I always wondered why he and Elissa never hooked up, considering they seem to spend every waking moment together and clearly love each other. But Elissa always brushes me off when I pressure her about it.

She tells me that despite Josh being an attractive, heterosexual man, she doesn't feel *that way* about him.

Of course she doesn't. God forbid my sister would actually choose to go out with a nice guy for once instead of the constant string of douches she seems to attract. I've only met a few of the guys she's dated over the past few years, but I've universally wanted to punch each one in the head. My sister is gorgeous, ambitious, and intelligent. Why the hell she doesn't have some guy worshipping at her feet, I'll never know.

"Lissa!" Cassie appears beside me and envelops my sister in a giant hug. "How can I miss you so much when I see you at work every day?"

Elissa squeezes her back. "Well, me bossing you around at the theater is hardly quality time together. Plus, my stupid brother always keeps you to himself. Selfish."

I roll my eyes. "As if I have a choice. Cassie and I are onstage together for nearly the entire performance. There's no way for me to not monopolize her."

Elissa steps back from Cassie and turns to me. "And what about after the show? When you abduct her into your dressing room and proceed to make noises that my entire crew complains they can never unhear? What about then?"

I clear my throat, pick up her bag of food, and peek inside. "Your famous mac and cheese? Cool."

Josh laughs as I pull the casserole dish out of the bag and sniff it. "Nice evasive maneuvers, man. Very smooth."

I flip him the bird before winding my arm around Cassie, and we all head into the living room just as Mom bustles out of the kitchen. She proceeds to hug and kiss all of us within an inch of our lives, even Josh. She's still wearing her apron and has flour smeared on her face and arms, but it's clear she's never as happy as when she's cooking for her family.

"Dinner will be ready soon," she says before brushing some stray hair off her forehead. "So everyone relax, grab a drink, sing some carols, and I'll call you when it's done."

"Do you need some help, Mom?" I ask.

She kisses my cheek. "You can come grab the eggnog. And

don't you dare add more alcohol to it like you did last year. I had a headache for days."

"Killjoy."

I'm about to follow her into the kitchen when my phone buzzes in my pocket. I pull it out and take a quick look at the message.

<Hey, what are you doing?>

I quickly look around to check on Cassie's position. She laughing with Elissa, which is good. I hate how guilty I feel about not telling her about this, but I know it would only lead to trouble.

I'm about to put my phone back into my pocket when it buzzes again.

<Are you at your parents' tonight as usual? I'm in the neighborhood. I could drop by and say hello. Your parents used to love me. I'm sure your future wifey wouldn't mind. Unless she can't handle the competition.>

I type in a quick reply and when I turn around, I notice Cassie staring.

Shit.

I can't let her know what's going on. She's touchy enough about Vanessa as it is. I paint on a smile and act casual.

Cassie tilts her head and studies me. "Everything okay?"

"Yeah, Marco just texted to wish us both a merry Christmas. I told him we send our love and we'd see him on New Year's Eve as usual."

"Huh. Okay." She moves into me and subtly runs her hand over my ass cheek. "Have I told you tonight how sexy you are? Because you are. Very ... sexy." She leans in and whispers in my ear. "We could go up to your room and cuddle. And by 'cuddle' I mean make out aggressively until one or both of us comes."

I glance over at my dad, chatting with Josh. I have no issue getting down and dirty with Cassie in any location, even my childhood home, but being aroused in full view of my family would be weird. Cassie has other ideas though and seems determined to rattle my resolve. I jump a little when she grazes her hand across my crotch. No one else can see it, but still.

"Hey, there," I whisper. "My father and sister are right over there, in case you'd forgotten."

"I know. But you're just too damn attractive."

I grab her hands and bring them up to my chest. "Let's just leave these here for a while, okay? Where I can see them."

Lately, Cassie has been insatiable. I'm not sure if it's nervousness about tonight, or the wedding, or the whole Vanessa thing, but there's something making her act out, and for once it's not me. I mean, my woman isn't backward about demanding sex at the best of times, but now she seems to be functioning on an entirely different level.

I've asked her time and again if she's okay, and she swears she is. Even though I have the urge to press her, I know that would only lead to resentment on her behalf. This is how Cassie works. She'll stew in her thoughts for a while before inviting me into the issue. It just takes patience on my behalf. If that means I have to endure her jumping me several times a day in the meantime, then goddammit, that's what I'm going to have to do.

I lean over and give her a lingering kiss. "Hold that thought. I'll be right back."

She pouts a little as I leave.

I hurry into the kitchen and set a tray with warm eggnog and some glasses. On the other side of the bench, Mom smiles at me while fussing with the presentation of her platters.

Every year she makes enough food to feed half of Manhattan, which means she sends us home with loads of leftovers. I'd give her shit about it if I didn't love her food so much.

While her back is turned, I sneak a crab cake and shove it into my mouth.

God. So good.

I'm about to grab another when Mom says, "Take one more, and you lose a hand."

I chuckle and go kiss her cheek. "If you don't want me to steal your food, then stop making it so delicious." When she gives me a rueful smile, I sneak another crab cake.

"Anyway," I mumble with a full mouth, "I'm a growing boy. I need energy."

That's true. Though I consider myself a pretty fit guy, Cassie's wearing me out. Her sexual revolution also includes trying positions I've only seen in really old, really porny books. The result is fantastic sex but an exhausted Ethan. I feel as if I've gone ten rounds in the UFC octagon. Muscles I didn't even know I had are aching.

Mom puts the finishing touches on her freshly made bread rolls before unpacking the bag of food Cassie brought.

"Two dishes this year, sweetheart? I see your usual potato au gratin, but what's this? Green bean casserole? Great! It's been a while since I've had that. I'm looking forward to it."

I open my mouth to warn her that Cassie made it, but if I can't laugh at her getting drunk on spiked eggnog, then I'll have to get my fun another way.

"Yeah, make sure you load up your fork, Mom. You won't have tasted anything like it before." *Not unless you've licked the inside of a nuclear reactor.*

I kiss her on the forehead before taking the eggnog out to the living room and serving it to everyone. After the first sip, we can all tell it's way too light on the alcohol, and Dad doesn't waste any time topping up our glasses with some of his most expensive brandy.

Cassie sips at her glass cautiously.

"You okay?" I ask.

She nods and steps closer to me so she can whisper. "Just making sure I don't get drunk in front of your parents. I'm struggling with my self control tonight, and sloppy-groping you under the dinner table might not be the best way to impress my future in-laws."

"Maybe not, but it would sure as hell impress me."

I lean down and kiss her cheek. Then her ear. Then the side of her neck. There's something taboo about being turned on by her in my childhood home, so of course I now have an erection roughly the size of the Freedom Tower.

I wrap my arm around her waist and pull her against me. The pressure of her body helps a little, but I'd have to get a whole lot closer for true relief. Her eyes go wide when she registers how hard I am.

"Ethan," she whispers and glances briefly over to where my dad is chatting with Elissa and Josh before looking down at my crotch.

"If you rub that thing on me again, I won't be held responsible for what I do in front of your family. For the sake of my dignity, and what little modesty I have left, put it away."

I stroke her back and grind just a little. "Where exactly should I put it? I have a few ideas, but I'd like to hear yours."

She looks at me in a way that screams she's aroused and pissed. Probably pissed because she's aroused. That combination isn't helping me be less turned on.

"Ethan, I'm not kidding. Stop looking at me like I'm tonight's main course and deflate that thing. De-stiffen it. Un-woodify it. Anything. Just stop making me want you in front of your family. Otherwise, I'm going to have to resort to the one method I know will make him go away." She looks toward the front hall.

I chuckle. "Tell me you're not talking about having sex in the downstairs bathroom while my family sips eggnog."

"Of course not," she says with incredulity before tugging down my head so she can whisper in my ear. "I was thinking more like in your bed upstairs. That wooden headboard is pretty sturdy. It would be great for gripping while I ride you. Just saying."

"Jesus, Cassie." I drop my head onto her shoulder. "You gotta stop saying things like that. I'm aching like a son-of-a-bitch over here."

She picks up a nearby magazine and fans herself. "You think your boner hurts? Let me tell you, when a girl gets super turned on, everything swells and aches and throbs. It's more than painful. It's torture. And being like this when I can't do anything about it only makes it worse."

I step away from her and run my fingers through my hair. I thought we were kidding around, but now that she's conjured an image of her riding me in my childhood bed, I can't get rid of it. I've never had sex in that bed. It's seen plenty of hand action over the years and a small amount of heavy petting, but never the full show. I'd like nothing better than to take Cassie upstairs right now and remedy that.

"You know," Cassie says as she runs her fingers over my pecs. "You could make an excuse that you want to show me something upstairs. We could be done in five minutes. Less if you put your mouth on me."

I'm about to crack and do what she wants when Mom calls, "Okay, everyone. Take your seats. Dinner's ready."

Dad carries in a platter holding a huge bird, and the rest of the table is covered in platters of delicious-looking food. Everything smells so good, I'm momentarily distracted from my need to be inside Cassie.

Everyone takes their seats as Dad carves the turkey, but when Cassie goes to follow, I grab her hand and pull her back to me.

"You're pure evil for getting me this turned on right before dinner. Be prepared for punishment later."

"Fine by me," she mutters.

"Also ... how about we not tell anyone you made the green bean casserole until after they've tried it? It'll be a surprise."

She glances at everyone sitting at the table. "Okay, sure. That could be fun. I can't wait to hear what they think."

It's only now I realize this whole thing could backfire. I've been thinking about how funny it will be to see my family's reaction to her food, but I forgot she'd be here to witness it. If they react how I predict, she'll be crushed. As we take our seats, I try and figure out how to best handle the situation.

Mom piles our plates with steaming turkey while Dad fills our wine glasses. Then various platters get passed back and forth as we stock up with sides.

When Cassie's casserole gets to me, I load up my plate. Maybe if I take most of it, there won't be any left for the others.

"Hey," Elissa says. "Stop bogarting the beans. You know they're one of my faves."

I reluctantly hand over the bowl. Elissa takes a generous serving before giving it to Josh.

"Looks great," he says. "We all know my version of cooking involves reheating takeout, so I always look forward to a Holt banquet. You guys make my stomach happy."

I cringe when he spoons three large portions of beans onto his plate. I'm guessing a stomach pump isn't on Josh's Christmas list, but after tonight, that might change.

"So, what's new, kids?" Dad says as the beans make their way down to him. "Tell us all about what's going on."

Elissa clears her throat. "Well, I have some news. Although I don't think Ethan and Cassie will like it."

Everyone stops what they're doing to look at her. She sits up a little straighter and shares a look with Josh. "A few weeks ago, Marco asked if I'd be interested in coming on board his new project, a modern retelling of *The Taming of the Shrew*. I said yes."

Cassie looks disappointed. "Wait, so you're leaving us? Our show?"

Elissa nods. "Yeah. I'm sorry. I've loved working with you guys, but now the show's settled, I need more of a challenge. I've recommended Talia Shapiro to take over as stage manager."

A flash of anxiety hits me. It's been four years since I've performed in a show not run by my sister, and I guess I've gotten used to having her there. Of course, I'm not enough of an asshole to deny that she should spread her wings and move on, so even though I'll miss seeing her every day, I'm glad her career is flourishing.

"Congrats, little sister," I say. "That's fantastic news."

She looks at me expectantly. "That's it? No arguing? No trying to change my mind?"

I smile. "Nope. I think you've made the right decision. Sounds like a great opportunity."

Elissa exhales in relief. "Oh, thank God. I thought for sure I'd have a fight on my hands. And you're right. It's an amazing offer. Plus, I finally get to work with Josh again. He's on board as my assistant stage manager."

Josh puts his hands in the air. "The dream team is back together. Hollah, bitches." He immediately looks contrite. "Sorry, Maggie. You're not a bitch. You're delightful." He catches my dad out the corner of his eye. "You, too, Charles. Elder Holts are exempt from hollering."

Mom smiles at him and places her hand over Elissa's. "Well, I'm thrilled you and Josh are working together again. The show sounds great. When do you start?"

"In February. Plenty of time to train someone to replace me."

Cassie sighs. "Well, I hate the idea of losing you, but if you insist on being all selfish and popular, I guess I'll admit it's a great opportunity. Who are they getting for Kate and Pertruchio?"

Elissa goes pale and takes a quick sip of wine. "Uh, actually, that's a big secret, but I guess it's okay to tell you guys. We found out yesterday they've secured two of the biggest movie stars in the world for the lead roles. Angel Bell and ... uh ... Liam Quinn."

"Quinn?" I say. "Really? Wow."

Cassie's mouth drops open. "Wait, Liam set-my-panties-aflame-with-his-hotness Quinn is your star? Are you kidding me?"

"Hey," I say and grab her thigh beneath the table. "Husband-to-be, sitting right here."

She waves me off. "Oh, please. Your hotness leaves Liam Quinn for dead, but he's still a veeery attractive man."

Elissa shrugs and drinks more wine. "If you say so."

She's not fooling anyone, least of all me. I remember how she and Quinn had some sort of doe-eyed mutual appreciation society going on when we were all doing *Romeo and Juliet* for the Tribeca Shakespeare Festival six years ago. Back then, I was Mercutio and Quinn was Romeo. That was the year before a certain brown-haired actress showed up at the auditions for The Grove and upended my entire world. So, yeah, even though Quinn moved out to L.A. and ended up becoming a megastar who now commands millions of dollars per movie, considering how everything turned out with Cassie, I figure I got the better deal.

"Wow," Cassie says. "I can't believe they got Hollywood's golden couple to do Broadway. Surely their schedule is jam-packed with looking fabulous and showing off their perfect love. I wonder if one of the producers had to sell a kidney to afford their fees."

Elissa shrugs. "Probably. But they're predicting their combined star power will break all box office records, so I guess they'll earn it all back."

"As long as Angel doesn't fall in love with me at first sight and break up with Quinn, of course," Josh says before tearing into a bread roll.

Elissa smiles at him and shakes her head. "Yeah, that's a real danger. Maybe I should make you wear a bag over your pretty face to prevent that from happening."

Josh puts his arm on the back of her chair and leans forward. "You honestly think a little paper will protect her from the power of all of this?" He gestures to himself. "You're dreaming, lady. I mean, I'll *try* not to break up one of the most popular couples in the history of Hollywood, but I can't promise anything. The heart wants what it wants, and I predict Angel Bell's heart wants a hot-geek assistant stage manager who can recite the Gettysburg address in Klingon if he's had enough booze."

Elissa suppresses a laugh. "Of course she does. It's every girl's dream."

Josh glares at her. "The sarcasm is hurtful, Lissa. Hurtful and unnecessary. Bah humbug to you, too."

Now, everyone laughs, and I'm touched to see how Cassie gazes at my sister with clear adoration. Even when Cassie hated my guts she loved my sister, and Elissa couldn't be happier that one of her best friends is going to become her sister-in-law.

"Well, little sister," I say and raise my glass. "Congrats on the new job. I hope you have a great time; even though looking at Quinn's ugly mug every day will probably make you sick to your stomach."

She blushes and gives me a small smile. Considering my sister hardly ever blushes, I'd say that rehearsal process with her and Liam is going to be as entertaining as hell.

"To Elissa and Josh, and their new endeavor," my dad says as we all toast. "And merry Christmas to all Holts." He gestures to Josh and Cassie. "Especially those who are honorary, or Holts-to-be."

Beneath the table, Cassie takes my hand, and I squeeze it. I get a strange sense of possession every time I think about her being my wife. It's not some sort of douchey sense of entitlement. More like a manifestation of what we've always known to be true: we belong to each other. I don't *need* to stand up in front of my friends and family to confirm that, but I want to. Considering I was the guy who used to believe that true love was a ridiculous concept, it's important for me to show just how much Cassie has changed my life.

We all chat quietly as we eat, but in an effort to protect Cassie from the inevitable backlash over her cooking, I make sure to keep an eye on what everyone is putting in his or her mouth. Unfortunately, Mom gets to the beans first. If anyone is going to be brutally honest, it's her.

I hold my breath when she takes a mouthful. She chews for a few seconds before her eyes go wide. Then she swallows and moans in what I can only assume is pain.

God, I'm a terrible son. I should have saved her from this torture.

"Ethan, that green bean casserole is—" There's a slight groan in her voice.

Dammit, she's going to say it's disgusting. Cassie will be heartbroken.

"Mom, wait –"

"-- absolutely *delicious*." She beams at me. "Much better than you usually make."

For a moment, I swear I've misheard. "Uh ... what?"

Mom eats some more, and then everyone is scooping the beans into their mouths, and I'm sure this is what it feels like to be in a horror movie, because I have no doubt that in about thirty seconds, they're all going to go full Linda Blair in *The Exorcist*.

"Wow," Elissa says as her eyes roll back into her head. "So good!"

"Absolutely," my dad agrees. "Restaurant quality."

Even Josh moans in pleasure. "Dude. Forget Angel Bell. I'm marrying this casserole. That's legal in New York, right?"

What the hell? I tried that casserole before we left Cassie's place. It tasted like the unholy love child of thousand-year-old-eggs and congealed grease. Actually, that's not fair. Certain types of congealed grease are tasty. That casserole was like a pile of boiled Odor Eaters, topped with slivered almonds. At least, I hope to God they were almonds.

I look around at the four faces currently smiling in rapture over Cassie's dish. Could I have been wrong about her cooking this whole time? Maybe Cassie is actually a genius chef, but my peasant taste buds are just too basic to recognize it.

I scoop some casserole into my mouth to test the theory.

As soon as I start chewing, the flavor hits me. Sautéed

mushrooms, beautifully breadcrumbed onions, beans cooked to perfection and bursting with some sort of tangy deliciousness I can't place.

"Jesus," I mumble. "What the hell?" I turn to Cassie, who's smiling smugly. "You made this?"

She shrugs. "Like cooking is hard or something?"

"But, I tasted it before we left. It was the worst thing I've ever had in my mouth, and that's coming from the man who had to endure Zoe Stevens' tongue on more than one occasion."

She laughs. "Well, what you ate earlier was an especially bad version I made so I could see the look on your face. You don't think I knew how much you hated my cooking? Please. Your distaste was about as subtle as a gorilla with a hangover. So, for the past few weeks, whenever you thought I was going to yoga with Tristan, I was actually coming here and having cooking lessons with your mom. She taught me how to make the perfect green bean casserole over a week ago. I came around yesterday, and we made this one for tonight. Pretty yummy, right?"

I feel myself tensing as that information sinks in. "So, the one I tasted this afternoon was —"

"A decoy. As were all the others you've had to endure over the past week. I'd feel bad, but sweetie, your face as you tried to hide how bad they were? I mean, those were some Oscar-winning performances, right there."

Snickers echo around the table as heat runs up my neck. I can't figure out if I'm furious or more turned on than I've ever been in my life.

"You made me eat terrible food as a *joke*?" I put down my knife and fork and stare at her.

Whatever she sees on my face makes her smile fade. "Uh ... well, it seemed funny at the time. Now, not so much."

"Swapping sugar for salt?"

"Honest mistake." She leans away from me and lowers her voice. "The first time."

"And all the other times?"

She cringes. "Comedy gold?"

I turn to my mother, who's watching with amusement. "And

you," I say. "You were in on this? You swapped out her horror casserole just to mess with me?"

Mom gives me a warm smile. "Oh, sweetie, it was just a bit of harmless fun."

"Harmless?" I say, my voice rising. "Did *you* eat any of her food?"

She screws up her face. "Oh, God, no. The smell alone made my stomach scream and run for cover."

My dad stands to refill our wine glasses. "Should I have any idea what's going on right now?"

"Just torturing, Ethan, honey," Mom says. "You know, for giggles."

I run my fingers through my hair and exhale. Evil goddamn women. If they continue to gang up on me when we're married, I'm in for a world of hurt.

"Wait a minute," Elissa says, staring warily at her plate. "Cassie cooked the beans?" She looks at me in panic. "Why the hell didn't you warn me? Do you want me to die? Because I've eaten her cooking before. It could happen."

Cassie's mouth drops open. "Hey! Not cool. Not untrue but not cool."

"Babe," Elissa says, "you know I love you, but in college you served me chicken that was black on the outside and raw on the inside. I'm lucky I didn't end up in the emergency room. I'm just saying that your food should come with a warning label. Like, *Consume at your own risk*, or *Stomach hazard ahead*. Informed choices and all that."

"Well, technically," Cassie says, "it doesn't need a label, because your mom cooked most of it. She made all the individual parts, and then I mixed them together. Maggie says that mixing is one of my strongest culinary talents. That and opening packages."

"You're amazing at that," Mom adds in her usual helpful way.

Cassie smiles. "Look, I know I'll never be a great chef, but at least I'm trying, right? And even if I didn't *technically* cook the beans, I still get credit for the joke."

Josh piles more beans onto his plate. "Well, I don't care if the Flying Spaghetti Monster cooked these. They're my life now, so if you could all keep it down, we'd like some alone time."

● ● ●

After a few more minutes of dinner conversation, The Great Green Bean Casserole Sting has been forgotten, and we're all back to enjoying the feast.

As Mom and Dad talk with Elissa and Josh about their new show, Cassie puts her hand on my thigh and leans over.

"Sooooo." She gives me a nervous smile. "On a scale of one to the Red Room of Pain, how much do you want to punish me right now?"

I take a sip of wine. "Oh, you broke the scale, lady. It's a tangled mess on the floor."

Her fingers tighten on my thigh before traveling closer to my crotch. "But it wasn't all bad, was it? I mean, I made up for all of the horrible food by rewarding you with ..." Her hand moves higher. "You know ... *dessert*. Right?"

I'm flooded with memories of her spread open in front of me, her sweetness on my tongue. I clear my throat as ninety percent of the blood in my body rushes to my cock. "So, are you saying that if you hadn't tricked me into eating Satan's leftovers, you wouldn't have given me ... dessert?" I raise my eyebrow. "Seems to me that would have been foolish, considering you got just as much out of those *dining* sessions as I did. If not more."

She stares at my mouth and licks her lips. "Well, yes, you are very good at dining. Like, crazy good. If you ever failed as an actor, you could become a professional diner. Which leads me to ask, are you planning on having dessert later?"

Before I can answer, my mother chimes in. "Really, Cassie, you have to ask? Have you met my son? He eats dessert every chance he gets. If he could get away with it, he'd have it three meals a day for the rest of his life. The boy is insatiable."

Cassie blushes and smiles to herself. "I've noticed." When Mom goes back to her Elissa discussion, Cassie whispers, "And that's why your son is the hottest man on the planet."

Her fingers are now dangerously close to the painful hardness in my crotch, and it's all I can do to stop myself from grabbing her hand and pressing it against me. I clench my jaw while trying to think of something else. Anything but how incredible it would feel right now to tear off her panties and slide myself inside her tight, warm —

"Earth to Ethan."

"Huh?" I look over to see Elissa staring at me.

"I asked if you and Cassie have had a chance to look at that list of reception venues I sent. If we want to lock down a good place, we'll have to book ASAP. Most of them are snapped up twelve months in advance."

I wipe my mouth with my napkin, in case of accidental drool, and shift in my chair. "Ah, yeah. We've seen a few. We like The Roof Garden the best so far. Spectacular views, and the menu seems great."

"Cool. Well, let me know as soon as you've decided, and I'll adjust my to-do list."

I almost laugh. I've seen her to-do list. It's a three-ring binder as thick as a telephone book, with more color-coded tabs than I care to count. Knowing Elissa, this will be the most efficiently managed wedding in the history of ever.

We chat more about the wedding as we finish our dinner, and even though Mom keeps it together, I notice her go quiet and blink a lot. I'm not surprised. This is a woman who bawls her eyes out watching the finale of *The Bachelor*, for God's sake. I can only imagine how intense her reaction will be when she witnesses her first-born marrying his one true love. Maybe I should warn St. Patrick's to have some life preservers on hand in case her tears flood the church.

"Everyone had enough to eat?" she asks as she swipes her cheeks with her napkin. "There's plenty of turkey left if you want seconds."

Josh leans back in his chair and rubs his stomach. "Maggie, if I eat one more mouthful, you'll be finding pieces of me all over the dining room. But thanks for an awesome meal. Your daughter hasn't cooked for me in weeks."

"I cooked for you last night," Elissa says. "You licked your plate and made a crack about not having to wash up, remember?

Then I punched you in the arm for being gross and made you wash up."

"Oh, yeah," Josh says. "How could I forget such a sexually charged exchange?" He whispers to Dad, "It's kind of embarrassing how much she wants me, right? It must make you uncomfortable to have her flirt so brazenly right under your nose."

Dad claps him on the shoulder. "I'm mortified. Now, who wants some more wine before we tackle dessert?" Everyone puts up their hands. Thank God we all took cabs.

My phone buzzes with a text. I ignore it. Then it buzzes a second time, and a third.

With a sigh, I grab my phone and subtly check it beneath the table.

<Seeing you again was amazing. Couldn't believe our old chemistry is still as strong as ever. I know you feel it, too. Saw how you looked at me at lunch. Like you want me.>

There was another message, followed by a picture.

Jesus.

<Just so you know what you're missing out on. Call me if you want a real woman for a change. You know I can be discreet.>

I take my time to tap out a long and extensive reply, and when I look up, I notice Cassie's frowning at me.

"Marco again?"

"Uh ... yeah. He gets so needy at this time of year."

She nods and goes back to the conversation, but I can see she's tense. She suspects something.

I make a mental note to level with her as soon as we get home. It's only a matter of time before she sees right through me anyway. I guess I'll have to 'fess up and face the music, even if it's something she doesn't want to hear.

FOUR

CASSIE

Over and over, Ethan runs his fingers up into my hair, then down to where the back of my dress sits between my shoulder blades. His touch always makes me instantly aroused, but tonight my mind can't shake this feeling of unease. Ever since our run-in with Vanessa, he's been off. Then there was that phone call he doesn't know I overheard. *"Can I see you this week?"* And now he's texting someone he's pretending is Marco, when I know damn well Marco can't stand texting.

So that leads me to believe there's something going on with Vanessa, and the thought of him having any communication with that hell beast drives me insane. Is he making plans with her? And if so, I hope he has a valid funeral plan, because I'm going to freaking kill him.

I can feel my blood pressure increasing, and I realize I have to stop. I'm making a lot of assumptions with zero facts, and that's never worked out well for us in the past.

I need to get to the bottom of this, and fast.

I lean over and whisper, "Just so you know, I'm semi-drunk and horny as hell, so you can either drag me upstairs and take care of this problem, or I'll have to resort to self-service in the bathroom."

As expected, those words snap his last ounce of restraint, and with a low growl, he pulls me to my feet.

"Uh, Cassie and I will be back in a minute." He guides me out of my chair. "She wants to see some old pics of Quinn as Romeo and me as Mercutio. Back in five. Ten at the most."

"No problem," his mom says as she starts to clear the table. "I'll have dessert ready when you get back. Come on guys. All of this can be cleared."

Everyone joins her in carrying plates and platters into the kitchen as Ethan takes off and practically drags me upstairs to his room. If there's one thing I've learned over the years, it's that whenever sex is on the line, Ethan is sure to show glimpses of why he was a track champion in high school.

As soon as we're inside his room, he shuts the door and pushes me up against it.

"I've been waiting for this all night."

He leans in to kiss me, but I put my hands on his chest to stop him.

"Ethan, wait. We need to talk."

He looks disappointed. "I thought you brought me up here to treat me like a sexual object. Were you deceiving me, Cassandra Marie Taylor? Because that's not the least bit cool."

"Well, I think that's hypocritical from the man who's been keeping important facts from me."

Now he looks confused.

"I need you to tell me about your lunch with Vanessa."

"You said you didn't want to hear about that."

"I know, but it turns out, I do. The thought of her alone with you drives me crazy, and even though I've been trying to put it out of my mind and move on, I can't." My voice is rising in pitch, even though I'm trying to stay calm.

"Cassie, it's fine. I'll tell you everything, okay? Is that why you're upset?"

I look down at my hands on his chest. "I overhead your phone call to her the morning after we ran into her. Jesus, Ethan. You couldn't even wait twenty-four hours to suggest meeting up? Is she who you've been texting all night? Because I know it's not Marco. And trust me when I say that if a single lie comes out of your mouth right now, I'm going to beat the crap out of you with your mother's baby Jesus candlesticks."

All of a sudden, my pulse is racing, and I can't get enough air. Then I'm gripping the front of his shirt so tightly, my knuckles are white.

Dammit. I wanted to stay calm and discuss this like an adult, but even thinking him hurting me again brings me to the verge of a panic attack.

Ethan pushes my hair away from my face and strokes my cheek. "Cassie, just breathe. Nothing bad is happening, I promise. I'll tell you anything you want to know."

"Ethan ..." My voice shakes. "If you're leaving me to go back to her, just tell me. I can deal with it. I'm a big girl."

Of course I'm lying. If he leaves me again, I'll never recover.

"Cassie." He pulls back and looks me in the eye. "I'm not leaving you. Ever. Take some deep breaths."

I close my eyes and concentrate on breathing in through my nose and out through my mouth. Each exhale calms me a little more. When I'm almost back to normal, I look up at Ethan and shake my head.

"Ethan, I —"

He bends down and gives me a soft, deep kiss that calms me even more. He understands how it feels to have your brain continually whisper the worst possible scenario, so he knows how to handle it.

When he pulls back from the kiss, there's still tension in my muscles, but at least I'm no longer shaking.

"I love you," he tells me, quietly. "I'm counting down the days until I become your husband. Why the hell would you think I'm leaving you?"

"That phone call. The morning after we saw Vanessa. I'm sorry I eavesdropped. That was wrong, but I —"

"That call was to Dr. Kate. I called to tell her about what happened and how it affected me. I know you don't like me bothering her out of office hours, but I thought running into the woman who destroyed me was important enough to break that rule. Vanessa was a huge part of my therapy sessions, so Kate knows how much crap I went through to get to the other side. She suggested we should schedule some time together since she hadn't seen me for a few months. That's who I was arranging to meet."

"Dr. Kate?" I let out a short laugh. "Oh. Yeah, that makes more sense."

"You thought I was talking to Vanessa?"

I nod.

He gives me a heartbreakingly tender look. "Sweetheart, I didn't even have solid plans to see Vanessa until you told me it would be a good idea. I mean, I knew I wouldn't get any real closure from her, but when you said it would be the healthy option, I thought you were right. I needed to face up to my past. Confront the monster under my bed. Unfortunately, it turned out to be a giant waste of time."

"Why?"

"Well, when I told her how much damage she'd done, she offered to make it up to me with a quickie in the restaurant bathroom."

I clench my fists as what he's just said sinks in. "The fuck?!"

"Yeah. And she actually said that if I'd been better in bed, she wouldn't have had to go to my best friend for sex in the first place. So, that killed my ego."

Fury fills my brain. "*You* need to be better in bed?! Is she freaking kidding? Was she even sleeping with the same man I am? Because if *you* were any better in bed, my orgasms would kill me!" I step away from him and pace the length of the room. What a ridiculous goddamn claim. "That woman is a complete moron."

"This is why I was glad when you said you didn't want to know. She'd like nothing better than to see you like this. I have no doubt that's why she started texting me."

I stop dead and stare at him. "What's she been saying?"

He pulls out his phone and brings up her messages before handing it to me. "I'm warning you, it's pretty bad. Just know that this is what she does. She pushes people's buttons. It makes her feel powerful. The whole thing boils down to insecurity and jealousy."

I hold my breath as I read what she's written. "What the ...? She threatened to come here tonight?"

Ethan nods. "She's just as delusional as she always was."

I exhale when I see Ethan's reply: <*Please stop contacting me. Like I said, I wish you all the best with your life. Now please leave me to mine.*>

Wow, that's polite. It also uses more words than, "Fuck off, manipulative cow," but whatever. Ethan's clearly more evolved than I am about this woman. I scan the next collection of texts.

"What the hell?" The bitch has the nerve to say they still have chemistry and then sends a full-length *picture* of herself in lingerie?!

That's it. I'm going to kill her. I'll do it slow, too. She won't die for days.

I squint at the screen. *Wait a second. I have that exact set of bra and panties. Ethan bought it for me.*

I scroll down and snort when I read Ethan's reply.

<*Vanessa, sorry you thought there could ever be anything between us again. There can't. I hate to say it, but you're not a good, kind, or particularly well-adjusted person, and I'm having trouble remembering what I ever saw in you. I apologize for my bluntness, but considering the nature of your recent texts, I figure you need a dose of cold, hard facts to banish any misconceptions you may have. The truth is I'm lucky enough to be deeply in love with the most spectacular goddamn woman on the planet, and as tough as this may be to hear, she looks waaaay hotter in that Chanel ensemble than you. So, goodbye Vanessa, we won't be speaking again. And to prove how not-interested I am in keeping in contact, I'm blocking your number. Take care and Merry Christmas. Ethan.*>

The passion in his words makes my throat close up. I've never seen a more perfectly worded smackdown. I look over at him. "You know, I do look better in that lingerie.

He gives me a smug smile. "Yeah, you do."

I walk over and slide the phone back into his pocket. "So, I guess you're not leaving me for her?"

"Jesus, sweetheart, why would I do that? Besides the fact that you're the love of my life, she's a goddamn sociopath." He puts his arms around me. "But you know what? Even with her mind games and manipulations, I'm not angry about what she did in the past. I mean, I've imagined what I'd do if I ever ran into her, and honestly, most of those scenarios involved me running into her with my car. But when I was faced with the actual woman standing there, all I felt was ... grateful."

Okay, wasn't expecting that. "Why grateful?"

"Because if it hadn't been for her, I wouldn't be who I am today. And I really like who I am. I mean, despite what you keep telling me, I know I'm not perfect —"

"Lies," I say and wind my arms around his neck.

"And I still tend to be an asshole on the regular, but I'm a *happy* asshole." He cups my face and rubs his thumb over my cheekbone. "An asshole who's lucky enough to be marrying the most beautiful, sexy, talented, *incredible* woman in the world. And in a way, I owe that all to Vanessa."

He leans down and kisses me, and his mouth is warm and sweet, and affects me in too many ways to describe. In that moment, I know for sure that he never kissed Vanessa with this much passion.

When he pulls back, we're both breathless.

"I'm sorry," I say. "For doubting you. For being a paranoid mess."

He presses his forehead to mine. "Don't apologize. In this situation, paranoia is normal. But trust me when I say that you never have to worry about me having feelings for someone else. As far as women go, I have tunnel vision. All I see — all I *want* to see — is you. And as for Vanessa, I actually feel sorry for her, because she's never going to know a love like ours. She's incapable of it, and that's a fucking shame. Because everyone should get to feel how I feel about you."

His expression turns serious, and goosebumps flare across my skin, and even though his voice is quiet, I can feel the heat of his intensity.

"How I love you, Cassie? It's like heaven and hell all wrapped up into one. I love you so much I worry that my chest will crack open most days. You know that old saying when life is good, that your cup runneth over? That's how my heart feels. It could be the size of a planet and still not be big enough for all the love I have for you."

"I feel the same way." I take a breath, bracing to voice something that has always played on my mind. "But Vanessa has one thing over me I can never compete with. She was your first love. And no matter how much I hate that, I can't do anything about it."

He's silent for a moment, and when I look up, I watch his expression morph from sympathy to determination, before he levels me with a steely gaze.

"Cassie, listen to me when I say this, because truer words have never been spoken. *You* are my first love. I didn't even know the meaning of the word until you crashed into my life, and I wouldn't change that for anything. You made me a better man, and every part of me loves you more than I can even describe. Compared with you, I didn't even *like* Vanessa."

The joy I feel is visceral and intoxicating. After so many years of thinking I'm his second choice, I'm beyond relieved to find out I've been wrong.

He tightens his arms around me when he sees my expression. "Cassie, you are my *first*, my *last*, and *every* love in between. How do you not know that by now? You're my *one and only*. And that's something no one else will ever be. And if you don't believe my words, then I'll sure as hell make you believe my actions."

When he kisses me, it isn't gentle. He tangles his fingers into my hair and pulls my head back so he can cover my mouth with his. I gasp when our tongues touch, and that only makes him kiss me more deeply.

A low moan echoes in his throat, and it breaks the last thread of my self-restraint. Within seconds, I'm unbuttoning his shirt with clumsy, rough fingers.

"Ethan, you're my one and only, too. And that's why I need you to take away this ache inside me. Now, please."

His hands become rough and needy. "You're okay doing this with my family downstairs?"

"As long as they don't walk in on us. Will they be suspicious that we've been up here for so long?" I tug the last button free on his shirt and rip it open before kissing his neck.

His entire body goes rigid with pleasure.

"Cassie," he moans as I steadily work down to his chest. "The number of fucks I give about anything that isn't your mouth right now is in negative digits."

I spin him around so his back is against the door. "Good. Because I've been waiting for this all night."

He buries his hands in my hair as I cover his body in kisses. Lips, tongue, and light teeth travel over the planes of his chest and down his abs. I use my hands to explore all the areas where my mouth isn't, and it's not long before his pants are hanging open and I'm sliding my hand into his boxers.

"Jesuuuus. Cassie ..."

He squeezes his eyes shut and leans his head back against the door as I stroke, applying firm pressure. He's so lost in what I'm doing, he doesn't even notice me sinking to my knees until I take him in my mouth. Then his eyes snap open, and the muscles in his jaw clench as he stifles a moan. Keeping quiet is never easy for either of us, but I can tell he's trying. I understand why. It's one thing for his family to suspect we're up here screwing each other's brains out. It's another for them to get vocal confirmation.

As I continue to suck, I can tell it's getting more difficult for him to stay quiet. When I add my hand to the mix, he lets out a loud grunt.

"Shhh. If I have any chance of looking your family in the eyes when we get back downstairs, they can't know what I'm doing right now. If you can't keep quiet, I'll have to stop."

He looks down and wraps my hair around his hand. "If you stop, Santa will put coal in your stocking instead of the raging orgasm ordered from your fiancée. Better not risk it."

Now, there's an effective threat. I go back to work but make sure to keep Ethan's gaze the whole time. I know how much that drives him crazy.

He watches in wonder as he slides in and out of my mouth, and when the urge for him to make noise becomes unbearable, he pushes air out between his lips on an extended, "Ffffffffffff."

"Are you trying to tell me something, Ethan? Fffff, what?"

He pushes out a breath as he leans his head against the door. "Ffffuck!"

Fast as lightning, he picks me up and throws me onto the bed. We both ignore the loud crash when I land. The dark mischief in his eyes makes me scurry back toward the headboard as he advances on me.

"Underwear off," he says in a dangerous tone that makes me shiver. "Now."

Yes, sir.

I barely have time to slide off my thong before he's pushing up my dress and pressing me down into the mattress.

I grip the duvet as he teases me with his fingers.

"Honestly," he says, "I'd like to spend some time with my face buried between your thighs, but I know the clock is ticking. In a few minutes, Mom will call out that dessert is ready, and when that happens we'll have about ninety seconds to plant our asses in our chairs before she comes looking for us."

I pull him closer. "Well, by then, I plan to be neck deep in a post-orgasm high, so you'd better get to work, lover boy."

A growl rumbles in his chest as he pulls down his jeans and boxers and settles between my legs.

"Grab the headboard and hold on," he says. "Because this could get rough."

I do as he says, and then, with impatient hands, he grips my hips and pushes into me.

Dear God in Heaven. I'll never get tired of how it feels to have him inside me. He grunts as he presses all the way in, and the sensation of being filled so completely makes me gasp.

"Don't ever doubt that you're my one and only, Cassie. Never doubt it again."

Then he starts to move, and even though his usual technique is to take his time with my pleasure, that's not what this is. When we get home, I know he'll make love to me for hours, but right now, we need to fuck. And judging from Ethan's dark determination, he aims to put everything with Vanessa firmly in the rearview mirror and reclaim me in the most primal way possible. Prove to me that as far as he's concerned, no other woman exists.

His intensity takes my breath away.

As he slides in and out, hitting a little harder each time, I squirm beneath him in an attempt to bring him deeper. I'm trying to be quiet, but despite my best efforts, my moans are escalating in pitch. When Ethan speeds up, I have to clench my jaw to stifle the sound. He helps by filling my mouth with his tongue.

I kiss him greedily, not even caring when moans spill out as his thrusts hit my sweet spot.

"Ethan! Oh, God ..." I'm whispering, but I might as well be screaming. He knows the edge in my tone. The plaintive, desperate plea. He slides one hand under my ass to get a better angle, and then I'm a helpless passenger on the train to O town. I throw my head back as our hips connect, again, and again, and again, and when I'm hovering on the edge, I can't resist sliding a hand between us to launch myself all the way over. It only takes a few seconds before I'm gone. I stop breathing when my orgasm hits, and Ethan grabs the headboard in desperation as I arch beneath him. His thrusts get faster and more erratic until his entire body tenses up, and when he comes, he presses a long, strangled moan into my neck.

We stay there for long, pleasure-filled seconds, and after we've both ridden out the aftershocks of our orgasmic high, Ethan collapses onto the bed beside me and enfolds me in his arms.

I run my fingers through his damp hair and sigh. "Do you know the best thing about what we just did?"

He looks down at me while trying to catch his breath. "What's that?"

"I know for damn sure Vanessa has never had an orgasm like that in her life, and what's more, she never will. Because the only man who can deliver that kind of expert sexage belongs to me."

His expression morphs into pure joy as he grazes his fingers over my face. "Damn straight, he does. Forever and always."

Seeing how he's looking at me now - how he's always looked at me - I can't believe I ever doubted him. He said his heart is too small to hold all of his love, but that's not right. His heart is so big, it also takes up space in my chest. In moments like this when he stares at me in wonder and his eyes sparkle and burn, I can feel his heart inside me, pressing against mine in perfect synchronicity.

He's right. *First love. Last love. And every love in between.* That's what we are to each other. Now and forever.

FIVE

ETHAN

When Cassie and I can finally breathe again, we fix ourselves up and head back down to my family. Cassie had to do a quick repair job on her hair and makeup to cover most of the damage, but apart from a very faint hickey on my neck, you'd never know we'd just had hot animal sex on my twelve-year-old duvet.

Note to self: spill something on that duvet before you leave tonight, so Mom is forced to wash it.

Apart from the great sex, I'm relieved we finally resolved the Vanessa issue. Now Cassie knows exactly where she stands as far as my heart is concerned, and I aim to never let her forget it.

"Perfect timing," Dad says, as he lays out fresh plates for dessert. "Your mother was about to send out a search party."

"Did you find the pictures of you and Liam in *Romeo and Juliet?*" Josh asks, and I swear I see him exchange a look with Elissa.

"Uh, no, actually. I thought they were in my bottom drawer, but I must have moved them when I collected my journals."

"Oh, sure," Elissa says with a knowing smile. "That makes sense."

Josh winks at Cassie. "Oh, well. If you still want to check out pics from that production, Elissa has a whole set at our place. Quinn was shirtless for most of the show, so naturally she has several copies, all stashed in different locations in case she needs some 'alone time'."

Elissa elbows Josh. "If you want to live to see the New Year, Kane, I suggest you stop talking. Now."

We all take our seats again, and Mom appears with platters of decadent desserts. My mouth waters. Mom wasn't wrong when she said dessert was my favorite meal. If it has chocolate or cream or custard, my mouth is all over it.

Immediately my brain screams that I've never tried food play with Cassie. Jesus. Need to rectify that ASAP.

After twenty minutes of eating our own weight in sugar, Dad stands and holds up his glass. "To my darling Maggie, for always making Christmas special. I don't know what we'd do without you."

"To Maggie!" we all toast. I lean over and kiss Mom's cheek. "Great dinner, Mom. Thank you."

She touches my cheek and smiles. "Any time, sweetheart. You know that."

We all adjourn into the living room where Tribble is on her bed, snoring loudly after eating a mountain of leftover turkey. Beside her, taking pride of place in the room is the giant tree Dad searched half of New York to find. Clearly for him, size does matter. Mom has decorated it beautifully with hundreds of designer decorations and tiny blinking lights.

"Okay," Dad says, rubbing his hands together. "Who's going first?"

Every year the Holt family does this whole thing where we open each present, one at a time. In between are stories and jokes, and Dad clicks away with his camera so we have fifteen thousand photos to commemorate the event.

This year, Josh is part of the fun. Elissa gives him a new pair of Captain Kirk pajamas. He's so happy, I think I see a tear.

Dad presents Mom with what looks like an incredibly expensive set of chef's knives. She cradles them to her chest as if they were a precious newborn baby.

I give Dad the usual, which is his favorite brand of single malt whiskey. He gives me a one-armed man-hug before presenting me with Sir Lawrence Olivier's biography. Yet another example of how far he's come. In past years, a subscription to a medical journal would have been common.

Cassie and I present Mom with a watch from Tiffany. It's the kind of luxury she'd never buy for herself but something she absolutely deserves. Mom cries as she hugs us.

When all the other presents are given out, only Cassie and I are left to exchange gifts.

I hand her a sparkly gift bag filled with tissue paper. It's my version of wrapping. Years ago I tried to wrap my beloved copy of *The Outsiders* after getting the author to personalize it for Cassie's 21st birthday. Although she adored the gift, Cassie mocked my pathetic wrapping skills for months afterward.

She takes the bag from me and hands me a neatly wrapped rectangle. I hold it up excitedly. "Wow, a pony? You shouldn't have."

She pushes me in the chest and smiles. "You're hilarious. Open it, wise guy."

I tear off the paper, and when I register what I'm holding, my chest tightens.

"Seriously?" I ask. "This is your gift? Have you been snooping? Or is this another joke?"

Cassie frowns. "No. Why would you think that?"

I point to her gift bag and smile. "Look inside."

She pushes through the layers of tissue paper until she pulls out the book I bought her. It's exactly the same one I'm holding.

"I bought it months ago," I say, as she stares at it in disbelief. "I couldn't think of a more perfect present for you."

A delighted smile spreads across her face before she glances over at the book's twin in my hands. "Great minds think alike."

If I ever wanted concrete proof we're soul mates, I just got it. I've never been one for religion, or even spirituality, but with Cassie I have no doubt we've known each other before this life. I'm also certain we'll know each other after it. In a hundred different lifetimes, I'll always find her. She's my other half. My *better* half.

How the hell did I get so lucky?

"There's an inscription," she says shyly, like she's embarrassed for me to read it in front of everyone.

I open the book to the title page and silently read the message in her familiar handwriting:

To my darling Ethan,

I wanted to get you something special for our first Christmas together, so here it is. The reason I chose this book was because no matter what life throws at us, you'll always be my Romeo. Despite your distaste for the character, if it wasn't for this play, and yes, your despised namesake, we might not be where we are now.

After all, he facilitated our first kiss, my first O (in front of Erika, of all people. I still can't believe we did that!), as well as countless Shakespearean declarations of love that allowed us both to uncover our true feelings.

Back then, Romeo held me tenderly when you pushed me away, and he showed me the heart of the man you were beneath all your high walls and prickly armor.

You always thought you were a bad Romeo, but in my mind, you were perfect. I fell in love with you so many times during that show, and these days I fall in love with you more every day. So if that's your version of a bad Romeo, I'll take it. Even with everything we've been through, I'd do it all over again just to be where we are now.

I know a lot of people spend their whole lives looking for their 'happily ever after', but not me. Having a happy ending would imply our tale is over, and I know that's not true. Our epic love story will fill volumes before it's done. It will spill from bookshelves, take over rooms, and burst from more libraries than we can count. And every book, every page, and every word will tell of my boundless love for you.

Thank you for being my (bad) Romeo.

With all my love,

Your grateful (if slightly broken) Juliet

I swallow hard. She's never written anything like that for me before. Her words make my heart do that thing where it grows so full, it presses painfully against my ribs and beats double time. I look up to find her staring at me.

"Do you like it?"

I wrap my arm around her waist and kiss her. "It's perfect.

You're perfect."

She strokes my cheek. "I'm really not, but I'm glad you think so."

"I love you, Cassie."

"Not as much as I love you."

Despite Josh and Elissa making gagging noises in the background, and my mother sniffling quietly as Dad pats her shoulder, I kiss Cassie again, softly and slowly, like she's a dream from which I never want to wake.

In reality, that's what it's like to be in love with Cassie Taylor. I'm living out all of my fantasies with the woman of my dreams.

I couldn't ask for anything more.

When we get home, I spend a couple of hours showing Cassie exactly what she means to me, and then we lie in bed, naked and weary as we flick through one of our new books.

Cassie looks up at me and sighs. "Do you think that if we hadn't been cast as *Romeo and Juliet*, we never would have gotten together?"

Her head is on my shoulder, her body pressed against the length of mine. As we speak, she absently traces the outline of the love heart on the book's cover.

I stroke her arm. "I don't know. I'd like to think fate would have forced us together some other way, but I guess we'll never know. One of the reasons I was so pissed about being Romeo was because I knew that as soon as I played a love scene with you, I'd be a goner. Up until that point, I'd fooled myself into thinking I could deny my feelings indefinitely. But after that first kiss backstage in the theater?" I shake my head. "Done. Ruined. Completely blind to every other woman on the planet, forever."

Cassie smiles. "Did it ever occur to you that Erika knew exactly what she was doing when she cast us together?"

I let out a short laugh. "All the time. That woman constantly manipulated us into being intimate, so we'd have to face our connection. Which reminds me, I'm due to send her my annual 'thank you' gift basket. It's the least I can do."

Cassie traces my lips with her forefinger. "If I profane with my unworthiest hand this holy shrine, the gentle fine is this: My lips, two blushing pilgrims, ready stand to smooth that rough touch with a tender kiss."

As she recites Romeo's lines, she gazes at me like I have the power to make the world turn. I'll never get tired of her looking at me like that. Ever.

I lean down and taste her lips. She kisses me back, warm and eager, and it's not long before I pull back, dizzy and intoxicated. As much as I'd like to make love to her again, it's almost sunrise, and we silently agree that a few hours of sleep are preferable to no sleep at all.

When she snuggles into my chest, I put my arm around her and stroke her side. After a few minutes, her breathing evens out and her body goes limp.

I look down at her sleeping like an angel in my arms and smile.

"My bounty," I whisper, "is as boundless as the sea. My love as deep. The more I give to thee, the more I have, for both are infinite."

And with that, I kiss her forehead and drift off to sleep. As usual, I dream only of my sweet, astonishing Juliet.

Part Two:
The Naughty List

ONE

YOU'D BETTER WATCH OUT

November 26th, Present Day
Kodak Theater
Los Angeles, California

If there were an award for dealing with gross incompetence without murdering someone, I should be winning it right now. I'm not usually a violent person, but the epic fuck-uppery with which I'm currently dealing isn't normal.

"Miss Holt!" I turn to see Ainsly, our harried production assistant, scurrying toward me. "There's a car blocking the loading dock, and the florist is trying to deliver a whole truckload of arrangements for the red carpet."

"Put a call over the loud speaker. If the car isn't gone in five minutes, have it towed."

"Got it."

"And why isn't this stage cleared? We have to start rehearsals in an hour."

"Oh, well ... I did tell the mechs they need to hurry."

"And?"

"They ... uh ... well, they laughed at me."

Of course they did. She's pretty, blonde, and polite. The macho pinheads who run the rigging clearly need a petite blonde bitch to sort them out.

"Okay, Ainsly. I'll handle it. Where's James?"

"Not sure. I saw him talking to the publicist about red carpet arrivals about an hour ago but haven't seen him since."

James is the new assistant stage manager I hired when my best friend abandoned me, and although he talks a good game, I've barely seen him all morning. I have no idea what he's doing, but I'm damn sure he's doing it half as efficiently as Josh would have.

"Fine," I say, as I make a mental note to add James to the list of people I want to assault. "Get those dressing rooms finished, okay? Can't have the biggest A-list celebrities in Hollywood dealing with dirt and grime like normal people."

"Yes, Miss Holt."

I sigh and rub my eyes as she disappears into the throng of people bustling around backstage.

Tonight is the inaugural celebrity benefit concert for Liam's dyslexia charity, The James Quinn Foundation, and not only is Liam overseas filming in Mongolia of all places, I'm having to cope with a super tight production schedule in an unfamiliar theater without my right-hand man. I haven't had to deal with this kind of pressure without Josh for so long, I'd forgotten how much I hate it.

I shoot off a quick text. *<You suck, Kane. You know that, right?>*

Then another. *<These L.A. people don't know enough about me to be afraid. They're inefficient and disrespectful. Not. Cool.>*

After a few seconds, my phone vibrates with a response. *<Then school them. You're Elissa Fucking Holt. Make them remember that name.>*

I roll my eyes. Sure. Like that's easy to do. I've spent my whole career in New York, building relationships and training crews. Here in L.A. I'm just some bossy blonde chick from Broadway.

I tap out another text. *<Can't believe you'd rather be with Angel in Australia instead of overworked & underpaid with me. That's hurtful, Joshua. You promised our friendship wouldn't change when you left NY. Liar.>*

My phone buzzes. *<Stop whining and get to work. All those spoiled stars aren't going to rehearse themselves.>*

Even though Josh has been living with Angel in L.A. for a while now, he recently chose to go on location with her for a few months so they could pat koalas or whatever when Angel's not filming. Talk about selfish. Just when I need him the most.

I stride across the stage, careful to avoid half-constructed set pieces and low-hanging lighting bars as I approach the group of burly men chatting and laughing near the fly ropes.

"Gentlemen, I need this stage cleared in five minutes."

The largest of the men gives me a cursory nod. "Yeah, yeah, sweetheart. Keep your panties on."

I stop dead. *Oh, no he didn't.*

"What did you just say to me?"

He turns and gives me a more thorough assessment, and this time his gaze lingers on my boobs long enough for me to imagine flaying him alive before burning his carcass.

"I said, we'll get to it when we get to it." He sneers. "Now run along and yap at someone else, short stuff."

I plaster on my sweetest smile to hide the hot anger crawling up my neck. "Oh, I see. Sorry to have bothered you. By the way, what's your name, big guy?"

His demeanor changes to one of outright lechery. "It's Tom, babe. As in Tom Cat." He links his thumbs through his belt loops in a way that screams, *ME MAN. HAVE PENIS. WOMAN BE IMPRESSED NOW.*

I laugh. "Well, that's just perfect." I beckon him closer and lower my voice. "So, let me tell you how this is going to go, *Tom Cat.* You're going to apologize to me for being a nauseating chauvinist douche, right before you get your crew to clear this stage. Then, you'll set those lighting bars in record time, because if you don't, not only are you going to be fired and blacklisted by every single theatrical producer I know, and believe me, I know a *lot*, I'm also going to tear off your puny, shriveled balls and use them as the centerpiece in the finale. Are you feeling me, sport?"

Tom's eyes glaze over in anger, and I have a strong feeling this guy has definite erectile issues. "Now, you listen here, missy—"

"*No*, Tom, you shut your Neanderthal mouth and listen to *me*. As far as you're concerned, this theater is the Sacred Church of the Kickass Bitch, and I am your Goddess, so you have three seconds to do exactly as you're told or face my unholy wrath. It's your choice."

He gives me a final glare before turning back to his men. "Fuck you, lady."

"Suit yourself."

I grab my walkie-talkie and give a quick order to security before walking over and addressing his men.

"Okay, gents, here's the deal. Tom is about to be thrown out of the theater in a most ungracious fashion for being a disgusting, disrespectful stain on society. So if you want to avoid joining him, here are my rules: you do what you're told, when I tell you to do it. If you don't, you're fired. If you call me anything other than 'Miss Holt', you're fired. If you behave like anything other than *complete gentlemen* from here on out, you're well and truly goddamn fired. Are we clear?"

Tom makes a scoffing sound and gives me a condescending look. "They're *my* guys, sweetcheeks. If you get rid of me, they'll follow. Have no doubt."

I look at the men calmly. "If that's the case, no problem. You're all welcome to join Tom in the unemployment line. I'll have a new crew here within the hour. The decision is yours."

Without another word, the men scurry away to do what's been asked of them.

I look at Tom in smug triumph. "Oh, wow, Tom Cat. Your men decided to work without you. It's a Christmas miracle! Thanks for playing. Better luck next time. Now, get the hell out of my theater."

He takes a threatening step toward me, and I immediately judge the distance from my closed fist to his crotch, while calculating how much force I'd need to drop him to his knees. Looks like all of those self-defense lessons Liam gave me before he left are finally going to pay off.

Just as I'm getting ready to throw down, two security guards arrive to escort Tom to the exit. I wave to him merrily as he leaves, ignoring the sexist obscenities he mutters under his breath.

Cool. One problem down, several hundred to go.

My phone buzzes, and I look down to see a text from Liam.
<5 days>

A tingle runs up my spine. It kind of ridiculous that he can do that to me with a couple of words on a screen. I wonder if it's normal that when I read his texts, I can hear the deep rumble of his voice in my head. It gives me goosebumps.

Another text pops up.

<To be clear, that's 5 days until I can see you. And kiss you. And strip off your goddamn clothes with my teeth, so I can put my mouth all over you. ALL over you, Liss.>

Another shiver. I really have no time to indulge in replying right now, but God, I want to.

I sideline filthy thoughts as I head backstage to check the dressing rooms.

Liam keeps texting. *<Do you know how much I miss you? Because seriously, this is hell. I need to be with you. And inside you. Now.>*

I fan myself with my clipboard, as I mentally run over the dressing room checklist. Evil man. He knows I'm working. And that I'm probably stressed out. This is his way of distracting me, and yeah, it's working.

<I want to fuck you right here in my trailer. It's freezing outside, but in here, you could be naked 24/7. I'd take such good care of you. Provide you with hot and cold running orgasms, morning, noon and night.>

Dear *God*. I can't remember the last time I orgasmed. I've tried a few times since he's been gone, but my body won't cooperate. It's mourning him with the passion of an Italian widow.

<Do you want me to make you come, Liss? Because I will. Over and over and over again. I'll do it until you pass out.>

My face is burning by the time I check the final dressing room. To be honest, the damn room could be filled with toxic waste and a jukebox dedicated exclusively to Billy Ray Cyrus, and I'd have no clue. I can't stop fantasizing about Liam making me come.

Another text: *<How do you want me to do it? With my mouth? My hands? My cock? God, my cock misses you.>*

"Miss Holt?" I turn to see Ainsly looking at me with concern. "Are you okay? You're all red."

I let out a breath. "I'm fine. Get moving on the production

riders, okay? This room should have—" My phone vibrates again.

<My cock wants you to kiss him. And lick him. And slide down onto him. He's aching for it. My entire body is aching for it. I want to be surrounded by you, Liss. Tight, and warm, and—>

"Miss Holt?"

"Uh—" I blink as I drag myself away from my phone to check the list on my clipboard. My vision is blurry as my brain flashes up mental images of my hot-as-hell fiancée, naked, hard, and servicing me in ways that make my legs forget they have bones.

"Miss Holt? You were saying what I need to get."

"Uh ... right. Yes. An espresso machine. And a bowl of M&Ms with all the green ones removed."

"Sure. I'll get on that. Can I also get you some water? Or something to eat? You don't look well."

She's not wrong. I'm lovesick. And Liam deprived. And orgasmically challenged. None of that is healthy, dammit.

"You're right, Ainsly, I'll grab a sandwich and be back in five, okay? You keep going on these rooms."

"Sure, I'll be here."

I almost sprint to my office. It's true I have a sandwich in my bag, but what I'm really hungering for isn't food. When I get inside, I lock the door and lean back against it. My fingers shake as I jab Liam's name for Facetime.

Within seconds, he appears on the screen.

Sweet giddy Christ, he's shirtless. It should be a crime to be that attractive.

I'll never get used to the sight of Liam's naked chest. What's more, the roll he's playing calls for long hair, so he's wearing messy extensions and braids that make him look like the Viking God of Extreme Hotness.

It takes me a few moments to adjust to the bout of dizziness the sight of him inflicts upon me.

"Hey," he says. I know that voice. The one that means he's so horny, he can barely speak.

"You're killing me, Quinn, you know that?"

He leans closer to the camera. "I can't help it. You look beautiful, by the way. Show me your underwear."

"Liam, everything is in chaos here. I have no time to—"

"*Now*, Elissa."

Jesus. I can't argue when he orders me around like that. It's too arousing.

I quickly lift up my shirt to show him my plain black bra.

"Fuck, yes." He licks his lips. "Don't suppose you have time for a quick strip tease? Or even better, a slow one?"

"Sadly, no." His face falls as I drop my shirt. "But just for the record, are you currently naked?"

He smiles before standing to show me an elaborate pair of leather pants that are caked in fake blood and embellished with fur. "Nope. Just lounging around in my nifty thrifty killin'-pants. They're surprisingly comfortable."

As bizarre as it sounds, my blond-ish, blue-eyed hunk is playing Genghis Khan in a big-budget and historically inaccurate blockbuster.

Ahhh, Hollywood. Casting white people in ethnic roles since forever.

The only reason Liam even considered the role was because James Cameron was directing, and he's Liam's idol. I'd never seen Liam fanboy, but the day Cameron called to ask him to do the project, Liam's blush was off the charts. It was both adorable and hot as hell.

"Those are some sexy pants, Mr. Quinn," I say with a smirk. "They make your junk look even more epic than it already is."

He sits again and raises an eyebrow. "You like the leather pants, huh? Well, play your cards right, and I'll take them off for you."

Man, if only. "You have no idea how much I want that right now, but I'm behind schedule as it is. Seeing you naked isn't going to help me focus on anything except how much I miss you."

He leans forward, and even with the low-quality satellite feed, I can see the longing in his eyes. "Liss, I miss you so much I can't see straight. I'm going insane here. It's like I've got this weird, clammy fever, and the only cure is to be with you again." He lowers his voice. "I need you. I've almost forgotten how you feel."

"I know. But the wait is almost over, right? Then we'll have four weeks of total bliss together. No theaters. No movies or publicity. Just you and me."

He smiles. "That's the only thing keeping me going right now. I can't wait."

"Are you ever going to tell me where we're going?"

"No. But trust me when I say you're going to love it."

"If I have no idea of our destination, how will I know what to pack?"

He lets out a dark chuckle. "As long as you're there, screw everything else. It's not like you're going to need clothes. I intend to keep you naked the entire time."

I slump into the chair next to my desk. "Yes, please. Naked. You. Some food and water so we can keep up our strength. That's all I need."

There's a knock on my door, and James says, "Oh, hey, Elissa. Uh ... you might like to come see the lighting designer. The entire grid just crashed. Power overload or something."

I bite back a grunt of frustration. "You have the backup drive, James. Take care of it."

"Uh, yeah, about that. I kind of forgot to back it up. Do you have a list of the cues? We'll have to program them all in again."

I clench my jaw. "I'll be right there."

Footsteps move away from the door as I turn back to my phone. "I have to go. No rest for the wicked."

The disappointment is clear on his handsome face. "I'm sorry I'm not there to help out, but the show is in good hands. You're going to rock this. And when I get back, I'll thank you by showing you all the things I've been fantasizing about for three long months. Prepare yourself."

"Well, now I'm intrigued."

Through the screen, the intensity in his gaze makes me shiver. "Good. Because not all of them are gentle."

My entire body shudders with anticipation. "Tease."

"That's on the list. And believe me when I say that even though I adore you more than anything on the planet, I'm going to enjoy hearing you beg."

There's another knock on my door. "Miss Holt? It's Ainsly. There's a problem with the red carpet, and Hugh Jackman is here for a meeting about his hosting duties." There's a pause. "Um, and George Clooney's people called to say he'll be an hour late, so we'll have to move him to later in the show. And there's someone here to see you who wouldn't give me his name but keeps telling me what to do."

"Shit," I say as my mind races. "Okay, Ainsly. I'm coming." I take one final look at Liam. His face is so close to the camera, I want to stroke it. "I'm sorry."

"Go," he insists. "I'll talk to you tomorrow."

"Okay. I love you."

He gets the same wistful smile I always see when I say those words to him. "I love you more. Have an amazing show. Bye."

I hang up and sigh before pushing my hair out of my face and wrenching the door open. The previous bustle of the backstage area seems to have sped up, and when I get to the stage, I'm pleased to see that the chaos has been cleared and the set is almost done.

"Thank God."

When James hurries past me, I grab his arm. "Hey. What's the situation with the lighting?"

He looks flushed. "Uh, all good. Some guy showed up and managed to get back all the cues."

"Some guy?"

"Yeah. Brown hair. Glasses. Kind of bossy."

I freeze as a familiar voice pipes up behind me. "Man, I leave you alone for five seconds and everything goes to shit. Thank God I took pity on you and jumped on a direct flight from Sydney yesterday morning. Feel free to now express your gratitude. I'll wait."

I turn to see a most unexpected and welcome sight. Josh is standing there with a duffle bag in his hand and a shit-eating grin on his face. Apart from Liam, I don't think I've been more grateful to see someone in my entire life.

I stride over and throw my arms around him. He drops his bag and wraps me in a tight hug, and dammit, having him here is so comforting, I well up like a regular human, not at all like the emotionally controlled boss-lady I've spent years becoming.

Stoppit, Elissa. You cannot cry in front of your crew. You've made them fear you exactly the right amount to be useful. Don't undo that.

I take in a shaky breath and push down tears as Josh tightens his arms around me.

"Missed me, I take it?" he whispers.

"You have no idea how much."

"Yeah, well, you doing your best to crack several of my ribs right now is giving me a clue. Be gentle with your bestie, please. He's a delicate and precious flower who just happens to live in the body of a mid-twenties hipster god."

"So when you texted me before ...?"

"I was in a cab coming from the airport. I knew this gig would be a nightmare without me. Plus, Angel is busy filming, so I had nothing better to do than to come back and save your ass."

I make a scoffing noise. "Make no mistake, Kane. I could have handled this without you, but I'm still glad you're here. I suspect you also came running back because you missed me like crazy and got bored being Angel's personal assistant. Am I right?"

"Crazy talk. You know how much I adore fetching coffee and taking phone messages. It's what I live for." He pulls back and looks down at me. "Angel sends her love, by the way. She really misses you."

"I miss her, too." I can't believe how much. Angel feels almost as much of a sister as Cassie does, and even though not seeing her for months is hard on me, I can tell Josh is already struggling with their separation.

"Josh ..."

He steps out of our hug and waves me off. "Alright, alright, no more talk. Just give me all the information I'll need to kick this show in the balls. We're burning daylight, here."

I smile as I hand over my clipboard. "Go for your life, babe."

Just then James walks by, and Josh steps in front of him. "Hey there, chuckles. Give me your headset."

James's face drops. "What? Why?"

"Because," Josh says as he claps him on the shoulder, "you've failed to even come close to filling my freakishly large shoes. So hand over the wearable tech, and go help Ainsly get those dressing rooms ready. Before you know it, we'll be neck deep in celebrity egos and pushy managers, and I need you running point."

James looks at me in confusion. "Who is this guy?"

I smile. "He's who you should aspire to be if you want to make it in this industry. Now, do as he says and move your ass."

James turns bright red as he hands his headset and pack to Josh before scurrying off into the wings.

Josh shoves his clipboard under his arm as he slides on the headphones and clips the pack to his belt. "You honestly thought that doofus could replace me? I see your delusions have gotten worse since I left."

"He came highly recommended."

"Oh, please. Look at him with his stupid messy haircut and Dolce and Gabbana glasses. He looks like an idiot."

"Josh, he looks almost exactly like you. I think that's half of the reason I hired him."

He scoffs. "You're insane. He's a total geek."

"And you are ...?"

"A *hot* geek. There's a difference."

"Of course. Silly me."

He grabs his bag and straightens up. "Right. We have a show to rehearse, so let's go fuck this sheep."

"Um ..."

"Yeah, I met some New Zealanders in Sydney. They blessed me with a new catchphrase."

"Excellent. Let's go."

After dropping Josh's bag off in my office, we head toward Hugh Jackman's dressing room.

"First order of business," I say, "is to brief our illustrious host."

Josh tries to hide his excitement. "Cool. Should I tell him I'm currently wearing my Wolverine underoos in his honor?"

"You absolutely should not."

"Killjoy."

"Also, don't say anything about fucking sheep."

He suppresses a smile. "No farmyard intercourse references, either? Wow. Seems like you got all fancy since I left." He pauses then says, "Did I mention I've missed the crap out of you?"

"Yeah, yeah. Stop your gushing. It's getting embarrassing."

As we head upstairs to the luxury dressing rooms, all of my

anxiety about the concert melts away. It may be one of the biggest and most complicated shows I've ever run, in an unfamiliar theater with an untested crew, but as long as Josh is by my side, it's going to be a walk in the park.

Backstage Batman and her Robin are on the case.

TWO

YOU'D BETTER NOT CRY

November 27th
The Los Angeles Home of Liam Quinn
Los Angeles, California

The next morning, a dull pounding in my head wakes me, and I try to will it away by snuggling into my pillow. Yeah, like that ever works.

It's my own stupid fault. I had way too much champagne at the after party last night, and now, I'm paying the price. At least I have most of the day off before I have to fly back to New York.

I stretch out and sigh. It blows my mind that I can starfish in Liam's massive bed and not even touch the edges. I've worked in theaters smaller than this thing.

While I've been here in L.A., I've been staying in Liam's house in the Hollywood Hills. Even though his New York apartment is huge by Manhattan standards, it still has only three bedrooms and four bathrooms. This extravagant monstrosity has eight bedrooms, ten bathrooms, and the most stunning view of L.A. from the infinity pool that I've ever seen.

The best feature about this house? The dedicated cheese fridge in the kitchen. When I saw that Liam had stocked it with all of my favorites, I had a major cheesegasm. If I still harbored any doubts about his feelings for me, that cheese fridge put every one of them to rest. Only a man who is butt-over-balls in love buys his woman that much quality *fromage*.

I roll onto my back and stretch. Maybe I'll cook up some mac and cheese for breakfast. It's the one food my stomach can tolerate when dealing with a hangover.

"Good morning, beautiful."

What the ...?

I open my eyes and turn to see Liam staring at me from my laptop, which is sitting open on a pillow. He's lying in bed too, and he has his head propped up with his hand in such a way that his bicep is bulging.

All of a sudden I'm wide awake. "Hi, yourself, sexy man. What time is it there?"

He looks over at the clock on his nightstand. "Almost eleven at night. I have to go soon. We're shooting at dawn, and my driver will be here to collect me in half an hour. Just wanted to spend time with you before I leave."

"Hmmm, waking up to you, even digital you, is something I've missed. I hate your shooting schedule."

"Me, too."

I adjust my position so I can see him better. "I have this vague memory of nodding off during our sexy Skype session last night. That wasn't real, right? It had to be a nightmare."

"I wish. I was actually in the middle of some of grade-A dirty talk when you just flopped onto your pillow and started snoring. Your hand was still down your pants, for God's sake. It's clear you're not attracted to me anymore." He grips his chest as if he's in pain. "It's okay. I knew this day would come, but I guess I didn't expect it to be so soon. Oh well, we've had a good run. You can have the apartment, but I'll sue if you don't grant me joint custody of the cheese."

"Ha! You're dreaming if you think you're getting that cheese without a fight, pal. May I remind you that the last time we visited your parents, I stole pictures of you in high school with what looks suspiciously like a mullet? If you cross me, I'll pass that shizz along to TMZ without a second thought."

He slaps the bed. "Dammit, woman! Do you really want to put our beautiful, impressionable cheese in the middle of this nastiness? You'll scar it for life!"

"Okay, fine. I'll bury the mullet. But I'm doing it for the cheese, asshole. Not you."

His dark scowl sends shivers up my legs. "Fucking fine, you shrew. But this is going on the naughty list."

I try not to smile. "The naughty list?"

"Yes. It's a list of your transgressions, and it's getting pretty damn long, I can tell you."

"And what constitutes a list-worthy transgression?"

"Lots of things. Disagreeing with me. Disobeying me. Being thousands of miles away where I can't touch you. Being so beautiful you make my chest ache. Looking at me how you're looking at me now, when you know damn well it's going to make me hard as a rock. The usual."

"I see. And the point of writing it all down is ...?"

"So I know exactly how much I need to punish you when we're finally together."

"Am I going to enjoy this punishment?"

"If I allow you to, yes. So watch your damn step, or I'll make your life miserable. No orgasms for you!"

I smile and hug my pillow. God, he's sexy when he pretends to be angry. Why on earth do I find that so hot?

"Well, if it helps," I say, "I'm sorry I fell asleep. You know how dozy I get when I drink. I actually nodded off in the cab on the way back from the party. If Josh hadn't been there to help carry me inside, our lovely Russian driver who smelled like vodka and cabbage would probably still be circling Hollywood boulevard, earning a huge fare."

"Wait a second, back up. Josh is there?"

"Yeah, didn't I tell you that last night?"

"No. You muttered something about how the show was amazing, and you raised eight million dollars for the charity, which is incredible by the way. Then you got all flirty and ordered me to strip. Too bad it wasn't much of a show, considering I was only wearing boxers, but still, you seemed to enjoy it."

"Oh, yes. I really did." Liam getting naked is pretty much my favorite thing on the planet, half asleep or not.

"I thought Josh was in Australia with Angel."

"He was, but he came back to help me out."

Liam smiles. "Seriously? That's great. I felt bad that you were handling everything by yourself, but knowing Josh took some of the load makes me feel less like a useless, abandoning bastard. Is he heading back to New York with you?"

"Yeah. His mom has guilted him into coming home until the new year."

"Well, if he needs his space from Ma and Pa Kane, he can always stay at our place. I'd feel better knowing there's someone taking care it when you leave." He pauses. "Speaking of leaving ..." He leans forward. "Four days, Liss. Four eternally long days until we're together."

"Can't you at least give me a hint at where we're going?"

"Okay, one clue. Bring your bathing suit."

I pull my knees up to my chest. "Seriously? There's a blizzard in New York right now, and even here in L.A. it's freaking cold."

He raises an eyebrow. "Then I guess you can cross L.A. and New York off the list of possible destinations, can't you?"

Damn him and his ability to keep a secret.

"So, it's going to be hot where we're going?"

"In more ways than one. On a related note, I also want you to bring an entire suitcase of lingerie. The sexier, the better."

I laugh. "Sure. I'll get right on that."

He leans forward and lowers his voice. "I'm not joking, Elissa. Go shopping. Use the credit card I gave you. Spare no expense. I want a whole selection to choose from."

"Liam—" I sigh. "I have no idea about that stuff. I've never worn anything but simple black and white underwear."

"I know. And as unbelievably hot as that is, I want to see you in something different. Feel free to be creative. I want you to torture me with your sexiness." His gaze drops down to where the shadow of my nipples can be seen through the white collared shirt I wore to bed. "Well, more than you already do, anyway. You look better in my shirt than I ever did."

"I respectfully disagree, but I do like that it smells like you."

"I'm glad that you're comfortable wearing an eight-hundred-dollar shirt to bed." He swallows and lets out a tight breath. "But, Christ, I wish I was there to tear it off you."

I sit up and make a show of undoing the top button. "Why tear it? I'll happily remove it if you ask nicely."

He sits up and licks his lips. "Hell yes. Take it off. Now."

"But, you didn't say please." I toy with the second button.

"Elissa ..." His voice is low with warning. "Unless you want another entry on the naughty list, I'd strongly suggest you remove that shirt, ASAFP."

I give him my most teasing smile as I undo the final button. Then I crawl up onto my knees and make sure I'm in prime position in front of the camera before holding the shirt open and giving him an unobstructed view of my breasts.

He groans as he curls his fingers into the sheet in front of him. "Maybe I should rethink the whole lingerie plan. If this is how you affect me in a man's shirt and plain white panties, the sight of you in something designed to drive men out of their minds might actually kill me. My cock has never been harder."

"Quid pro quo, Mr. Quinn," I say, my voice betraying how much his arousal thrills me. "Let's see the proof."

With a smug look, he adjusts the angle of his camera and pulls down the sheet to show me exactly how naked and hard he is.

Oh. Wow.

Good God, his dick is glorious. Thick and long, it curves in a perfect arc pointing up to his abs. Even though I love seeing my effect on him, I also feel sorry for him. His erection looks so tight and swollen, it must be painful. That doesn't prevent my body from going from zero to *I need to have him inside me now* in less than two seconds.

"See what you do to me?" he says. "I need relief, Elissa. Touching myself isn't even in the same universe as having you touch me. It's barely worth my time, anymore."

I slump onto the bed. "I know what you mean. I've given up, too. The other night I tried for so long, my hand cramped up."

Liam moves the camera so I can see his face again. "Wait a

minute. Your *hand?*"

"Yeah. You were expecting me to use some other part of my body to masturbate?"

He looks confused. "No, but don't you girls usually have certain ... devices to help you out?"

"Devices? You mean vibrators?"

"Well, yeah." He looks so embarrassed discussing the matter, I almost laugh.

"Sorry to tell you this, but I've never owned one."

"Why not?"

"I don't know. In college, Cassie and Ruby tried to drag me to a sex shop, but I wasn't interested. Maybe that was a mistake, because they both purchased super amazing vibrators they raved about for the next two years. According to them, Buzz and Woody rocked their worlds."

Liam tries not to smile. "Buzz and Woody? Really?"

"Yes. They're the main characters in *Sex Toy Story* - a touching tale that's been ribbed for her pleasure."

He chuckles. "I bet. So you've never even tried one?"

"No, but I don't consider I've missed out on anything. I mean, my hand may be low-tech, but it's pretty damn talented."

"Oh, I believe me, I know."

"Right? And now that I have People's *Sexiest Man Alive* as my live-in fuck-buddy, I have no need for anything else, do I?"

There's a beeping noise, and he feels around the bed before picking up his phone and checking the screen.

"Shit. My driver will be here in fifteen minutes. I'd better shower and try to deflate my dick before he gets here, or he might get the wrong impression about how pleased I am to see him." He glances up at me. "Speak to you tomorrow?"

"Absolutely."

He sighs. "Four days, sweetheart. Just remember that."

"I will."

We exchange I love yous and sign off, and when he disappears from the screen, I button up my shirt and flop back down onto the bed.

Four days. I can last until then. No problem.

My body screams that I'm a filthy liar, but I figure if I just ignore it, the dull ache inside might go away.

I'm considering having a cold shower when there's a knock at the bedroom door.

"Hey. You finished your disgusting sex call with Quinn yet?"

I pull the sheet over my legs and smile. "Yes. Come in."

Josh enters, and with a tired grunt, he throws himself onto the bed beside me. "Please tell me you have pain killers."

I grab some Advil and a bottle of water off my night stand and hand it to him. "Go for your life."

"Thanks. Considering this hangover is all your fault, providing relief is the least you can do."

"Hey, I told you to stop drinking after your seventh beer. It's not my fault you didn't listen."

Josh pops two pills into his hand and uncaps the water. "I have no memory of that. I do, however, remember Miley Cyrus touching me in strange and inappropriate ways while you laughed your ass off."

"Can you blame me? The look on your face was priceless. You kept yelling that Angel Bell was your girlfriend so you were off the market, but that just seemed to make Miley want you more."

He nods as he throws the pills in his mouth and chases them with a gulp of water. "Sometimes, being this attractive is a curse."

"I wouldn't know."

He laughs. "Of course you wouldn't. You're hideous. I have no idea what Quinn sees in you. How is he, anyway? Still all tall and good-looking?"

"Yeah, but he seems exhausted. I think he's looking forward to our vacation even more than I am."

"I bet. I still can't believe you're letting him organize everything. I remember when I tried to plan a surprise party for your sweet sixteenth. The second you found out, you took over."

"Well, sure, but that's only because you were doing everything wrong."

"In other words, different from how you would do it."

"I stand by my definition of *wrong*."

"Uh huh."

I shove him in the arm. "If you stop giving me shit for five seconds, I may be inclined to make mac and cheese for breakfast. You in?"

His whole face lights up. "God, yes. I haven't eaten carbs in weeks. Angel thinks they're the work of the devil. Get that pasta in my face hole, STAT."

• • •

Half an hour later, we're sitting at the kitchen bench stuffing our faces with creamy, cheesy goodness when the intercom sounds.

I press the video button to the front gate and see a man leaning out the window of a delivery van.

"Hello?"

"Delivery for Elissa Holt."

"Oh. Sure, come on up." I press the button to open the gate then grab some cash from my purse and hand it to Josh. "Could you tip him? If I go I'll have to put on pants, and I don't need that kind of negativity in my life right now."

"Sure," he says and takes the cash. "Since you made me breakfast, the least I can do is facilitate your pantslessness." He looks around. "Now, if you could just provide me with a map of how to get to the front door, I'll be on my way."

I smile and point down the hallway. "Go that way for a few miles, then turn left. If you reach the bowling alley, you've gone too far."

Josh laughs. "Funny." When he reads my face, his smile drops. "You're not joking, are you? Quinn has a goddamn bowling alley in this place?"

"Yep. And a movie theater. And an entire room dedicated to gift wrapping."

"The fuck? Big on presents, is he?"

"This house used to belong to some TV producer whose spouse was the ultimate Hollywood housewife. There was also a huge room that housed her extensive range of designer handbags, but Liam converted that one into a gym."

"Really? So, now his handbags are homeless? Tragic. At least he can wrap presents to his heart's content."

"Don't laugh. The previous owners only left because they decided this house wasn't big enough for them. They ended up moving to an even more ridiculous McMansion that featured *three* gift wrapping rooms."

"Well, now you're just making shit up to mess with me."

"Not at all. True story."

Josh makes a disgusted noise. "Just when I think rich people can't get any weirder ..." He goes toward the hall. "I'll be right back. Maybe. If you don't hear from me in a few hours, send out a search party."

As it turns out, he's only gone for five minutes, and when he returns, he's carrying an enormous gift basket wrapped in polka dot tissue paper and topped with a giant red bow.

"Just a hunch," Josh says, "but I'm guessing it's a mix tape." He places it on the bench and hands me a small envelope. "It came with this."

I pull out the card.

Darling Liss,
Now you can see what all the fuss is about. I'll expect a full report when I see you.
Enjoy.
Love, Liam.
Ps. Bring this stuff on our trip. I want to see what you've learned by then.

"From Quinn, I take it?" Josh asks, trying to read over my shoulder.

"Uh ... yeah."

"So, come on," he says as he starts tearing away the tissue paper. "Let see what's he's sent. Maybe it's a puppy!"

"Josh, wait—"

Before I can even finish the sentence, the paper falls away to reveal an impressive range of sex toys, including half a dozen vibrators of various shapes and sizes, something that looks like a butterfly headband, and a bunch of porn in both magazine and Blu-ray form.

Josh's eyes widen as he notices a particularly large and realistic-looking dildo. "What the ever loving fuck?!" He covers his face and backs away. "My eyes! My poor, innocent eyes!"

I laugh and pick up one of the Blu-rays. "Well, that's what you get when you unwrap someone else's gift, Mr. Nosy."

Josh peeks through his fingers. "What the hell is wrong with your man, Elissa? Most guys send flowers or chocolates. Maybe jewelry if they're hankering for a blow job. But Quinn sends you half a sex shop? Has he no respect for my delicate sensibilities?"

"I don't think he expected you to see it."

"Clearly. Freak."

"So I take it you've never sent Angel a giant latex dong? Sheesh. Some boyfriend you are."

Josh crosses his arms over his chest and glares. "Do you think I'm stupid? Why the hell would I give her something that *big*, that can do things no natural penis can?"

"Like what?"

He grabs one of the vibrators. "Check this out." He presses a button, and the tip of the thing starts rotating one way, while the body rotates the other. The whole shaft buzzes with powerful vibrations. "See? No man can compete with that. This can reach erogenous zones scientists haven't even discovered yet."

"Should I ask how you know this?"

He turns off the vibrator and throws it onto the counter. "One of the girls I used to date always insisted I finish her off with one of these pieces of crap, no matter how much amazingness she'd experienced with Magic Mike. Seems a regular penis didn't cut it for her. It was humiliating. Quinn has no idea he's just opened himself up to being second best for your vagina, forever."

I laugh, because seriously, I don't think Liam will ever have any competition where my vagina is concerned, but as close as Josh and I are, I don't think saying that would help right now.

Josh rubs the back of his neck and looks around. "So, now that we've experienced yet another session of oversharing in our long and glorious friendship, can we do something fun? Wanna go bowling?"

I think about it for a second. "That depends. Do I have to put on pants?"

"Nope, but be warned, you may want that extra protection when I *kick your ass*."

"Dream on, Kane. Dream on."

Without warning, he lunges forward and slaps my ass, hard. Then he runs down the hallway toward the bowling alley, chuckling like an idiot all the way.

I grab the largest dildo from the gift basket and race after him. *Oh, it is ON.*

THREE

BETTER NOT POUT

November 30th, Present Day
The Home of Charles and Maggie Holt
New York City, New York

"Ethan, come on."

"No."

"Seriously? Your baby sister tells you she needs your help, and you refuse? What kind of a monster are you?"

"The kind who isn't discussing this any further. Go ask Cassie."

"I did! She told me to talk to you, since you're the expert. She's just the mannequin."

My brother ignores me and continues unpacking boxes of Christmas ornaments in preparation for our family's annual tree decorating party. Well, it's not so much a party as all of us struggling to shove as many decorations as possible onto the giant tree Dad has squeezed into the living room. Then when we all go home, Mom will take everything off and redecorate it with mathematical precision. God forbid the distribution of the tinsel should be even vaguely uneven.

This is why I love her.

Since Josh and I got back to New York a few days ago, I've

been doing final preparations for my Christmas getaway with Liam, but there are some things I can't do without help. It's too bad my buttmunch of a brother is refusing to play ball.

"Ethan, *please*."

"No."

"Why not?"

"Because you're my *sister*. It would be weird and wrong."

"Oh, for the love of God, you two, stop bickering." My mom gives us both the stink eye as she brings in another box from the hallway closet. "It's like having teenagers in the house again. What on earth are you arguing about, anyway?"

Ethan shoots me a look. "Nothing, Mom. Don't worry about it."

"Yeah, it's all good, Mom. Ethan's just being a dick."

Mom narrows her eyes at us then shrugs. "Fine. I didn't want to get involved anyway. By the way, Ethan, your father wants to know if you can get us tickets to a show this weekend?"

"Sure. I can get anything you want."

"How about Hamilton?"

Ethan grimaces. "Except that. Can't get tickets without selling a body part or family member. Wait, let's try selling Elissa and see what happens. They can only say no, right?"

I laugh and throw a clump of tinsel at him. "You're an asshole."

"Elissa—" Mom clucks her tongue in response to my unladylike language. She's lucky I resisted the urge to call him a fucking asshole.

"Hey, Mrs. H," Josh says from where he's watching TV on the couch. "Awesome homemade croissants. Got any more?"

Mum puts down her box. "Sure, honey, I'll get you some. Anything to get away from the bickering."

Josh's face lights up. "You're the best, Maggie. Have I told you today how pretty you look tonight?"

Mom rolls her eyes and heads into the kitchen. She secretly loves spoiling Josh, and he exploits it every chance he gets.

"You could help out, you know," I say as my evil bestie turns back to the television.

"I'd love to," Josh says, "but I'm carb-loading right now. Angel will be back from Australia in January, and I want to ingest enough processed crap before then to give diabetes to a whole platoon of vegans. I have no time for frivolous Christmas chores."

"So Angel won't be back for Marco's New Year's Eve party?" I ask.

He takes a swig of his beer and flips through the channels. "Nope. I can't believe I'm finally in a relationship on New Year's Eve and don't get to kiss the hell out of her at midnight. What the hell is wrong with this world?"

"I'll kiss you, sweetheart," Ethan deadpans. "You just have to promise to not use tongue."

Josh smiles at him. "Aw, come on, big fella. Don't be shy. You know you want the tongue."

Ethan mimes vomiting onto the nativity scene before turning to unpack another box. I'm about to hassle him again about my favor when Cassie appears in the front hall. As usual, whenever his new wife is within a three-mile radius, everything else ceases to exist for my brother. I can't believe it was only a year ago they were upstairs banging like teenagers while we cleaned up Christmas Eve dinner.

It seems being married hasn't dulled my brother's endless fascination with Cassie. He watches her cross the room with the same level of pride as parents watching their child compete in the Olympics. If it wasn't so stinking cute, it would make me want to throw up all over our collector's edition Rudolph figurine.

"So," Cassie says to me as she gives Ethan a smile. "Did my man help you out? Are you all set?"

"Not even a little bit. He said it would be weird."

Cassie turns to my brother. "Ethan, your sister needs you. It's your duty to help."

"Honey, don't ask this of me. I beg you. I'll be scarred for life."

"Oh, please. Liam wants her to buy sexy lingerie, and no one knows more about that than you."

Ethan puts his arms around her. "Believe me, she could wear a canvas sack and Quinn would still lose his shit. Anything she chooses will be fine."

"Ethan, come on." Cassie's tone tells me my brother's already lost this one. "If you do this, you and Liam can bond over buying your women stupidly impractical intimate-wear. Wouldn't it be nice to share your hobby with a friend?"

Ethan drops his head onto her shoulder and sighs. "Fine. But let the record show I'm not at all comfortable helping my baby sister buy underwear that will make her man want to do filthy things to her. My therapy bills are expensive enough as it is."

"Noted." Cassie runs her fingers through his hair and leans in to whisper, "And, as a reward, you can pick up something up for me."

Ethan's whole posture changes. "Seriously? My ban is lifted?"

"*One* item," Cassie clarifies. "Not the whole store. Our credit cards are still recovering from the last time you went on a binge."

Ethan grips the back of her neck. "Yeah, but it was worth it, right?"

"Maybe." Cassie presses again him, and my disgusting brother kisses her so passionately, I get full visible tongue. God, he's gross.

When he's done violating his wife's mouth, he grabs the box of tinsel from my hands and drops it onto the couch.

"Okay, let's go. We've got an hour before Mom serves dinner and I want to have my brain bleached of the whole experience by then."

I turn to Josh. "Want to come?"

"Where are you going?"

"Lingerie store."

"Will you model stuff for me?"

"Nope."

"Then I'm out. Have fun, though."

I grab my purse, and after Ethan throws my coat at me, we head outside to grab a cab.

● ● ●

Considering it's the holiday season, we make good time, and fifteen minutes later, we're walking into La Perla on 5th avenue.

I gape as I take in the opulent store. My God, I've never seen underwear this pretty. All of the mannequins are like lady-shaped presents, waiting to be unwrapped.

As soon as we enter, both ladies behind the counter spot Ethan and light up like Times Square, before nearly tripping over each other to get to him.

"Mr. Holt! Welcome back."

"We haven't seen you for a while."

"Please let us know if you need any help."

"Anything at all."

I don't know if they're eager because they usually earn a crapload of commission from his epic purchases, or because he's tall, semi-famous, and according to most women, handsome. Either way, I roll my eyes.

Ethan acknowledges the women with a wave and a smile before turning to me and giving me his serious face.

"Okay, listen up, short one. This is how it's going to work. I'll choose a bunch of stuff for you. At no time will you question my choices, comment on how they'll look on your body, tell me your actual bra size, or describe how Quinn will react when he sees you in them. When I'm done choosing, I'm gone. If you want to try on stuff, that's your business. I don't want to know what you buy. In fact, as far as I'm concerned, you leave without buying anything and spend your entire vacation wearing a chastity belt and a turtleneck. Are we clear?"

I put my hands on my hips. "You do realize I'm not thrilled about this, either, right? But at least you know what you're doing. I have no clue."

"Yeah, I'm used to that. Let's go." He stalks up and down the racks of lacy, frilly, delicate garments, and it looks utterly bizarre to see my giant, macho brother surrounded by such delicate prettiness. Every now and then he stops and grabs something before shoving it at me, and after ten minutes my arms are overflowing. When I start struggling, one of the hovering assistants takes everything and places it into a dressing room. By the time Ethan's done, the dressing room is overflowing with bras, underpants, bustiers, slips, and super-flimsy bodysuits.

He hold onto a beautiful navy bra and panty set with matching garter belt and pantyhose.

I give him the side eye. "Cassie said *one* item, Ethan."

He hands everything to the clerk, along with his credit card. "Semantics. It's one *outfit*. Not my fault it contains four items." The woman carefully wraps everything in layers of tissue paper before placing it into a fancy cardboard bag and handing it to him. "Now, if you'll excuse me, I have a wife to dress up and then strip bare."

"First of all ... ew. Remember what you said about me and Liam? I also don't want the mental image of you defiling my friend. And second, have you forgotten that Mom will be serving dinner in ..." I check my watch, "half an hour? So, unless you and Cassie intend on doing the dirty upstairs again, any ravaging will have to wait until you get back to your place."

Ethan scowls. "I hate waiting."

"Hey, you have nothing to complain about. For you it's a few hours. I've been waiting *three months* to be with Liam."

He gives me his most sarcastic expression. "You're right. I have no idea what it's like to have to wait for sex. Oh, except for those *three years* I waited for Cassie." He raises an eyebrow at me.

I grunt in defeat. "Fine. You win. This time."

"And every time, little sister. How do you not know that by now?" He gives me a quick peck on the cheek. "Okay, this has been fun, in a twisted kind of way, but now, I'm leaving. I'll see you back at Mom and Dad's."

"Yep. See you then."

I watch the two clerks physically deflate as he leaves. I don't think I'll truly ever understand what women see in my brother. I mean, I love him, but if they had to put up with an 11-year-old Ethan farting into their pillow every night before bed, there'd be no way they'd look at him with those sappy heart-eyes.

With my brother out of the way, I head into the dressing room and grab the nearest bra to examine it. God, these things are flimsy. There's absolutely no support. If I wore this under a T-shirt, my boobs would jiggle like water balloons.

Working methodically, I divide everything into categories. Not that it helps me make a decision. Even though each garment is undeniably beautiful, I have no idea what will turn Liam on. Should I follow Ethan's lead and do the garter belt thing? Or would Liam prefer the leather-look bustier and matching thong?

Ugh, this is impossible.

I quickly strip off my clothes and pull on a delicate blood-red slip that's completely translucent apart from some strategically placed lace flowers over my nipples.

Is this really what men want? It's totally impractical.

There are also three slip dresses of varying lengths and transparencies. Which one do I buy?

As if my thoughts have magically travelled to Mongolia, my phone lights up with Liam's number.

I answer and feel my stress melt away as soon as he appears on the screen.

"Hey, handsome."

He gives me a tired smile. "Hi, beautiful." His face is covered in dirt, and he has his hair and extensions pulled up into a messy bun. On the whole, I disapprove of the whole man-bun movement. For me, it's up there with male jeggings and dress shoes without socks. But on Liam, I can't deny the bun looks hot as hell.

"How's filming going?" I ask.

He wipes a hand across his face and sighs. "Slowly. We only have a few scenes left in the final battle, but the weather has been screwing us. That's one of the downsides of filming in frozen tundra. We're at the mercy of random blizzards."

"See? This is what happens on a James Cameron movie. You could have shot in a nice warm sound stage in Canada and added CG snow. But noooo. It had to be authentically Mongolian, even if the guy playing the baddest middle-eastern bastard in history is an Irish kid from Hoboken."

He chuckles. "Yeah, well, apart from the weather, it's been an amazing experience, even if it has kept me away from you. So, what are you doing? Are you at your parent's place?"

"No. I ducked out to run an errand before dinner."

"Oh? So where are you?"

"Well, I'm trying to do what you asked, but it's turning out to be more difficult than I thought." I prop up the phone on the plush chair in the dressing room so he can see what I'm wearing.

"I need your help. Do you like this one? Or ..." I grab the

other two slips. "One of these?" I hold up the other two in turn before grabbing the leather bustier. "Or would you prefer this? Or ..." I scoop up a kaleidoscope of jewel-colored bras and panties. "These? I mean, the choices are endless. Do you want sweet or slutty? Pretty or edgy? Demure slips, or thongs so tiny you'll need a pair of tweezers to remove them from my butt? Seriously, honey, I have no idea what you're after." I throw up my hands and wait for Liam's response. After a few seconds, I lean forward to check the screen, thinking the connection has dropped out and his image has frozen. Turns out Liam has frozen of his own accord. His mouth is open, and his gaze is raking all over me and the see-through lingerie I'm almost wearing.

"Liam?"

"Uhhh ..."

I wait again. He still doesn't say anything. "Liam? Can you hear me?"

"Yeah, I can hear you. And see you." He rubs the whiskers on his chin. "Fuck me, Liss, I can definitely see you."

I read in a Cosmo once that pretty underwear can make a woman feel powerful, but I never understood the concept until now. The way Liam's looking at me? I could ask him to do anything right now, and he'd agree.

"Okay," I say. "So, which one should I get?"

He closes his mouth and swallows. "All of them. Every goddamn one."

I laugh. "Sure. I'll just buy out the whole store." His piercing gaze makes it clear he approves of the idea. "You're serious? Liam, come on."

"Elissa ..." He brings the phone closer to his face. "Do you love me?"

"Of course."

"And do you want to make me happy?"

"You know I do. But these things are so overpriced. I mean, look ... this one costs—" My mouth dries up as I register the number printed on the price tag. "Jesus Cheese-Loving Christ! Fifteen hundred dollars?! Are you freaking kidding me? For what? A scrap of netting and lace? That's ridiculous!"

I hear footsteps, and one of the sales assistants calls out, "Is everything alright in there, miss?"

I want to yell that no, everything is not alright. Their stupid undies cost more than what I used to pay in rent, for God's sake. Instead, I say, "I'm fine, thanks. All good."

When the footsteps retreat, I turn back to Liam. "Honey, seriously, the cost of all of this ..." I gesture to the catastrophe of underwear around me, "... it could feed a small African nation for a year."

Liam looks at me with an air of supreme obstinance. Coupled with the scruff, the bun, and the dirt-smeared face ... yeah, he definitely looks like a sexy Genghis Khan, ready to do bad things to me if I disobey. I've never really had a thing for historical figures before, but I wouldn't complain about going a few rounds between the sheets with Liam's version of a warrior king.

"Elissa," he says, and his voice is as primal as his appearance. "I promise that when we get back from vacation, I'll donate a fat chunk of cash to whichever African charity you choose. But right now, I'm going to need you to pick up every bit of lace, satin, and leather in that goddamn dressing room and charge all of it to the credit card I organized for you. Understand?"

I drop everything on the floor and sigh. I can tell arguing would be futile. "Yes, master."

Liam makes a noise in his chest. "You need to call me that more often."

I pick up the phone and bring it up to eye level. "Oh, you like that?"

"No. I fucking love that." He's looking at me so intensely, it gives me chills. Then he shakes his head and chuckles. "Wow. I think I've been living this character for way too long. I need to get back to civilization and stop behaving like a caveman. Okay, I gotta go shower. You heading back to your parents' place?"

"Yeah. I'd much rather watch you shower, though."

"Don't worry. Soon, you'll get to shower *with* me."

"Can't wait. Will you still have those hair extensions when I see you?"

He raises an eyebrow. "I was going to get them removed after our last scene, but if you want me to keep them in ..."

I feel like a schoolgirl admitting a secret crush. "Maybe. And the beard. Just for a few days, at least. Long enough for you to pretend I'm half of eastern Europe and thoroughly plunder me."

A slow, sexy smile spreads across his face. "I think that can be arranged."

As we stare at each other, the sexual tension builds, and we realize that because of his shooting schedule, this is the last time we'll see each other before we reach our vacation destination.

"I love you," he says. "I'll see you soon."

"I love you, too. Travel safe."

When I hang up, a wave of emotion rises up in my throat, and I have to take a few deep breaths to stop myself from crying. When he gets home this time, that's it. I'm nailing his feet to the floor. He's not allowed to leave me like this again. I miss him too much.

It doesn't help that I've been wearing his engagement ring for nearly four months now, and we haven't made one single wedding preparation. While I adore him being my fiancée, I want him to be my husband.

After shaking off my emotional mood, I change back into my clothes and carefully gather up my pile of overpriced scraps of fabric. When I take it to the counter and inform the girls I'll be buying everything, dollar signs light up behind their eyes.

Merry Christmas, girls. Get a bottle of Bollinger for yourselves, courtesy of Liam Quinn.

As I'm waiting for the redhead to ring up the purchases, the tall brunette studies me. "Hey, have we met?"

I smile politely and shake my head. "I don't think so."

"Really? Because you look familiar. You've never shopped with us before?"

"No. My brother shops here enough for the both of us."

"Uh huh." She continues to stare, and it makes me want to be anywhere else. Of course, wrapping a million pieces of intimate wear in tissue paper takes forever, so it seems I'm stuck here for a while. To get away from the unwanted scrutiny, I wander over to a rack labeled *Bridal*. There are lots floaty, pretty things in white, cream and pastels. Maybe I'll come back here before my wedding night and pick up something special. Or if my husband-to-be has his way, I'll take the whole damn rack.

"Liam Quinn!" the brunette exclaims suddenly.

"Excuse me?"

"You're the girl who was on the red carpet with Liam Quinn a few months ago. The one he dated after he broke up with Angel Bell." She turns to the redhead. "You know, I'm still not over that. They were so perfect for each other. I never saw it coming."

The redhead nods. "Right? I cried when I heard. I still can't believe they're not together. The way he used to look at Angel? That was *true* love."

I clear my throat. They turn as if they've forgotten I was there.

"Oh, sorry," says the brunette. "So, was it fun? Dating a movie star? Did he break your heart? Is it painful to talk about?"

I walk back to the counter and pick up my purse. "Are we almost done here?"

The brunette nods in sympathy. "I understand. It's hard to let someone like that go, right? I mean, the man is gorgeous. Did you kiss him? Is he a good kisser?"

"Chastity, stop," the redhead says, giving me a sideway glance.

Seriously? She works in a store that reeks of sex, and her name is Chastity? Oh, the irony.

"The poor thing probably didn't even date him," the redhead whispers before looking at me with genuine concern. "I'm sorry about her. She gets carried away with romantic fantasies. You don't need to tell us anything. But just out of interest, did you win that date? Like on a call-in radio show or something?"

See? This is what I get for banning Liam from talking about our relationship in interviews. I thought I was making it easier on myself, considering my one appearance on the red carpet led to me shutting down all of my social media to avoid the vilest cyber-bullying I've ever witnessed. It blows my mind that Liam's fans claim to only want what's best for him but then threaten violence on the woman he loves.

God, people are weird.

When Liam saw how much hate I got for 'replacing' Angel, he

agreed it was probably best to keep our relationship on the down-low, at least for a while.

However, now that these two glamour models are staring at me like I'm a bug on a windshield, I kind of wish I'd retained my Liam Quinn bragging rights.

"Nope," I say. "I didn't win the date. Liam and I are old friends. We've known each other for years."

"Ohhhhh," says the brunette, as if a light bulb went off. "That makes more sense. I mean, yeah. You and him?" She laughs, and the redhead joins her. "As if, right?"

The redhead finally finishes up with her wad of tissue paper and hands me my bags. "Well, if you ever see him again, tell him he's always welcome to shop here. We'll give him a *special* discount."

I wonder if slapping a smug store clerk would get me another entry on Liam's naughty list. If he'd witnessed this little exchange, I'm sure he'd cheer me on. I push down a flash of anger and fix them both with my fiercest glare. Within a second, their smiles drop.

"Actually," I say. "I'm going on a four-week vacation with Liam tomorrow." I hold up my left hand and waggle my massive diamond ring. "And this chunk of ice is what he gave me the day he asked me to marry him. Pretty freaking awesome, right?"

The brunette blinks for a few seconds before stuttering, "No. No way."

The redhead doesn't even bother trying to speak. She just gapes.

"Yes way, Chastity." I give her a smile. "So, Merry Christmas to me." I stride toward the door, but just before I reach it, I turn back to them. "Oh, and to answer your question, yes, he's an amazing kisser. Better still, he fucks like a god." They both gasp. "Goodnight, ladies, and thanks for your help. Enjoy that commission, won't you?"

With that, I pull the door open and step out into the freezing weather. Unfortunately, my triumphant exit is marred when I slip on a patch of ice on the sidewalk and fall heavily onto my ass.

Dammit.

Like a true badass, I climb to my feet and proceed to strut

down the sidewalk like I'm a six-foot-tall supermodel with three percent body fat, rather than a five-foot-three stage manager with a cheese addiction.

Looks like I was wrong about pretty underwear. It can make you feel powerful after all.

FOUR

I'M TELLING YOU WHY

December 1st
The Apartment of Liam Quinn
New York City, New York

"Lissa, would you stop pacing? You're giving me motion sickness, which is ironic since I'm not the one going on a trip."

I flop down on the couch next to Josh and sigh. "I'm sorry. I've never taken a trip where I haven't planned out every detail. I'm nervous. "

"You're hiding it well. I couldn't tell by the way you circled the apartment fifteen times while you rearranged your luggage, or by the twenty times you checked your passport." He pushes his glasses up his nose. "I know it's not midday yet, but maybe you should have some wine. Or a Valium." Josh taps something into his tablet and squints at the screen. "Goddamn sonuvabitch."

"What?"

"Nothing."

"Sure, you always swear at technology and glare like you want to murder it. Spill, please."

He leans back and tilts the screen so I can see. It shows an entertainment website featuring a dozen photos of Angel in

Australia, apparently sharing an intimate night out with her leading man. They're laughing and hugging, and in one, it looks like they're about to kiss. The headline reads, *"Hollywood's Sweetheart Finds Love Down Under with New Prince Charming."*

"Josh—"

"I know you're going to tell me it's not what it seems, and they're just working together, but fuck, Lissa. I can't stand seeing her with him. I really can't." He slams the tablet onto the coffee table and strides into the kitchen.

"Why so jealous? You weren't like this when she was pretending to be in love with Liam."

"That was different." He opens the fridge and grabs a beer. "Back then, I didn't think I had a chance with her, so I had nothing to lose. Now, I have everything to lose, and it freaking terrifies me." He rips the cap off the beer and takes a long swig. "Watching her lust after that guy on set every day ... seeing her kiss him and have sex with him—"

"*Pretend* to lust. *Pretend* to have sex. She's just doing her job, honey. You know that."

"Lissa, you don't understand. This guy, Julian ..." he takes another swig of beer. "I've never wanted to beat up someone so much in my life."

"Why? Is he an asshole?"

He laughs. "Not at all. And that's the problem. He's seems like a nice guy. Funny. Friendly. Has a killer collection of comic books. He even agrees that Captain Kirk would destroy every other Starfleet captain in the Star Trek universe."

"And, that's bad because ...?"

He walks over and sits beside me. "Don't you see? He's *me*. He's the tall, handsome, hot-bodied version."

"Josh, you're six-feet tall. That's not exactly short. And you're handsome."

"Yeah, but I'm normal-person handsome. He's *movie star* handsome. Why would Angel stay with me when he has everything I have and more? He's a hot geek in the body of Greek god."

"That's ridiculous. Angel was with Liam for *years* and didn't lust after him once, and yet from the day she met you, she wanted to jump your bones. Have you considered that she doesn't go for the Greek god type? Maybe she likes her hot geeks ... well ... geeky."

He takes a breath and lets it out. "I suppose."

"If your main concern is that this other guy is ripped, then fight fire with fire. Hit the gym. You have a great body. It wouldn't take much to create definition."

He narrows his gaze. "Did you just suggest I work out? Because if so, who are you, and what have you done with my best friend?"

"Hey, just trying to help. Liam's private gym is right down the hall. You wouldn't even have to leave the apartment."

Before he can hit me with a smartass response, there's a knock at the door that's so loud, I jump.

Josh puts down his beer and gives me a grin. "Sounds like your ride's here."

He opens the door to reveal a large black man wearing a charcoal suit. "Good afternoon, sir. My name is JT, and I'm here to collect Miss Holt."

"Hey, JT," Josh says, offering him a high five. "Loved your last album, man. Very cool."

The man looks at Josh without a hint of a smile. "Sir, I believe you're confusing me with Mr. Justin Timberlake. It's a common mistake. However, he's a funky white boy, while I'm a professional driver. We're different people."

Josh nods. "Ahh, I see. Sorry for the confusion."

"No problem. Happens all the time." He looks past Josh to me. "Good afternoon, Miss Holt. Are you ready to go?"

"As ready as I'll ever be." JT collects my bags as I go to hug Josh. "Bye, bestie. I'll try to call from wherever I end up to let you know I've arrived safely."

He squeezes me. "Have fun. When you get back, I expect to hear all about it, with the sex stuff edited out, of course."

"Wow, expect a short story, then."

He makes a disgusted noise then steps back, and I wave as JT escorts me out of the apartment and down to a stretch limo.

When I climb inside, I gasp. The entire car is filled with hundreds of fresh roses.

I'm not usually one for girly stereotypes, but this?

Well played, Mr. Quinn. Well played.

I open the card on the seat and read the message.

Darling Liss,

I'm not sure if you got the memo, but I intend to pamper the hell out of you on this trip. Too often, you neglect yourself to take care of others, me included. Well, now it's my turn to take care of you. Please don't fight it. You deserve this.

There's champagne to your left, and caviar to your right, and when you get to the airport, there'll be a surprise waiting for you.

Be prepared to get naked.

I'll see you soon.

All my love,

Liam x

A naked surprise at the airport, huh? Oh, please let it be him. Traveling together would be so much better than being stuck on a plane by myself.

I take two big mouthfuls of champagne before leaning back into the plush leather seat.

Well, I guess this is it. Let the adventure begin.

• • •

A moan vibrates in my throat, and I'm ashamed I'm unable to stop it.

"God," I say, my voice hoarse with pleasure. "So good."

"You're so tight," a husky voice says from above. "Let me know if I hurt you."

I exhale and try to relax. "It hurts, but it feels good. Don't stop. Please."

"As you wish, ma'am."

The large female masseuse digs her thumbs into the base of my spine, and I moan again. I've never had a massage before. Well, not by a professional, anyway. Liam massages me all the time, but he never gets far before he feels the need to massage places he can't reach with his hands.

When we reached the airport, JT handed me another note directing me to go to the first class lounge. I fully expected to find

Liam here, gorgeous and smug. Instead, I found Jane. Right now, I'm not sure who I love more. Jane and her magical hands are the bomb. She goes to town on my shoulders and neck, and I'm so blissed out I nearly lose consciousness.

Over the next two hours, she works on my entire body, even my hands and feet. When she's done, another woman enters the dimly lit treatment room to give me a manicure and pedicure, while a third lady carries out a facial. Then, just when I think I can't get any more relaxed, I'm rudely brought back to reality by a small Chinese woman who gives me a full leg wax and a *very* thorough Brazilian.

Despite the pain, I'm glad everything is neat and tidy for my time with Liam. There's nothing like being completely hairless to make a girl feel like rubbing herself all over her man.

When my flight is called, I'm so high on endorphins, I feel drunk. Maybe that's why I walk out of the lounge straight into the path of a poor, unsuspecting man striding past the doorway. I squeal as we collide, and even though he drops his backpack in an effort to keep us upright, when it becomes clear gravity intends to make us her bitch, he gallantly twists, so he takes the brunt of the impact.

He grunts as his back hits the floor, and half a second later I fall heavily onto his abdomen and somehow manage to jerk my knee into his groin.

"Fuck me!" He turns onto his side and cups his man parts. "Oh, fuuuuck meeeee."

"I'm sorry!" I scramble off him and pat his shoulder in sympathy. "I didn't mean to. I'm so sorry."

He pushes out a tight breath between his teeth. "S'okay. I'm fine." He grunts again and rolls to the other side. "I didn't want to have children anyway. I hear they're overrated. Messy. Loud. Very expensive."

He curls up into a sitting position, and once he catches his breath, he holds out his hand. "I'm Scott, by the way. And I assume you're a hurricane in human form."

I shake his hand and laugh. "That's me. But you can call me Elissa."

"Painful to meet you, Elissa."

He squeezes my hand, and I'm little uncomfortable with how openly he's flirting. Doesn't he know I'm with the world's most amazing man and therefore have no need to flirt ever again?

Oblivious to my indifference, he keeps a hold of my hand as he stands and helps me up. After I get my purse and he grabs his backpack, we turn back to each other.

"So, where are you jetting off to, Hurricane Elissa? Some unsuspecting island nation that won't recover for months?"

"Uh, good question. I'm not exactly sure. I'm flying to Brazil, but after that, I have no clue. My travel plans are a better guarded secret than Area 51."

"So, either you really trust your travel agent, or someone made the travel arrangements for you."

"That second thing. My fiancée, actually."

He grips his chest. "Oh. Ouch. And here I was thinking I had a really cool story to tell our future children about how I met their mother."

I give him a sympathetic smile. "Sorry."

"It's okay," he says with a shrug. "I'm used to all the cool women who knock me over in airport being unavailable. Story of my life." He drops his head and smiles. "I'm also headed to Brazil. I'd say I'll see you on the plane, but ..." he points to the first class lounge, "seems like your fiancée has you with the cool kids at the front of the bus. I'll be slumming it at the back." He gives me a wry smile. "Anyway, I'd better go. I have some cheap alcohol to stock up on before we leave. Maybe I'll see you on the other side."

"Yeah. Maybe."

"Goodbye, Hurricane Elissa. Happy travels to you." He holds out his hand again, and I shake it.

"Bye, Scott. It was nice meeting you."

With a wave, he strides off in the direction of the duty-free stores, and I saunter toward the departure gate.

FIVE

HE SEES YOU WHEN YOU'RE SLEEPING

It's a truth universally acknowledged that once you fly first class, you're forever ruined for any other type of travel. This was my first experience sitting at the front of the plane, and I couldn't believe that during my ten-hour flight I feasted on gourmet food, slept in a bed complete with designer sheets, and even had a shower. All while soaring thousands of feet above the earth.

Incredible.

When I book flights for myself, I always travel economy, because I can't justify the outrageous expense of business or first class. Of course, Liam has no such qualms. No wonder he always looks happy and refreshed after he travels.

When I get off the plane, I briefly see Scott in the immigration line looking exhausted and more than a little miserable. Ah, the curse of economy. He gives me a solemn wave as I pass, and I wave back. Then I lose sight of him.

After collecting my luggage and heading through customs, I find a good-looking silver-haired man in a collared shirt and slacks holding a sign that reads, "Miss Elissa Holt."

"Hello?"

His face lights up. "Miss Holt! Hello. You're even more beautiful than the picture Mr. Quinn sent. My name is Luis. Please, let me take your suitcase."

He takes control of my luggage and leads me outside to where a slick town car is waiting.

"Luis, how long until we get to our destination?"

"Oh, not long, if the wind is kind to us."

"Wind?"

He nods sagely.

"Don't suppose you can tell me anything about where we're going?"

"I'm afraid not. Mr. Quinn was specific about it being a surprise."

I sigh and close my eyes. "I hate surprises."

• • •

Okay, so, I have to admit, this surprise is pretty awesome.

For the first time in my life, I'm in a helicopter, and it's amazing! Luis turns out to be a pilot, and he gives me a running commentary on the region and its people as he flies us along the Brazilian coast.

After a while, we head out to sea, and he points to an island in the distance. "That's where we're going."

"The island?"

He nods.

The green shape gets bigger as we approach, and when we're right over it, I press my head against the window to get a better look.

Either I'm crazy, or that island vaguely resembles a love heart.

In the center, there seems to be a large lake, and around the edges are pristine, white beaches.

"It's beautiful."

Luis nods. "Mr. Quinn thought you would like it."

"Is there a resort down there? I can't see it." I can just imagine sitting out by a pool while a bronzed Brazilian waitress brings me a drink with an umbrella and half a pineapple poking out of the top.

"No," Luis says. "Apart from my wife and I who take care of Mr. Quinn's house, the island is completely uninhabited."

I turn to Luis. "Liam owns a house there?"

"Well, yes, but only because it came with the island."

I stop breathing as his words sink in. "Luis ... are you telling me that Liam—" God, this is too bizarre to even say. "Liam bought an *island*?"

Yep, sounds just as ridiculous as I thought it would.

Apparently Luis doesn't think so, because he gives me a warm smile. "He bought it a couple of months ago. For you. He calls it *Bliss*."

My lungs tighten. "Let me get this straight. Liam bought an island."

"Yes."

"For me."

"Yes."

"And he called it Bliss?"

"Yes."

A shrill giggle bubbles out of me.

Sweet Holy Mother. Most girls are lucky if they get dinner and a show. My man bought me a baby continent.

I giggle again and realize there's a strong possibility I'm losing my grip on reality.

"He must love you very much," Luis says as he banks the helicopter down toward the island.

My island.

Feeling like my insides are going to explode, I say, "Yeah."

Luis takes us down over a wide grassy area before expertly landing on a bright yellow helipad.

I know I should be asking more questions about Brazil, but I'm still caught up in the whole, 'My fiancée's idea of a grand romantic gesture is purchasing an entire land mass.'

Despite his protests, I help Luis load my luggage into a waiting SUV, and then we're hurtling through the underbrush of a tropical rainforest.

After a while, we come to a clearing where a neat white cottage sits. "This is where Alma and I stay," Louis says. "If you need anything at all, you call us. We're available twenty-four hours a day."

"Okay." Sure. My island. My staff. Makes perfect sense.

A few hundred yards down the road, the jungle gives way to reveal one of the beaches I saw from the air. Above it sits a stunning contemporary mansion, seemingly built out of glass and stainless steel. It's so beautiful, it takes my breath away.

"It used to belong to a Sultan," Luis says. "He spared no expense in the construction."

"Why did he sell?"

A shadow crosses Luis's face. "He was a superstitious man. Claimed the house was cursed."

"Cursed?"

Luis shrugs. "Every time he stayed there, something bad happened. Personally, I think the man was a little crazy, but at least he sold it to Mr. Quinn for a bargain price."

"Did Liam know about the whole *cursed* issue?"

"Yes. But I'm sure you know that Mr. Quinn isn't afraid of such things."

True. Liam isn't afraid of much at all. Except clowns, which is totally justified. Clowns are the work of the devil.

"Ready to see your new home for the next few weeks?" Luis asks with a smile as we pull up near the giant front door.

"Sure," I say. My trip has been already so full of unbelievable experiences, might as well add another one to the list.

• • •

Jesus Harold Christ. You've got to be kidding me.

"*Senhorita?*"

When I was growing up, I'd often flick through Mom's copies of *Home Beautiful*. Every time I read the features on the homes of the rich and famous, I couldn't believe the amount of opulence with which some people lived.

"*Senhorita* Holt?"

Every one of those millionaire playgrounds looked like fixer-uppers compared to this place, with its open plan layout and floating wooden staircases. The entire front of the building is plate glass to make the most of the stunning ocean views. The decor is contemporary but comfortable, and it feels so familiar, I wonder if I've seen pictures of it before.

"*Senhorita.*" A warm hand touches my arm, and I turn to see Luis's wife, Alba. She was waiting when we entered the house, and is now staring at me in concern. "You've been standing still for a while. Are you all right?"

I nod. "Sorry, Alba. Just trying to take everything in."

"You like the house?"

"Very much."

"Mr. Quinn thought you would. I can give you a tour if you'd like."

"Sure."

Over the next fifteen minutes, Alba shows me through the house as she highlights all of the features, including a state-of-the-art entertainment system, the well-stocked library, a massive sandstone balcony, complete with pool, and a gourmet kitchen that would make my mother scream in delight.

When she shows me upstairs into the main bedroom, I'm speechless. In the middle of the room is the largest four post bed I've ever seen, but unlike the heavy wooden versions I'm used to, this one is made of laser cut metal, so the posts look as though they're made of shiny 3-D lace. It's beyond beautiful.

"Wow."

Luis brings in my luggage and sets it by the foot of the bed. "Would you like us to unpack for you, Miss Holt?"

"Uh, no. That's fine, Luis. I can do it myself." The mere thought of anyone seeing the sheer volume of lingerie in my suitcase gives me cold sweats. They'd think I was some sort of sex maniac. I mean, it's true in regards to Liam, but no one needs to know that.

"If there's nothing else you need," Luis says, "we'll leave you to relax."

I go to give them both a cash tip, but Alba waves me away. "No need, Senhorita. Mr. Liam has taken care of everything."

"So it seems. Do you know when he might be arriving?"

They share a look. Then Luis pulls an envelope from his jacket and hands it to me. "Perhaps this will explain."

They both smile before taking their leave. When they're gone, I open the letter.

Darling Liss,

By now I'm sure you've already had a tour of the house and island. I hope you like it. When I think that we're going to be alone together with no one pointing, staring, or taking our picture for a whole month, I get stupidly excited. Total and absolute privacy is the only gift I want this Christmas. Screw the usual presents. Being with you is all I need. I hope it's okay that I've organized to have my gift a little early.

If everything goes to plan, I'll arrive on the island just before dinner tonight. So relax, have lunch, get Luis to show you the waterfall and have a swim. I'll be there soon, and goddammit, sweetheart, I can't wait to see you.

All my love,

Liam x

PS. Did you see the size of that bed?

Oh, the things I'm going to do to you on that thing.

I smile and flop back onto the feather-soft duvet. He'll be here soon. Thank God. The wait is almost over.

• • •

After having a shower to freshen up, I slip into one of the new bikinis I bought especially for the trip. Even though I could count on one hand the amount of times I've worn any sort of bathing suit, I'm surprised how comfortable this one feels, despite it being on the skimpy side.

I cover up with a floaty sarong tied around my neck before heading down to the main living area. Alba is in the giant kitchen, cooking something that smells delicious on the fancy glass cooktop.

"Perfect timing, Miss Elissa. Lunch is ready."

"You didn't have to do that, Alba."

"Oh, it was no trouble. Plus, Mr. Quinn didn't hire me just for my pretty face. I love to cook."

She turns off the stove and spoons a steaming dish of meat onto a waiting bed of rice. "This is called *feijoada*. It is popular in Brazil and my husband's favorite."

I perch on one of the stools that sit along the front of the massive marble island as Alba places the plate in front of me.

"It smells fantastic."

She smiles before turning away to clean up.

Turns out, it tastes even better than it looks, and I try to act like a lady while I shovel it into my mouth. I don't think I fool Alba for a second, and she gives me a warm smile as she washes the dirty pan.

"Will you go to the beach after lunch? It's a beautiful day."

"Actually, Liam said I should check out the waterfall. Is it far?"

The pan slips from Alba's hands and hits the edge of the sink with a loud bang. When she looks over at me, she looks a little pale. "No. It isn't far. Luis can take you."

"Oh, I'm sure I can find it by myself if you point me in the right direction."

She picks up the pan and continues to wash it. "You should not go by yourself. There are wild creatures on the island. Best to have someone with you."

Wild creatures? What, like lions? And tigers? And bears? Oh, my ...

When Luis walks in, Alba has a hushed conversation with him in Portuguese. Whatever she says, Luis seems to reassure her. Then she smiles at him before coming over to collect my empty plate.

"Thank you, Alba."

"You're welcome, Miss Elissa."

"So," Luis says as he leans against the bench. "Alba tells me you'd like to see the waterfall."

"Yes, as long as that's okay. If you've got something else to do, I could—"

Luis raises his hand to cut me off. "My only concern is taking care of you, Miss Holt. Would you like to go now?"

"Sure."

Before we can leave, Alba takes a canvas beach bag from a nearby closet and hands it to me. "This contains a towel, hat, sunscreen, and bug repellent. The bug repellent is most important. Many mosquitoes in the rain forest."

I take it from her and give her a smile. "Thanks, Mom."

She laughs as Luis and I head out the door to the waiting jeep.

• • •

Dense foliage whips by on both sides of the jeep as Luis speeds through the forest. Heeding Alba's warning, I concentrate on rubbing thick bug repellent all over myself.

"Is there something wrong with the waterfall?" I ask.

He looks confused. "No. Why?"

"I just got the impression Alba didn't want me going there."

He chuckles. "My lovely wife listens to too many ghost stories, and she believes the waterfall is cursed."

"A cursed house *and* a cursed waterfall? Wow. No wonder Liam got this place for a song."

Luis laughs again. "Well, if you believe my wife, the waterfall is the source of the evil spirits who haunt the house. You see, this island has not always been so idyllic. Many years ago, it was the home of a particularly brutal tribe who believed their god would only keep them safe if they offered human sacrifices. There's a large stone altar near the waterfall, and legends tell us that was where the sacrifices took place."

"You don't believe it?"

"Oh, I do. When the Sultan bought the island, they cleared nearly a hundred sets of human remains from the area. I just don't believe that means it's cursed. But then again, my wife has a far better imagination than I. When workers were building the Sultan's mansion, they claim to have seen something in the jungle they called, *Espírito Vingativo,* or The Vengeful Spirit. They swore it sabotaged them on several occasions by moving their work tools or interfering with machinery." He gives me a quick glance. "Do you believe in these superstitions, Miss Holt?"

I shrug. "Not really. The only superstition I believe in is something called the ghostlight. You see, in most theaters, the stage managers leave a tall lamp in the middle of the stage when everyone goes home for the night. Some people think it's just for safety to stop people crossing a pitch black stage and plummeting into the orchestra pit. But a lot of theater folk believe that theaters are haunted, and the ghostlight allows the spirits to perform while no one is there. They think if the ghosts are happy, they won't cause accidents in the theater."

"Do you think that's true?"

"To be honest, I'm not sure. But I still put a ghostlight on every night when I'm running a show. Better to be safe than sorry, right?"

He smiles. "Right."

We turn off the road and head down a dirt track, and it's not long before I hear the sound of running water. As the car emerges from the forest canopy, I get my first look at the sapphire-blue lake I saw from the air.

"Wow. It's gorgeous."

Luis pulls the car over and cuts the engine. "Yes, it's a beautiful spot."

In front of us is a white beach, and on the opposite side of the circular lake is a tall, basalt cliff, over which is spilling a stunning waterfall. The lake is crystal clear, and I can't wait to see if it feels as good as it looks.

Luis leads me down to where a luxurious 'beach hut' sits by the water. By this point, I'm completely unsurprised to discover it's the size of a small house.

"There are drinks and snacks in the fridge here," he says as he opens the French doors to a spacious living area. "And also a full bathroom with spa. If you need me, just lift the handset over there and press the button. It will come straight to my phone."

"Thank you, Luis." I look around at the dark border of forest that surrounds the lake. "Alba said there were dangerous creatures here. Is that true?"

Luis shakes his head. "Not to my knowledge, and I've covered every square inch of this island over the past few months. There are some monkeys, the odd pygmy boar, and a whole bunch of reptiles, but nothing that should give you any trouble. Most of them will run a mile if they see you."

"Okay, cool. Just as long as there are no Elissa-eating jaguars or anything."

"Oh, there were a few of those," he says with a smile. "But I made sure to banish them before you arrived. You'll be perfectly safe." He points to the hut's phone. "When you get bored, just buzz me and I'll come pick you up."

"Will do."

He waves before jumping into the jeep and driving away.

I have a quick snoop around the hut, and after uncapping an ice-cold cola, I discover a small library of books.

"Excellent."

I grab a random book and take my drink and bag out to the beach. The heat of the sun isn't too bad, so I ditch my sarong, spread out my towel, and make myself comfortable.

Sitting in the sun is a bizarre experience for someone who spends most of her time in the dark. Even though I'm a semi-vampiric New Yorker, I could get used to this.

I'm five chapters into a terrible book about a zombie apocalypse when I hear a noise behind me in the trees. When I turn to find out what made it, I see a clutch of long-limbed monkeys studying me from high in the canopy.

"Hey, guys. Wassup?" They blink at me. God, they're cute. "FYI, avoid this book. It's terrible. Don't get me wrong, I'm going to totally keep reading it, but get ready for some ranting, okay? The author has zero clue about how to fight zombies. Total idiot."

More wide-eyed blinking.

"Okay, good talk. I'm going to have a swim now. Watch my stuff for me, alright?"

I drop my book and walk down to the water. Without thinking too much, I run and dive in. The cool temperature is a shock to the system after the warm sun, but at least it's refreshing. Feeling energized, I swim out into the center of the lake. Even out here, the water is so clear, I can see fish below me, as well as crabs and rocks on the sandy bottom.

In awe of the incredible location, I lie back and float for a while, enjoying my first real tropical experience. I'm just bummed I'm not sharing it with Liam. I pray the time passes quickly until he arrives.

After a few minutes of floating, the sound of the waterfall lulls me into dozing, and I close my eyes as all my limbs relax.

Balancing on the edge of consciousness, I lose track of time. When I open my eyes again, the sun is lower in the sky and has been dulled by a bank of dark clouds on the horizon.

"Okay, that doesn't look good."

I swim back to the beach and grab my towel. As I'm drying myself, I see that the monkeys are still in their spot, staring at me. I also notice my book and drink are missing.

"Alright, who's the thief?" I wrap my towel around my chest and head toward them. "I asked you to watch my stuff, and you steal it. Not cool, guys." They watch warily as I approach. "You can keep the drink, but how about you give back the book? I have to see how that train wreck ends, okay?"

Looking up at them, I can't see any evidence of my stuff. Maybe they dropped it.

I scour the ground before going farther into the forest to see if it's in the undergrowth. I've only gone a few yards when I see a break in the trees. It's a clearing, and smack bang in the middle is a huge piece of rectangular stone.

"Oh, wow. Could that be the creepy death altar? I think so."

I walk over to examine it. The top is smooth, almost glassy, and there's an indentation leading off one side.

"Probably to drain all the blood," I whisper to myself like a total creeper. I've always been fascinated with the macabre. Guess that's what comes from reading a crapload of Stephen King and Dean Koontz while I was growing up.

I run my hand over the surface. It's cold, but the temperature isn't what makes me shiver. I'm tracing my fingers over the blood channel when I hear a noise over to my right. I look up into the trees to see if my friendly neighborhood spider monkeys have followed me, but the canopy is empty. Then, I hear the noise again and realize it's not coming from above.

My breath catches in my throat when I catch a glimpse of what seems to be a figure standing there, watching me, half obscured by a tree.

"Luis?"

There's only the outline of a head, but even in the dim light I know it's not Luis.

The hairs on the back of my neck stand on end. "Whoever you are, I'm warning you, I've been trained to kill a man with my bare hands." Well, I've been trained to punch a man in the balls with deadly force, at least. Liam didn't get to the part where he transformed me into a walking weapon.

There's a hooting sound right above my head, and I glance up to see the monkeys also staring toward the mysterious figure. When I glance back, there's nothing there.

"Lost tourist?" I whisper to myself. "Or vengeful spirit?" Okay, that's too scary to contemplate, even for me.

With a tight whimper, I take off toward the beach as fast as I can, which isn't terribly fast considering my main form of exercise is walking to the fridge to get cheese.

I'm pushing through the last patch of bushes on the edge of the beach when a strong hand grabs my arm.

I scream and turn to see Luis's concerned face. "Miss Holt? Are you all right?"

"Luis! Were you just over near the altar?"

"No. There's a storm on the way, so I thought I should come get you. Why?"

"Nothing. I thought I saw someone in the forest."

He looks to where I've come from and frowns. "Well, we're the only people on the island right now, so I doubt it." He turns back to me. "Perhaps we shouldn't mention this to Alba. If she thinks you saw *Espírito Vingativo*, I'd never hear the end of it." He pats my shoulder. "I'm sure you just saw a shadow. Sometimes the light plays tricks with our eyes in the jungle."

"Yeah, I guess."

As I go back to the beach and grab my towel and bag, there's a rumble of thunder from the dark clouds closing in on the island. "Sure. A shadow. That's all it was. No problem."

Except shadows don't disappear when they realize they've been seen.

• • •

By the time I finish up dinner, torrential rain is pelting the plate-glass windows as lightning carves up the sky.

"Maybe you should stay here tonight," I suggest as Alba cleans up. "You're going to get drenched if you try to go home in this."

"Oh, I'll be fine. My Luis will be here soon. He'll take good care of me."

We both jump when the back door bangs open, and Luis appears in head-to-toe rain gear. He looks like Captain Nemo if he'd still been on deck when the Nautilus submerged.

He slams the door behind him and stands in the back hallway, dripping onto the tiles. "Okay, so ... it's raining."

Alma laughs. "Really? We hadn't noticed. I'm almost ready to go."

"Actually, I came early to give Miss Holt some bad news." He looks at me with a regretful expression. "I was meant to pick up Mr. Quinn from the mainland an hour ago, but because of this weather, the helicopter is grounded until it passes. I'm sorry."

My heart sinks. "Have you spoken to Liam?"

"No. I tried to call, but I can't get through. As soon as the storm dies down, I'll try again. It seems we won't be able to collect him until tomorrow."

I sigh. Of course this would happen. We haven't seen each other for a quarter of a year, so it's not like I'm dying of anticipation or anything.

Goddammit.

I take a giant mouthful of wine and swallow, hard. "It's not your fault, Luis. Thanks for letting me know."

"No problem. If I find out more, I'll call you."

"Thanks."

I feel deflated. I thought I'd finally be going to bed wrapped around my gorgeous man, but it seems I'm soloing it, yet again. God, I'm so tired of sleeping alone.

After Alba and Luis leave, I grab my wine, head upstairs, and go into the obscenely large bathroom to run myself a bath. Might as well make the most of my alone time. I dig through the cabinets to find bath salts and candles, and when the tub is full, I strip off and sink beneath the bubbles. It feels so good, I moan.

As the warm water relaxes my muscles, I close my eyes and listen to the storm raging outside. Knowing my luck, this stupid weather will set in for days, leaving Liam stranded on the mainland for God knows how long.

I wish I could talk to him. He'll be just as disappointed about this as I am. Maybe more. After all, I haven't been the one filming in a frozen wasteland for months. I'm sure he's more than ready for a solid dose of sunshine.

Hearing the wind howl outside, I fear the sun may never shine again.

I'm on the verge of dozing off when there's an extra bright flash of lightning, followed by a deafening crack of thunder. Three seconds later, the lights go out.

"You have to be freaking kidding me!"

With a grunt of frustration, I swallow the rest of my wine and climb out of the tub. This is ridiculous.

Moving carefully by candlelight, I pull on one of the fluffy, white bathrobes hanging on the wall and proceed to brush my teeth so roughly, my gums bleed. Feeling sorry for myself, I take a candle, go back into the bedroom, and climb into bed.

As I sink into the luxurious mattress, I feel like I'm surrounded by emptiness. A giant empty house. A huge empty bed. Empty arms where Liam should be.

I sigh and close my eyes, and I'm horrified when the words from Annie start echoing in my brain:

The sun'll come out ... tomorrow. Bet your bottom dollar that tomorrow, there'll be sun.

Stuff it, you perky ginger.

SIX

HE KNOWS WHEN YOU'RE AWAKE

I don't sleep well. Nightmares about being held down on a stone altar while *Espírito Vingativo* prepares to sacrifice me to the gods make me toss and turn for hours. The weather doesn't help. Even though the intensity of the storm lessens, the wind continues to howl around the house, making it sound like the island is screaming.

I don't know what time it is when I stagger to the bathroom, but the power is still out and the candles have burned down, so I try not to bump into anything in the darkness.

When I'm done, I head back into the bedroom. Just before I climb back into bed, there's movement out the corner of my eye, and as I turn, I see the outline of a man standing right in front of me.

"Jesus Christ!"

As soon as I open my mouth to scream, the shadow lunges forward and grabs me. My back hits the wall as a huge, wet hand closes over my mouth.

On instinct, I thrash against him, trying to get free, but he's tall and strong, and when he lays his weight against me, I can barely move.

"Hey, calm down. It's me. Shhh. It's just me."

His voice sends goosebumps up my spine the same instant the

lightning flashes to give me a better look at his face.

As recognition hits my brain, he lets me go and stands back. "Sorry for the scare. Didn't realize the power was out."

"Oh, my God, Liam!" I throw my arms around his neck, and he pulls me into a tight hug. His hair is down to his shoulders and soaked, and I feel the roughness of his beard as he presses his face into my neck.

"How did you get here?" I ask. "I thought you were stranded until the storm passed."

He tightens his grip and says, "If you think a little bad weather is going to keep me from my woman, then you're underestimating my desperate, pathological need for you."

I notice he's dripping onto the floor. "Wait, did you swim here?"

He chuckles. "Are you kidding? Even ducks are drowning out there right now." He strokes my back. "I might be desperate, but I'm not suicidal."

"Then how?"

"It's a long story, but just in case the Brazilian police come calling tomorrow to track down some crazy American who commandeered a luxury yacht, you know nothing." He pulls back and looks at me. "I can't believe I'm here with you. Jesus, Liss. I can't ..." He shakes his head. "You don't even know how I'm feeling right now. I've missed you so fucking much."

He leans down and cautiously presses his lips against mine. I inhale as a jolt of electricity hits me that's more powerful than all of the lightning outside. While we were apart, I thought I remembered how intense our chemistry was. How being with him lit napalm beneath my skin. I was wrong. Whatever thigh-tingling memories I had of how Liam Quinn affects me were a pale, sad imitation of the explosive, knee-buckling reality.

With a sharp inhale, he changes the angle of his mouth and sucks gently on my lips, first the top, then the bottom. Lord, how he tastes and smells. Perfect.

At first he's hesitant, like he doesn't remember how to kiss me. I don't blame him. It's been so long, I'm not sure I remember, either. But our instincts return quickly, and when that happens, our mouths open and tongues slide until we devolve into a mess of grasping hands and primal, desperate noises.

I try to feel him all at once. Reclaim the body I've been craving. He seems to do the same as he moves his hands into my hair and grinds against my stomach. The shape and feel of him is both brand new and completely familiar. Even though his wild hair and lumberjack beard are different, for the first time in months I feel whole. His lips are as intoxicating as they've always been, and the soft but insistent sweep of his tongue has me clawing for more.

"Your beard feels weird," I say as I pull back, breathless and dizzy.

"Yeah?" He looks down and tugs on the tie that's keeping my robe closed. "Good weird or bad weird?" He pushes open the robe and grazes his hands over my naked waist.

I suck in a breath and scrape my nails through his facial hair. "I'm not sure. Better kiss me again so I can decide."

This time when he kisses me, there's no hesitation. It's full on, one-hundred-percent turbo-charged Liam. He shoves my robe off my shoulders with rough hands and sets my body on fire with his fingers while his mouth throws gasoline on the flames.

I'm unprepared to feel so much so soon and grip his shoulders in an attempt to stay upright. My system goes into overload. It's gotten used to being bored and safe, not aroused so thoroughly I have real concerns I might pass out.

"So you like the island?" Liam asks as he charts a path of hot kisses down my neck toward my chest.

"It's amazing." When he cups my breasts, I have to lean against the wall for support.

"And the house?" He falls to his knees and kisses the side of my breast, then the top, then the nipple.

I squeeze my eyes closed and grip his broad shoulders. "Yeah, it's ... good."

He stops circling his tongue around my nipple and makes a noise. When I open my eyes, I find him staring up at me with a perplexed expression. "That's it? I search the world to find you the perfect island with the perfect house, and all you have to say about it is 'it's good'?"

I tighten my fingers on his shoulders. "Liam, I'm so turned on right now I'm flat out defying gravity, so maybe we can have a conversation about my vocabulary when I'm more lucid. For example, after you make me come."

"Then this conversation is never happening, because I'm going to spend the next four weeks making you come."

"Big talk."

"Don't think I'm serious?"

"I've yet to see the evidence."

"Fine. Prepare to have your mind blown. Then you can tell me how 'good' it is."

He closes his mouth over my nipple, and the wave of pleasure that hits me is so strong, I cry out. Not content with teasing one breast, he uses his hand on the other, and the effect is just as powerful.

"God, I've missed you girls," he mutters to my chest. "I'm pretty sure you've missed me, too."

My eyes have adjusted enough to see him in the dim light. I'm not going to lie, his perfect face framed by all that hair is freaking sexy. I push my hands into it and urge him to go lower.

He looks up and arches a brow. "Liss, if you want me to put my mouth on a certain part of your body, all you have to do is ask." He grazes his hands up the backs of my thighs until he reaches my ass, then squeezes as he lays open-mouthed kisses across my stomach. "Or if you're desperate, you could beg. That'd work, too."

I'm so high on pleasure and expectation, I'm having trouble getting enough air. It doesn't help when he nibbles on my hip.

I swear and press my head back into the wall.

"Liss?" He rolls a nipple between his thumb and forefinger. "Don't you have anything to say?"

"I..." I suck in enough breath to speak. "I'd just like to remind you that ... there's more to me than just my breasts."

"Oh, I'm aware. Believe me." He kisses the top of my thigh and traces one finger down from my belly button to where I'm aching so fiercely, it borders on pain. "As much as I adore your breasts, what I've been craving to taste lies a little farther south."

He grabs my left leg and pushes it over his shoulder, then closes his eyes and nuzzles me.

"Oh, God. Please, Liam. Please, please, *please*."

"Very nice begging. I approve." He puts his lips right against me and whispers, "Now be quiet and let me concentrate, because I aim to enjoy this."

Swollen and desperate, I'm nearly vibrating with anticipation when he unexpectedly lifts me up the wall. I squeal and grip his hair as he draws up to his full height, positioning my thighs over his shoulders.

"I've got you," he reassures me with a mischievous grin. "But if you feel the need to keep tugging on my hair like that, I won't complain."

Before I can process that he's somehow gotten sexier since I last saw him, he pushes his face between my thighs and finally lets me experience the full force of his magic mouth.

"Oh, sweet Jesus! Liaaaaam!"

He lifts and maneuvers me until I'm exactly where he wants me, before using his mouth to take control of my body like he was born to do it. Within minutes, he has me so wound up I'm on the verge of hyperventilation.

"Please," tumbles from my lips with embarrassing frequency as he drags me to the edge of my first orgasm in months.

"A little needy there, Liss?"

I groan and push against the wall to try and get his mouth back on me. "Liam ... please."

"Please, what?"

I'm so desperate for release, I let out a noise that's half laughter, half sob. "Please, don't stop."

He grips my waist with both hands before pulling me away from the wall and striding over to the giant bed. When he gets there, he throws me into the center of it like I weigh nothing.

After removing his t-shirt and throwing it on the floor, he gives me a dark smile. "If you think I have any intention of stopping before I give you the orgasm of your life, then you've forgotten who the fuck you're engaged to."

A sense of primal urgency quickens his movements as he

pulls off his shoes and socks and tosses them away. When he's barefoot in his jeans, he stops for a moment to stare hungrily at my nakedness. "Christ, you're beautiful. Now lay back, my darling wife-to-be, and spread your legs. I have work to finish."

Moving with determination, his chest and arms ripple when he grabs my ankles and drags me to the edge of the bed. Then he sinks to his knees and closes his hands around my hips before covering my inner thighs with hot, hungry kisses. Dizzy and helpless, I grip the duvet cover and try to keep breathing.

This time he takes it slower, but the build is even more powerful. He kisses me everywhere and nowhere, using light nibbles to drive me insane. It doesn't take long for him to have possession of every nerve. He's like a master fisherman, reeling in a giant Marlin a little at a time, pulling the line as tight as he can without breaking it.

When his mouth finally closes over me again, I'm so needy I nearly sob with relief. This time, I know he's not going to stop. He builds momentum like a boulder rolling down a mountain, increasing his suction as he slowly pushes long fingers inside.

God, it's too much. Too full. Too many layers of pleasure. I grip his hair and feel the low pulses of my orgasm begin to fire. All of my limbs tense, rigid with impatience, and I teeter there, paralyzed while my lungs seize in my chest.

"Liam ... Liam ... *Liam*." I say his name in ecstasy over and over again, and just when I think it's been so long since I've orgasmed that I've forgotten how, everything snaps and unwinds with such power, a strangled moan pours out of me.

For long, pleasure-filled seconds, my orgasm hits me in waves, and when it finally fades, I feel like I've melted into the plush mattress.

"Jesus, I've missed that." Liam sinks onto the bed beside me and strokes my hair away from my face as I try to regain my breath. Minutes later, my semi-lucid brain registers him scooping me up. When he lays me gently beneath the covers, I slip further into unconsciousness. He slides in beside me and presses his long, warm body against mine.

Instinctively, I curl into him, and he puts his arm around me and pulls me into his chest.

"Liam ... I—" I'm interrupted by a yawn that won't be denied.

I can feel him smile against my temple as he strokes my hair. "Sleep, Liss. We can do all of this again tomorrow, I promise. We're together now. That's all that matters."

I want to tell him I don't need sleep. That I want to pleasure him as much as he just did me, but the comfort of being wrapped in his arms is too intoxicating. Against my will, I succumb to the slow, steady drag of sleep.

As I drift off, I smile when a low groan of contentment rumbles in Liam's chest.

• • •

By the time I open my eyes, the storm has passed and the sun has come out of hiding.

What do you know? Annie was right.

I have to blink a few times to make sure I'm awake when I identify the warm piece of man-meat wrapped around me. He's here. Despite everything conspiring to keep us apart, we're finally together. With that knowledge, I smile so wide, my cheeks hurt.

We're facing each other with his arm beneath my head, legs tangled together. I can't describe how wonderful it feels to finally wake up next to the man I love. As for Liam, he still looks completely out of it. His eyes are moving beneath his eyelids, and his breath comes in short, shallow gusts.

I push myself up onto my elbow to get a better look at him. Even with his new Grizzly Adams makeover he's the most handsome man I've ever seen, but I also notice the dark circles under his eyes and the paleness of his skin. After his insane shooting schedule and having to fight through the storm, I can only imagine how exhausted he is.

I look down at his body and see a few bruises and some nasty scratches. I know by now they're a result of him insisting on doing most of his own stunts, and I'm as unhappy about that as his insurance company. But the one thing I know about Liam is that when he makes up his mind, there's little anyone can to do change it. His determination is just one of the many things I love about him.

"Noooo. No peas." He frowns and pouts. "Noooo, Ma, donwanem." I smile as he mumbles something unintelligible before flopping onto his back.

How he can be completely adorable and sexy as sin at the same time is beyond me.

I use his lack of consciousness to my advantage and carefully climb out of bed to go shower and brush my teeth. It's probably stupid to want to make a good early-morning impression considering where we are in our relationship, but I don't care. I want to smell awesome for him.

When I'm feeling fresh as a daisy, I wrap myself in a robe and climb back into bed to watch him sleep. As I study him, I wonder if it's normal to be this fascinated by one man. To be fair, he's no ordinary man. Even unconscious, Liam Quinn is strangely compelling to watch.

After a while, he starts mumbling again before throwing off the covers to reveal he's naked except for his navy boxer briefs.

Well, hellooooo, Mr. Quinn.

The dark fabric hugs every aroused inch of him, and when he starts to make noises that sound suspiciously porny, my resolve to let him sleep dissolves.

"As if any other woman would have lasted this long," I whisper to myself. "I mean, for the love of God, look at him."

I lean over and lift the waistband of his underwear. If I can just get them down without waking him, I can surprise him with a little good morning oral.

I hold my breath as I peel the boxers far enough down his hips to fully reveal his erection. Then I take a few moments to marvel at the glory of my future husband.

I'm about to run a finger down his length when a hand snaps out and grabs my wrist.

"And what the hell do you think you're doing, Miss Holt?"

I look over to find him assessing me with bleary eyes."Ahhhh, nothing. Just saying good morning."

"To my cock?"

"Well, he was awake, and you weren't. It would have been rude to ignore him."

"Of course he was awake. I was dreaming about you." He tucks himself back into his underwear. "Better stay back. You have no idea how close he was to exploding in your face. You could have been killed."

I raise an eyebrow. "Killed?"

"Well, okay, maybe not killed, but if he'd gone off in your eye, it would have stung like hell. Believe me, I know."

"Oh, really?" I suppress a smile. "You've friendly fired yourself in the face?"

He turns onto his side and props his head on his hand. "Of course. Most men have. It's not like that stuff always comes out at the same velocity. Sometimes it's like opening a warm champagne, and sometimes it's like that science experiment where you drop Mentos into a bottle of Pepsi, and the whole thing explodes in a huge geyser of stickiness."

I laugh and stroke his face. "You should trademark that name."

"Huge Geyser of Stickiness?"

"Yeah, just in case you ever decide to make a porno."

"Is that so?" In a flash, he flips me onto my back and presses both my hands into the mattress. "And would you star in this porno with me?" He tries to act serious, but I can see his mouth quirk.

"Of course. My porn name is Horatio Sixty-Second."

He closes his eyes and moans, "Holy shit, baby. That's so fucking hot."

I manage to get my hands free long enough to push him off. He laughs as he rolls onto his side.

"Listen," I say, and slap his chest, "I'll have you know that name's scientifically formulated. It's my first pet plus the street where I grew up. When I was five, I had a regal goldfish called Horatio Swimsalot the Third, and I grew up on 62nd street, so there. The name is legit."

He puts his hands behind his head. "Well, by that logic, my porn name is Wigglebottom Washington."

I burst out laughing. "Oh, my God. That's so perfect for you. Wigglebottom!"

He sits up and scowls. "How dare you laugh. Mr. Wigglebottom was a dignified cat. It wasn't his fault my brother chose that stupid name."

"Oh, really? What did you want to call him? Thor? Hunter? Brick?"

"Don't be ridiculous. No one calls their cat Brick."

"Okay then. Tell me your preferred pussy name."

He stares up at the ceiling. "I wanted to call him Fluffypants."

I nearly bust a gut holding in my laughter.

He rolls his eyes. "Go on. Let it out. Don't want you getting cancer or anything."

"Fluffypants!" I fall forward and laugh my ass off.

"That would have been a kickass name!" he says, indignant. "But then Jamie won rock-paper-scissors, and the poor little dude was stuck with Wigglebottom. He was humiliated."

"How old were you guys when you named him? Five? Six?"

"Fifteen. Naming our pussies was serious business back then."

At this point, I have no idea if he's messing with me or not.

"Well, personally," I say, "I don't think you can go wrong with either Wigglebottom or Fluffypants for your porn name. They both describe you to a tee."

"Why you little—" He goes to grab me, but I twist out of reach just in time and dash down the stairs toward the living room, thinking I have the advantage indoors. However, despite Liam's size, he's goddamn fast and catches me around the waist just before I reach the kitchen.

I squeal when he hoists me over his shoulder. "Liam! Stoppit! Put me down."

"Nope. You need to be taught a lesson, young lady, and I aim to be the one to teach you."

I paddle on his back before reaching down to cup his ass as he strides toward the huge modular couch. "Well, I suppose there are worse things than being disciplined by Wigglebottom Washington."

"Right. That's it." He sits on the couch and spreads me across his lap with me lying on my stomach. "You have so many entries on the naughty list by now, I've lost count. Time to pay the piper, lady." He flips up my robe up to reveal my bare bottom and smacks me firmly on both cheeks until my skin starts to burn.

"Liam!" I giggle as he strokes the areas he just hit. "That tickles."

"You sound like you're enjoying this a little too much." He smacks me again, harder this time, three times each side. It stings like hell, but I kind of like it. Feeling the strength of him holding me down and the firm slap of his hand ... wow. Definitely hot.

He strokes my butt again. "Now, are you going to behave? Or do you want more?"

I'm silent for a moment then say, "More."

His hand freezes. "What?" He sounds genuinely surprised.

I clear my throat. "I said, more, please." I pause. "Master."

The bite of Liam's fingernails as they curl into my butt cheek lets me know he approves. "Liss, are you sure?" He sounds excited but nervous. Seems like we're on the same wavelength about that.

"Yes. More, please," I say firmly.

He lets out an uneven exhale. "Okay, you asked for it. Don't move."

He slaps each ass cheek in turn, successively applying more pressure. I'm surprised how each sting shoots pleasure right through to my spine. I close my eyes and moan as my skin starts to swell and burn.

I'd always had a vague fantasy about Liam spanking me, but now that it's happening, it's even more glorious than I imagined.

When he finishes, he rubs my bottom gently. Right now, I don't want gentle. I want his fingers inside me. Rough and insistent. Hitting my deepest places.

Instead, he lets out a rough breath. "Have you learned your lesson? Or do I need to continue?" His voice is strange. It has an edge I've never heard before.

I'd actually like him to continue doing other things.

"Lesson learned," I whisper as my pulse beats double time. "Thank you."

He lifts me until I'm sitting on his lap, and then he grips the back of my neck and pulls my head down to his mouth. "Thank you ...?" His lips brush my ear, making me shiver.

"Thank you, *master*."

He makes a low noise in his chest, and for a moment I think he's going to throw me down on the couch and fuck me after all. But his expression morphs into deep contemplation, and he stands abruptly to set me on my feet.

"Are you okay?" he asks. "Did I hurt you?"

"Yes," I say, a little embarrassed. "But only because I asked you to."

"Fuck. Okay." He nods and thinks for a few seconds before stepping away from me. "I'm ... ah ..." He looks down the hallway. "I need to take a shower."

"Liam—"

"Could you call Alba and ask her to bring over my clothes? I dropped my suitcase off on the way here last night. Everything was soaked."

"Sure, but I—"

"I won't be long."

"Okay."

He strides over to the stairs and takes them two at a time until he's out of sight.

More than a little confused, I go to the kitchen and call Alba. When I hang up, I sit on one of the stools, careful of my tender behind.

Well, that took an interesting turn.

Did it freak him out that I asked to be spanked? I mean, our sex is rarely gentle, but this was something we've never done before. Maybe it was too different.

I rub my eyes. I wouldn't blame him if he was freaked out. I am, too. Even though I consider myself pretty tough as far as injuries go, I never considered I might have a thing for pain. What the hell does that say about me?

• • •

After Luis and Alba deliver all of Liam's freshly laundered clothes, we all bustle about setting up for breakfast on the balcony beside the pool. Liam comes down to help, freshly showered and wearing bright red board shorts that sit deliciously low on his hips. I don't miss the way

Alba's eyes widen when she sees him shirtless.

She shoots me a quick glance, and I nod, as if to say, "I know right? How dare he be so hot?"

When the preparations are nearly done, I dash upstairs and pull on another of my new bikinis before topping it off with a sarong.

By the time I come back down, the large wooden table next to the pool has been set with sparkling silverware and fresh flowers, and Liam is lying on a sun chair with his eyes closed. His hair has been pulled up into a ponytail, which highlights his cheekbones like crazy. Even though it's still early, his body is already glistening with a thin layer of sweat. It only accentuates his muscles.

I make a mental note to rub sunscreen on him later. After all, somebody has to do it.

He cracks his eyes open as he hears me approach, and when he registers what I'm wearing, his brows furrow, and he sits up.

"Nice sarong." Despite his words, his tone suggests he thinks the sarong is an asshole. "Where did you get it? And why does it want to hurt me by hiding your hotness from my eyeballs?"

With a patient smile, I stand in front him and untie the knot around my neck. Then I strike a pose and hold the sarong open so Liam can see my bikini. This one is deep blue with gold highlights.

Liam takes in a breath then exhales as he tries to look everywhere at once. Even though he gives my whole body a thorough appraisal, his gaze keeps coming back to my chest.

"Okay," he says, still staring at my boobs. "So, that's you in a bikini. Don't let this go to your head, but this is possibly the best thing I've ever seen in my life."

I smile. "What about the view out here? The ocean, the cliff, the pristine beach below us? It's stunning."

At last he makes it up to my face. "Liss, there's not a single thing on this planet as stunning as you. How do you not know that by now?"

As usual, he melts me with his words, but there's something else in his expression, and I wonder if he's still bothered by what happened earlier.

I'm working up the courage to ask him when Alba calls out, "Breakfast!"

Liam sighs in disappointment when I refasten my sarong, and he takes my hand as we go sit at the table where Alba and Luis have set out omelets, fresh fruit, tea, and coffee.

We eat breakfast in relative silence, content to take in the view. When we're done, Liam leans back and rubs his completely flat stomach, as if there were something there other than ripped abs.

"So, Miss Holt, how adventurous are you feeling today?"

I dab my mouth with the linen napkin, still thinking about the glory of Alba's cheese omelet. "Hmm, depends. On a scale from 'using a different brand of dental floss' to 'swimming with sharks', how adventurous are we talking?"

"Adventurous enough to get your blood racing."

I put my hand on his thigh. "Being with you is enough to get my blood racing, Mr. Quinn." His posture stiffens as I slide my hand up toward his crotch. "So as long as you're with me, I can do anything."

He smiles. "Right answer."

SEVEN

HE KNOWS IF YOU'VE BEEN BAD OR GOOD

I squeeze my eyes shut and grip Liam's hands. "Okay, so, it turns out I can't do this."

"What happened to 'I'm up for anything as long as you're there?'"

"That was when I was high on cheese omelet and safe on the ground. Now I'm fifteen thousand feet above sea level and sure to die."

"That's not even a little true. We're only sixty feet up."

"I thought you loved me."

"I do."

"Then why are you trying to kill me?"

"Stop being so dramatic. Just open your eyes." I shake my head, but he kisses me softly and whispers, "You're perfectly safe, I promise."

I crack one eye open and grip his arms. *"Let's go for a hike,"* he said. *"I know a spot that's beautiful at this time of day,"* he said.

Yeah, well, after arriving at the lake, we hiked up the cliff for nearly an hour before reaching this spot. And sure it's gorgeous, but now he wants me to jump off the edge to my certain death? No thanks. I'm firmly on the NOPE train to Fuck-that-ville.

"How about you open the other eye, too?"

I sigh and open both eyes. I never thought I had an issue with heights before now, but looking down into the water, I feel a sick dread fill my stomach.

"We're not that high, Liss. And I've jumped from here before. The water's plenty deep enough. It's a total rush. I think you'd really enjoy it."

I look over to the beach where we've left all our stuff. What I wouldn't give to be lying there reading a terrible zombie book and talking to the local wildlife. The spider monkeys are there again today, looking like Disney characters come to life.

Liam moves behind me and wraps his arms around my waist. "Listen, if you really don't want to do it, that's fine. No pressure. We can walk back down. I just thought you might like a challenge."

The thing is, I usually do. I don't know why I'm so hesitant about trying this. Guess I've never really given the idea of cliff diving much thought beyond, *Wow, that's a thing that looks like fun, as long as I'm not the one doing it.*

"Okay," I say and take a deep breath. "I'll give it a try. But you have to go first."

He kisses my shoulder. "No problem." With his usual grace, he moves forward and points to a rocky outcrop. "When you're ready, stand right here on the edge and jump out, not up. There are no rocks down below, so you'll be fine." He comes back over and takes my hands. "Ready to see how it's done?"

"Sure. Show me your stuff, Quinn."

He gives me a mischievous smile, drops my hands, turns on his heel, and runs full speed toward the edge. When he gets there, he launches off like a superhero. I'm in awe when he completes a perfect swan dive and lands head first into the water.

I run over to the edge and look down just as he breaks the surface to wave to me.

"See?" he yells over the sound of the waterfall. "Nothing to it."

I scowl at him. "Show off!"

Curse his superhuman physical prowess. Now I'm going to look like an uncoordinated fool in comparison. Ugh.

I walk over to the outcrop and take a deep breath.

Okay, Elissa, you can do this. Stay calm, jump out, and try not to flail like a skydiving octopus on the way down. Easy.

When I take a last look at Liam, he smiles at me in encouragement.

Okay, here I go. I'm doing it.

I bend my knees and prepare to push off, but then I straighten up and shake out my hands.

Okay. Yep. Here I go. I am a leaf on the wind. Watch how I soar. I bend my legs again, but when it comes time to jump, I shake my head and step back from the edge.

"Liss?" His voice echoes off the cliffs, and even from here, I can tell Liam is wearing a concerned expression.

"I can't, Liam," I call down to him. "I'm sorry. Why don't you swim back to the beach? I'll walk down."

He looks disappointed, but he smiles anyway. "No problem. I'll be waiting when you get there."

I mentally berate myself as I start the long climb down the rocky trail. *Way to wuss out, Elissa. Good job. You're supposed to be a badass who's not afraid of anything or anyone. Harden up, lady.*

One good thing about the trek back is that it's all downhill, so it only takes half as long to get down as it did going up. In just under twenty minutes, I've made it to the clearing with the altar and can see Liam a few dozen yards away, soaking up the sun.

I glance over to where I saw the shadowy figure. Of course, now there's no one there. Maybe it was a shadow after all. Or a man-shaped palm frond.

Gathering my courage, I cautiously walk over to get a closer look. "Hey, Mr. Spirit. If you're here, please don't murder me. That would bum me out."

When I reach the tree, I peek behind it. Nothing. Thank God.

I'm about to turn and leave when I see something bright under a fern a few feet away. I walk over and brush back the leaves to reveal the awful zombie book I was reading the other day. Next to it is an empty bottle of cola.

A chill runs up my spine.

"It could have been the monkeys," I tell myself.

Yeah, sure, it was.

Fighting the urge to run, I hurry through the clearing, hoping like hell I don't bump into anything on the way.

When I get to Liam, he smiles up at me as he squints against the sun.

"Hey, thrill seeker. Welcome back."

"Hey."

"You okay? You look flushed."

"Yeah, just creeped out by the murder altar back there. I keep imagining things."

He frowns. "Like what?"

I wave my hand. "Vengeful spirits."

"You've been speaking to Alba, haven't you?"

"A little, but it's fine. Just tell me there's no such thing."

He looks at me like he thinks I'm both crazy and adorable. "There's no such thing."

"Cool. Thanks." I flop down on the towel beside him. "So, on a less creepy note, sorry for not jumping. I'm a wuss."

"No, you're not. That was a tough thing to ask you to do. Most people would have balked."

"You didn't."

"Yeah, but I have more guts than brains. You're the smart one in our relationship." He leans over and kisses me. "Maybe we should develop your adventurous side with something a little less extreme."

"Like ...?"

He shrugs and feigns innocence. "Oh, I don't know. Maybe ... topless sunbathing?" When I give him a skeptical look, he gestures to his chest. "Look, I'm already doing it. You should join me."

"Seriously, Liam?" He's grinning like a teenager about to get his first glimpse of boob.

"What do you have to lose?" He gestures around us. "We're in a private spot, and you can avoid those pesky tan lines."

I do hate tan lines. Not that I've really had a tan before. "What if Luis comes to check on us?"

"He won't. I gave him and Alba the weekend off, so they could go to the mainland for their daughter's birthday. They won't be back until Monday morning. That means we have this entire island to ourselves for nearly three days."

When I hesitate, he makes chicken noises. Bastard.

Oh, game on, Quinn. I'm not chickening out this time.

"Okay," I say, and stand. "How about we take this a step further." I strip off my top and push my bottoms down my legs before stepping out of them. "You wanted me to ditch my clothes this trip. Fine. You got it."

Liam's eyes nearly bug out of his head. "Uh ... wow. Okay. So, wow. You're ... naked."

"Do you have a problem with that, Chicken McNugget?"

He swallows, hard. "Nope. No problem at all." He just stares for a few seconds, slack jawed and practically drooling.

"Liam?"

"Sssh!" he says, waving a hand. "Talking will wake me up, and this is the best dream I've had in a long time." He brings two fingers to his temple and squints like he's concentrating. "Dream Elissa, please walk around so Dream Liam can ogle you. Maybe get him a Dream Coke while you're at it."

Shaking my head, I head over to the beach hut. On the way I hear him whisper to himself, "Oh my God. It worked. I'm Obi-Wan Kenobi."

It feels weird being naked out in the open, but I kind of like it. Right now, the girl who's spent most of her life in the concrete jungle of NYC is feeling wild and free, and it's empowering.

I grab two Cokes from the fridge and head back to Liam. He's studying me with the intensity of an alcoholic watching someone pour him a drink. There's longing but also a little fear.

When I pass him his drink, he looks away with effort, and judging by his color, either the sun is starting to get to him, or he's blushing.

"Still cool with me being naked?" I ask.

He holds the cold bottle to his face. "Yep. It's ... good."

"Good? Hmmm. So turned on you're having trouble with your vocabulary, Liam?"

"Uh ... no. I'm ... good."

I enjoy his discomfort way too much as he tries to look at me and keep himself under control at the same time.

"Then how about some quid pro quo, Clarice." I uncap my

bottle. "If I'm going to be naked, it's only fair you are, too."

He takes a mouthful of his drink then wipes his mouth. "I don't think so."

"Why not?"

"Because it's different for me than it is for you."

I slap his shoulder. "Hey! Sexist, much? Why is it different?"

"You really don't get it?"

When I shake my head, he sighs and stands. Then he opens his shorts and pulls them down. As soon as his erection bounces free of the fabric, it points proudly to the sky.

Liam gestures to it with vague disgust. "*That's* why. I look like a goddamn rhinoceros." He glares down at his crotch. "Why can't you behave yourself, dude? Seriously. Just because Elissa's naked, you don't have to lose your shit. You're a disgrace to penises everywhere."

I'd laugh if I didn't find the sight of him erect so damn hot. "Actually, I think he's a penile role model. I know a lot of ladies would be thrilled if their men were packing that in their tighty-whiteys."

"You would think that. You're biased."

"I am, but that doesn't make it untrue." I stand and walk over to him as he kicks off his shorts. His breathing speeds up when I put one hand on his chest and trail the other along his length. "You know, if it's uncomfortable for you to be this hard, I could always release the pressure." I move closer, and he lets out a hiss when I press my stomach against him.

He grips my hips to keep me still. "You realize it's illegal for you to be this sexy, right? Torture of any kind is condemned in most countries."

"I thought you wanted me to torture you with my hotness. Isn't that what you said on the phone?" I move away a little, grab my sunscreen, and smear it on my newly exposed areas. When Liam sees me rubbing it on my breasts, he stops breathing. To really turn up the heat, I make my movements as sensual as possible.

"Uh ..." He shakes his head, as if to clear it. "Shit, I need to sit down. There's not enough blood in my body to deal with this." He sinks back onto his towel but keeps his eyes on me.

I cup my breasts and smear lotion over my nipples with my palms. I even add a little moan for extra measure. "I'm so glad we're the only ones on the island. That means if you ravaged me right here on the beach, no one would know."

His eyes glaze over. "Well, sure. But ... uh ... sex on a beach isn't wise. Sand will get into places it should never be."

"Then we use the beach hut. Wash the sand off first."

He squeezes his eyes shut. "You're evil. Sexy as hell but totally evil."

I kneel next to him and rub my lotion-slick hands across his chest. "No, evil would be leaving you to deal with that massive hard on all by yourself. I'm being a good girl and offering to help."

He flops back on his towel and presses the heels of his hands into his eye sockets. "Fuck."

When I straddle his waist and continue stroking down his abdomen, he makes a strangled noise. "Liss ..."

"Shhh. Liss is busy right now. You can talk to her later."

I slide down his body, so I can reach his erection. It's lying on his stomach, heavy and thick.

It's been so long since I've been up close and personal with him, I feel like Captain Ishmael finding the white whale.

Thar she blows.

I rub what's left of the lotion onto his thighs.

"You don't need to put sunscreen on my cock," he says, still hiding his face.

"Wasn't intending to. That would taste gross."

I lean over and lick him from the base to the head. He starts making low, long sounds and moves his hands from his face into his hair. "Jesus Christ ..."

When I suck gently on the tip, every muscle in his body tenses as he moans. I'd almost forgotten how sexy it is to hear him make those noises and watch him hang on by a thread, knowing I'm the one affecting him like that. It's even more empowering than jungle nudity.

"You like that?" I ask.

He tugs as his hair. "Too much. Way too much. I'm trying to not become a giant geyser of stickiness right now, Horatio, but you're not making it easy."

Smiling to myself, I slide him into my mouth as far as I can, and when I suck in earnest, he yells, "Fuuuuck!" so loudly, it echoes off the nearby cliffs.

He continues swearing under his breath as I fall into a rhythm, twisting my hand at the base while teasing the head with my mouth. Every pass of my tongue winds him tighter, and it isn't long until he's making noises like he's in pain.

"Elissaaaa. Fuck, how the hell are you doing that?" His voice is low and rough, and he grips my hair as he thrusts. I want to take him all in at this point, but there's no way I can. "God, Liss ... oh, shit ... ohhhh, Jesus, you're going to make me come."

Knowing exactly what he needs, I give one final suck before pumping my hand in long strokes until his back arches, and he comes in thick bursts across his stomach and chest. "Yes ... ohhh, God, yes. Lisssss ..." With each wave, he groans my name, and his breath comes in short, uneven gasps.

When he's done, he collapses so heavily, I wonder if he's passed out.

"Liam?" He doesn't answer, but his eyelids flutter. "You okay?"

"No." His voice is a groan, and he barely moves his mouth. "You killed me. Death by orgasm. What a way to go. Just leave me here to rot. The jungle will take care of me."

I snuggle into his side. "If you're less dead in a few minutes, want to go for a swim?"

"Sure. Sounds good."

"By the way, you should wash yourself off before that stuff dries. It'll set like glue. Also, I think I have sand in my vagina."

He chuckles, still with his eyes closed. "I did warn you."

"Shhh. Dead men tell no tales."

EIGHT

AND WHEN YOU'RE GOOD, HE GIVES YOU SEX

The rest of our weekend flies by in a blur of sex, food, and sleep, and by the time Sunday evening rolls around, I'm more than a little exhausted. Turns out, being naked around each other for an extended period of time is a sure-fire way to guarantee we'll behave like total nymphos. For the past two and a half days, we've had sex whenever and wherever we liked, and Liam's impressively short recovery time has often taken me by surprise. I still tingle when I recall how he'd bent me over the kitchen bench while we were making lunch. He'd fucked me so furiously, you'd never have guessed we'd already made love four times.

Now, we're in bed, watching eighties movies and eating ice cream, and I can't remember a time when I was happier or more satisfied.

"Hey," I say as Liam swirls some salted caramel around my nipple and licks it off. "Isn't there some big Christmas event on the mainland tomorrow night?"

He presses sticky caramel kisses to my chest and neck. "Hmmm, maybe. Why?"

"I thought we might go. Alba said there'll be music and fireworks. It sounds like fun. We could spend the afternoon there, see some sights and do some shopping, then go to the parade."

He leans on one elbow. "What if people recognize me? I came

here to get away from all that."

I stroke the side of his face. "No one will know you with all this hair. We'll be fine."

"I suppose." He scratches his beard. "Just don't let me go back to New York without getting a shave and a haircut. If my mom sees me looking like this, she'll cancel Christmas."

"Is Momma Quinn not a fan of beards and long hair?"

"In general, yes. On her son, no. She thinks they make me look 'uncivilized'."

I run my hand over his chest and down his abs, loving the way his body immediately reacts to my touch. "I happen to like you uncivilized. Feral Liam is hot. And clearly he's a fan of mine, because he's left his mark all over me."

He drops his gaze to my neck and my breasts before making his way to my hips, and at each location he studies the blemishes coloring my skin. Some are pale pink shadows and some are deep purple, but there's no denying they're all bruises, and remembering how I got each one makes me want him jump him all over again.

"You're really okay with all of this?" He caresses the four small bruises on my hip, which match the shape of his fingers, and I see that same concerned look on his face as when he spanked me.

"I'm more than okay. I enjoy being marked by you."

He looks up at me. "The other day when I spanked you, I was terrified I'd pushed things too far. I felt bad for hurting you."

"That's why you freaked?"

"Yeah."

I stroke his cheek. "For the record, I've fantasized about you spanking me for ages, and let me tell you, the reality was soooo much hotter."

"Hmmm, tell me more about what you find hot."

I put my ice cream down, and climb over to straddle him. "I like it when you're rough. And when you order me around. And when you hold me down and take me exactly how you want." I graze my fingernails down his chest and smile when I feel him harden beneath me. "In fact, maybe we should take things further."

"What do you mean?"

"Explore this new dimension of our sex life. Would you like

to maybe experiment with ... oh, I don't know ... ropes, perhaps? Handcuffs? Floggers?"

He pushes his pelvis up to rub against me. "Christ, Liss, just when I think I'm too exhausted to even think about having sex again, you find new ways to excite me. Fuck yes, to all of that. When?"

I raise myself up so I can reach between us and stroke him. With every firm pass of my hand, he moans and grips my hips.

"Well," I say, "while I was checking my emails this morning, I accidentally found out there's an interesting store on the mainland, and it happens to be in the same area where the Christmas festival is taking place. What a coincidence."

"Oh, you accidentally found that out?" he says, his breathing labored.

I position myself above him, still stroking him as I lean over to kiss his chest. "Uh huh. My fingers slipped on the keyboard and randomly typed *sex shop* into Google. It was so weird."

"That is weird. You know what else is weird? That you're not sliding down onto my cock this very second. That's very weird."

He tries to guide me onto him, but I keep myself just out of reach as I suck on his neck. "Surely you don't want to be inside me again. Aren't you bored with that by now?"

He grabs the back of my neck and pulls my head back so he can see my face. "Liss, trust me when I say that even if I lived a thousand lifetimes, I'd never get bored of being inside you." I squeal when he flips me onto my back, and then with a low growl in his chest, pushes deep inside me. I wrap my arms and legs around him to pull him even deeper.

"You're an incredible woman, Elissa Matilda Holt," he says, starting with slow, shallow thrusts that feel so good, I dig my fingernails into his back. "I can't believe you're mine."

I close my eyes as his thrusts get stronger. "God, Liam, I can't believe you think my middle name is ... Matilda. You're a terrible ... oh, yes ... fiancée."

He slides his hands into my hair and pulls my head to the side. "What is your middle name, then?"

"It's--" He circles his pelvis, and he hits something inside of me that makes me see stars. "Oh, God ... it's ... May."

He drops his mouth to my neck and nips and sucks where he's already marked me. "Noted, Elissa May. Now, do you want to keep talking, or...?"

"Nope. No talking. Just ... ohhh, fuck."

"You got it."

He puts one hand under my butt to give himself a better angle and proceeds to thrust with the focus and determination of a man on a mission to make his woman come as hard as possible. To my delight, he's not only successful, he's also not the least bit gentle.

NINE

LIAM, BABY

As I stand on the dock and stare at what's in front of me, I'm at a loss for words. Liam has surprised me, yet again.

"You're kidding me, right?" I say.

He stands with his arms crossed over his chest, looking smug as hell. "Not kidding. Very much serious."

"This is the yacht you 'commandeered' to get here the night of the storm?"

"Yep."

"So, you didn't steal it as much as took possession of it."

"Well, if you want to split hairs, then, sure. I commissioned it months ago and was going to surprise you with a proper christening before her first voyage. But that plan went out the window when I had to use her to get to you. So, yeah. I picked her up early."

The 'her' he keeps referring to is the most gorgeous luxury yacht I've ever seen. When he said we were taking a boat to the mainland, I expected it to be one of those cheesy tourist charters with cup holders in the seats, not this glistening testament to having too much damn money.

But it isn't the size or opulence that has me gobsmacked. It's the two words that are emblazoned across the bow in fancy, cursive letters: *Elissa May*.

"So, you knew my middle name all along?"

"Of course. What sort of fiancée would I be if I didn't?"

"And you named your boat after me?"

He puts his arm around me and sighs. "Elissa, it's a long maritime tradition for men to name boats after the women they love. Of course I had to scratch Angel's name off it first." He laughs when I elbow him in the ribs.

"You're not funny," I say.

"You know that's not true. I'm hilarious."

He takes my hand and leads me onboard, and I soon discover that the inside of the yacht is even fancier than the outside. It resembles a floating five-star hotel.

"If we ever get sick of the island," Liam says as he nuzzles my neck in one of the six bedrooms, "we can always sail around the coast for a while. Do some fishing. Be naked at sea."

After the tour, he casts off and points us toward the mainland, and it doesn't surprise me that seeing Liam drive several hundred tons of nautical machinery is crazy sexy.

"Where did you learn to drive a boat," I ask suspiciously.

"Dad's brother had a little fishing boat. Used to take Jamie and me out sometimes and give us lessons. It's not hard." He glances over at me. "You wanna try?"

I look out at the expanse of ocean in front of us. Guess there's no danger of crashing into anything. "Sure."

I step up to the big chrome wheel as Liam takes his position behind me.

"Just like driving a car," he whispers and wraps his arms around my waist. "Hands at ten and two, and keep your eye on the speed."

Even though I've never driven a car, I get the idea. I grip the wheel and follow his directions, and after a few minutes I relax enough to enjoy myself.

"See?" Liam says, sounding proud. "You're a natural." He points to a panel of brightly lit switches beside me. "Now, press that button."

"Okay."

As soon as I press it, Liam shouts, "Not that one, Liss! Jesus

Christ, we're going to die!"

My heart leaps into my throat for a whole three seconds before I realize Liam's shaking with suppressed laughter.

I whip around and slap him on the shoulder. "You asshole! You nearly gave me a heart attack!"

He turns me back to the wheel, then wraps his arms around me and kisses my neck. "Yes, but it was a sexy heart attack."

Despite the soothing press of his lips, my heart is still beating out of my chest. "What does that button even do?"

"I have no idea. I know the ignition switch and the speed gauge. That's it. My guess is that most of these panels are just for show."

I lean back against him and smile. "You're an idiot."

He lets me drive until we reach the marina on the mainland before taking over to bring her into dock. Then we take a taxi to a local restaurant Alba and Luis recommended.

Liam looks around nervously as we enter, worried he'll be recognized, but the maître d' and waitstaff don't bat an eyelid.

"See?" I say as he sips a local beer. "Nothing to worry about. Here, you're just some random hipster with a man-bun and a beard."

He glares at me. "I told you what would happen if you continued to call me a hipster, Elissa May, and yet you continue to do it. One might think you're asking to be spanked."

I try not to smile. "One certainly might."

He nods in satisfaction. "Then prepare to be punished when we get home."

Despite looking like he's in control, I don't miss the way he smiles to himself as he stares at me. "I had no idea I was in love with such a freak."

I grab his shirt front and pull him forward. "You fell in love with me *because* I'm a freak. And believe me, the feeling's mutual." I give him a long, deep kiss, and we're so wrapped up in each other, we don't notice the server waiting to deliver our food until he clears his throat.

● ● ●

After a delicious lunch of authentic Brazilian food, we make our way to a small shop with red, opaque windows, and if the two of us thought we were kinky before we went inside, we sure as hell didn't when we came out.

"Holy shit," Liam whispers as we walk down the street with our comparatively tame collection of handcuffs, rope ties, and various floggers. "Did you see that thing near the door?"

"Yep."

"What the hell, Liss?" As soon as Liam had spotted the chrome bar and cage, he'd gone white. It was labeled as a *cum-thru urethral plug*, and it was the stuff nightmares were made of. "Men put that thing up their cock? How? And why? And *how?* My dick ran for cover at the sight of it."

"Lucky you're a Dom then. Your penis can remain free of metal devices of any kind."

He nods, but he's still pale. I don't want to laugh at how traumatized he is, but I can't help myself. My big, strong man who doesn't blink at jumping off cliffs or participating in death-defying stunts is brought undone by a device that slides up a guy's pee tube.

Hilarious.

As we head toward where the concert and fireworks are happening, the area becomes more crowded. Street vendors hawk their wares, and kids beg their parents to buy them stuff. Bright, Brazilian music pours from nearly every doorway.

When we reach a broad piazza, there's a whole band there, fronted by a gorgeous group of scantily clad dancers in *carnival* costumes.

I turn to check Liam's expression and discover he's watching them with intense interest.

"Big dance fan, are you?" I ask.

He nods with a serious expression. "Their years of training and discipline are clear. They're athletes. I respect that."

"Also, their boobies shake when they move."

"That, too."

I laugh and tug on his arm. "Come on, big guy. You can buy me a drink."

I drag him to a nearby stall where they're selling something that looks and smells a lot like Sangria.

"Two please," Liam says as he hands over some money.

The woman smiles at him as she takes the cash, but then she does a huge double take. She immediately starts giggling and nudges the woman beside her, who's pouring the drinks.

"*O garanhão,*" she whispers to her friend, who promptly spins around to stare at Liam.

The second woman gasps and covers her mouth. "*Sim!*"

Liam drops his head. "I think our anonymity just went out the window."

The women hand over our drinks, and by the time we've walked to the other side of the square, there's a steady murmur of, "*O garanhão,*" as we pass.

When we've polished off our drinks, we stop at the front of an upmarket hotel and ditch our empty cups into a trash can. Liam looks around warily. I think he's as surprised as I am we're not being mobbed. Most fans go berserk when they realize who he is. Seems like the Brazilians are content to point and whisper about him from afar.

"I knew being anonymous was too good to last," he says, putting on his sunglasses. "Still, it could be worse."

I look inside the window of the hotel to check out the decor, but it's the reading material on a stand in the lobby bar that catches my eye.

It just got worse.

"Uh ... Liam ..."

"Maybe we should head back," he says. "If the mood changes, we could be in trouble. I feel too exposed here."

He's not wrong about that. "Liam—"

"What does *o garanhão* mean, anyway?"

I take his hand and pull him over to the window. "It means *the stallion.*"

He frowns. "Really? That's weird."

"Not when you see what I'm seeing."

I point to the magazine rack where there are various newspapers and magazines in both English and Portuguese, and every single one has a picture of Liam on the front cover, naked. And hard.

His erection has been covered by a black rectangle, but the size of it explains why all the headlines are screaming about *O garanhão*.

As soon as Liam registers what he's seeing, he goes whiter than he did over the pee tube. "Ohhhh, shit."

TEN

NOT-SO-SILENT NIGHT

"Goddammit." Liam's face goes from white to red as he stands in the lobby bar and flicks through the pictures in one of the magazines. As angry as he is about seeing himself naked, he's absolutely furious they've also printed pictures of me.

I'm not thrilled about that part, either.

"How the hell did someone get these?" he asks, flipping the pages hard enough to tear them. "No one knew where we were. I kept it a secret for that very reason."

"I hate to say it, but could Luis and Alba have—?"

"No." He shakes his head. "No way. Their references were impeccable. There must have been someone else on the island. A fucking bottom-feeding pap who somehow sniffed us out."

I sink onto the couch beside us, shocked and shattered. I didn't think it could get much worse than when we were photographed kissing in the alley when Liam was still pretending to be engaged to Angel. But wow, was I wrong.

Back then, I was the anonymous other woman. Now, my identity is crystal clear.

Not only are there naked pictures of me, there are several of me *fellating* my well-hung fiancée. They're from an angle that blocks the details of what I'm doing, but anyone with a brain can work out what's going on. They must have been taken the day we were at the lake.

"I saw him," I say, feeling so drained my voice has zero emotion. Liam sits beside me. "Who? The pap?"

I nod. "Remember when I mentioned seeing someone near the altar? I bet that was him."

"Goddamn fucking parasitic asshole." He crushes the magazine into a ball and throws it into the trash. "Stay here, okay? I have to make some calls."

He stalks over to the other side of the lobby and pulls out his phone.

I'm so preoccupied, I don't even notice the waitress standing beside me until she says, "Something to drink, senhorita?"

I nearly kiss her in gratitude. "God, yes, please."

By the time Liam returns, I'm halfway through a bottle of red wine. He grabs the glass I've filled for him and drains it in three gulps.

"Well, Stacey's on the case. She's going to get as many injunctions as she can, but there's not much we can do. This thing has so much traction, nothing's going to stop these pictures from being plastered all over the internet."

After the whole Anthony Kent debacle, Liam and Angel signed with one of Hollywood's most respected agents, Stacey Savage. She's smart, tough, and has connections everywhere, so if she can't kill the pictures, no one can.

When I refill Liam's glass, he guzzles that one, too. He looks wired.

"I wanted to take you on this trip to avoid crap like this," he says. "Not to drop you in the middle of it with me."

"My parents are going to see those photos," I say, staring at a stain on the carpet. "They'll be so proud."

Liam swears under his breath and rakes his fingers through his hair. "If I ever get my hands on the bastard who did this ..." He's gripping his wine glass so tightly, I'm afraid he'll break it. I pry his fingers loose and put it on the table.

Liam rubs his eyes. "Let's get out of here. We might not be able to outrun this story, but we can sure as hell ignore it. I've organized a security team to sweep the island before we get back. If the bastard who took those photos is still there, they'll find him."

He grabs our shopping bags as I finish my last mouthful of wine and leads me out of the hotel into a cab. Even as we drive away, I can still hear people calling out, "*O garanhão.*"

We've only been driving for a few minutes when my phone rings. I know without looking that it's Josh.

"Hey."

"Jesus, Lissa, are you and Liam okay? I can't go on the internet or turn on the TV without seeing way more of your two that I'm comfortable with."

I rub my temple. A headache is brewing behind my left eye. "We're fine."

"Well, yeah, that's obvious from the photos. Dayum, girl. Fine as hell!" When I groan, Josh says, "Too soon?"

"Way too soon."

"Sorry. But seriously, do you need anything? Alcohol? Valium? A heat-seeking pap missile?"

"God, yes to that last one." I glance at Liam who's staring stony-faced out the window. "I just hope the police find the guy before Liam does, or he could be up on some major grievous bodily harm charges."

"I tried to call your parents to warn them about what's going on."

"Did you get onto them?"

"Yeah, but I was too late. By the time I spoke with them, they'd been drinking heavily for over an hour."

"Shit." I lean my head back against the seat. "This just keeps getting better and better. I guess Dad will have no choice now but accept that his little girl is no longer a virgin and that Liam and I are more than just good friends."

I feel sick.

Josh tries to make me feel better by telling me that people are saying nice things about my ass, but it doesn't help. When we arrive at the marina I sign off and tell him I'll call him in a few days. Liam has gone quiet, and that's never a good sign.

After paying the cabbie, we head down to where the Elissa May is docked. Liam's in the middle of casting off when he stops dead and stares at the boat.

"What is it?"

He holds up his finger, and I follow his gaze to the cabin windows.

"The lights are on," he whispers. "I turned them all off before we left. That slimy asshole's on my fucking boat." He drops the rope and strides up the gang plank, fists clenched at his side. I follow, and hope like hell I can stop him from killing the guy.

As soon as we climb down the stairs, we hear banging around, as if whoever's there has just realized they've been busted. Liam storms into the master suite and grabs a man dressed in black by his throat before slamming him against the wall so hard, the floor vibrates. Liam's shoulder blocks the man's face from my view, so all I see is a mess of brown hair.

"Wait," the man yells, fear bright in his voice. "Please. Don't hurt me."

Liam slams him into the wall again. "Hurt you?! You're lucky I don't break your goddamn legs for what you've done." Liam grabs something from the man, and I jump as an expensive looking camera smashes to pieces as it hits the tiled floor. "Try to take your photos now, you piece of shit!"

"Liam—" I grab his arm to try and calm him down, but when I get close enough to see the pap clearly, I realize I recognize his face.

"Oh, shit. Scott?"

Liam's snaps his head around. "You know this guy?"

I'm so shocked, I can barely nod. "I ran into him at JFK. Literally. Knocked him over."

Liam turns to glare at Scott's terrified face. "You'd better explain yourself right the fuck now, or I'm going to take you out into the middle of the ocean and leave you for the sharks."

"Alright, alright," Scott says, holding up his hands defensively. "Just calm down, man, okay?"

God, does he have a death wish? Doesn't he know never to tell an enraged Liam to calm down?

Liam slams him into the wall again. "Talk!"

"Okay!" Scott's so scared by now, he's trembling. "My sister works at La Perla on Fifth Avenue. Elissa was in there last week, and she bragged about how she was going on vacation with you. My sister knew I was having a dry spell and needed to land some major pictures, so she passed the information along to me."

My stomach drops. With that information, I can see the similarities between him and Chastity.

I swallow my nausea. "How did you find me?"

"It wasn't hard. Everyone knows where Quinn's penthouse is. I staked it out until I saw you getting into a limo, followed you, watched you check in at the airport, and bought a ticket on the same flight." He looks between us. "Paps these days have more skills than most private investigators. Tracking people down is what we do."

"So," I say, trying to keep a lid on my anger, "you waited for me to come out of the first class club and then, what? Made sure I ran into you?"

He shrugged. "Basically. I hoped you had more information about your destination so I could do some planning, but Quinn was clever about keeping you in the dark."

Liam grabs Scott's shirt and talks through clenched teeth. "You stalked my fiancée? Are you fucking serious right now?"

"How did you find the island?" I ask. "There's no way you tailed our helicopter."

Scott glances at Liam briefly before coming back to me. "I followed your car to the private airfield, and after you took off I paid the clerk to get me a copy of the flight plan. Then I hired a boat to take me to the island."

Liam pushes Scott away in disgust. "I bet you're patting yourself on the back about this whole thing, aren't you? Smug as hell you're making big bucks from invading our privacy." Liam pulls out his phone. "Well, have fun spending that money in jail."

Scott's face crumbles. "Now, hang on. Let's not be hasty. Surely we can work something out?" When Liam ignores him and jabs some numbers, Scott grabs his arms. "Come on, man. Please! Tell me what to do to make this go away."

Liam shoves him in the chest so hard, Scott almost falls over.

"All right, you son-of-a-bitch," Liam says, his voice huge in the confined space. "Here's my deal. If you can you recall every one of those photos so no one will see them again, you're free to leave. Can you do that?" Scott's eyes dart back and forth as he tries to come up with an answer. When he can't, Liam scowls at him. "Didn't think so."

As Liam goes back to his phone, Scott's expression turns hard. "Okay, fine. You wanna play hardball? Let's go. Call the cops, and I'll charge you with assault."

Liam lets out a short laugh. "You think what I've just done to you is assault? Wrong." Fast as lightning, he punches Scott square in the face. Scott's nose explodes with blood. "*That's* assault. Go ahead and file a complaint."

Scott grunts as he clutches his nose and tries to stop the bleeding. "Jesus Christ! You're a maniac!"

"No," Liam says, his voice dark and intense. "I'm a man who caught a criminal burgling his yacht. The same criminal who trespassed on private property, so he could stalk innocent people. The authorities will not only throw your assault charges out of court, they'll give me a medal for smacking you in the mouth. Now, sit down and shut the fuck up, or I'll forget why I only hit you once."

Scott sits heavily on the bed and holds his T-shirt up to block his nose. When Liam turns away to talk on the phone, Scott look at me imploringly. "Elissa, please. Don't let him do this."

I walk over to him. "Don't you dare put this on him. You did this to yourself. You stalked us like animals and sold *naked* photos of us in our most intimate moments. You're scum. If you don't want to pay for your actions, then make better goddamn choices."

When I turn away, he stands and grabs my arm. "Elissa—"

I guess he didn't learn his lesson the first time. In a second, I simultaneously spin and drop to one knee as I punch him as hard I can in the crotch. He freezes, his face red with pain, before making a pained gurgling noise and crumbling to the floor.

Liam turns around and looks at me questioningly. I shrug. "Like you're the only one who gets to punch the bad guy?"

"I have no problem with you punching him. I'm just surprised you were actually listening in my self-defense classes. Good job."

Liam's praise makes me feel less sick about our situation, but I'm still furious that we've been put in this position.

At least Scott has the good sense to stay still and quiet until the police arrive.

ELEVEN

WE WISH YOU A MERRY SEXMAS

By the time we get home after filling out the police report, it's nearly two in the morning. Liam's quiet as we walk up from the dock to the house, and when we get into the bedroom, he sits on the edge of the bed and stares at the floor, looking shattered.

When I stand in front of him, he wraps his arms around me and rests his forehead on my stomach.

"You hungry?" I ask.

"No."

"Thirsty."

"I'm fine, Liss."

"I don't think you are."

He stays silent and hugs me. I hug him back. I never fully understood his paranoia about people following him before, but I sure as hell get it now. When the pictures came out of us kissing in New York, I felt stupid, because we'd let our guards down in a public place. But this? You can't get more secluded than an uninhabited island off the coast of a foreign country. This is a place where we should be able to feel safe and open. Instead, I feel violated. Vulnerable. More shaken than I'm letting on.

Scott took a beautiful, private moment between us and turned it into filthy tabloid fodder. There's no way someone could ever get used to that type of abuse, and poor Liam has been dealing with it for years. How is it legal that lowlifes like Scott can get away with this behavior? Worse still, how are they allowed to profit from other people's suffering?

Liam gives me a squeeze then pushes me back so he can stand. "I'll be back in a few minutes."

After he walks into the bathroom and closes the door, I sink onto the edge of the bed and drop my head into my hands.

How could I have been so stupid? If I hadn't been such an insecure idiot, I wouldn't have felt the need to brag about Liam to those girls in La Perla, and Scott wouldn't have found out we were together. I'm the one who practically led him to us.

Guilt squirms in my stomach. As angry as I am with Scott, I'm furious with myself. Liam has enough people intent on manipulating and exploiting him. He doesn't need me helping them.

I flop back onto the bed and close my eyes. Christ, what a mess.

Listening to the ocean should be soothing, but even it sounds angry with me. When Liam hasn't emerged from the bathroom fifteen minutes later, I figure he is, too.

I suck up my courage and knock on the door. There's the sound of running water. "Hey. Everything alright?"

"Yeah. You can come in."

When I open the door, I find him shirtless in front of the sink. Chunks of long hair lie strewn all over the floor, and his head looks like it's been run over by a lawn mower. What's more, his face is practically bald. He tilts his head up and scrapes the razor over the few remaining whiskers on his neck.

"I figured looking like my old self might be a handy disguise now that those pictures are out." He sighs. "I decided to torture myself and checked the damage from my phone. Did you know there are already memes of us? And some asshole has opened a twitter account called The Stallion, where he pretends my penis is tweeting. What the hell is wrong with people?" He finishes shaving before running his hand over his face and neck. When he's satisfied he didn't miss a patch, he washes his face and pats it dry with a towel.

"Liam?"

"Hmmm?"

"You cut your own hair?"

He rubs his hand over the uneven mess on his head. "Had to. I couldn't stand it a second longer. Did I do a good job?"

"Not at all."

He hands me the scissors. "Then by all means, Vidal Sassoon, fix it."

When he sits on the closed toilet seat, I stand between his legs and assess the damage. Can I fix it? I at least have to try. I've never given a haircut before, but I've watched enough of them to fake it pretty well. I even up the sides and back before tackling the top. By the time I'm done, it's not perfect, but I've definitely made it better.

Pity I can't say the same about our situation.

Liam just keeps staring at the floor, hands clasped together. It's weird seeing him clean cut again. It's even weirder that he's so quiet.

"Liam?"

He looks up at me as if he was deep in thought and had forgotten I was there. "Yeah?"

"I'm so sorry."

He shrugs. "I'm sure you did your best. Don't worry. It's only hair, right? It'll grow back."

"No, not about the hair. About this whole mess. I should have just kept my mouth shut. "

"Jesus Christ, Liss." He jumps up and brushes chunks of hair off his shoulders in quick, angry movements. "This isn't your fault."

He throws the towel on the ground and strides into the bedroom. I take a breath and follow. "Yes, it is. If I hadn't lost it with those girls in La Perla, none of this would have happened. I just got so damn angry about how they were looking down on me. They didn't believe there was any way you and I could be—"

He spins to face me, and his expression is hard. "Elissa, stop it. Don't you dare try to take the blame for this. It's on me. All of it.

I knew it would happen, but I was too fucking selfish to save you from it. I should be the one apologizing, not you."

With a grunt of frustration, he stalks over to the window and stares out at the ocean. His posture suggests he's bearing the weight of the world on his shoulders.

I decide I should give him a second to calm himself. After running his hands over his freshly cut hair, he takes in a deep breath and slowly lets it out. When he turns back to me, he seems calmer but no less upset.

"I want to tell you this scandal will blow over and nothing like this will ever happen again, but I can't. It *will* happen again. And again, and again, for decades to come. I've accepted it, but as long as we're together, you're going to be a target, and I can't fucking bear that." He drops his head. "This is *exactly* why I didn't contact you for all those years. Because I knew that if I gave into my feelings and brought you into my life, you'd end up paying the price for my fame. But I did it anyway, because I'm a selfish prick who wanted you at any cost."

"Liam, don't be ridiculous. I came of my own free will. You didn't force me. I knew what it would be like dating someone famous."

"That doesn't make it right. However you look at this, it's my fault. This career was my choice, not yours. You would have still loved me if I'd stayed a construction worker, for God's sake. You don't care about the money or the fame. As nice as it is to be able to shower you with extravagant gifts, I'd give it all up to protect you."

"Give up what? Fame? That's impossible. Even if you quit Hollywood tomorrow, you're still going to be recognized everywhere you go. You're the biggest movie star in the world, and people won't just forget that because you want them to."

"Liss, the whole world has seen you naked, for fuck's sake! Don't you see how screwed up this is?"

"Of course! But there's nothing we can do. You're *not* a construction worker anymore. You're a star. And I love you enough to accept the consequences of what that entails."

"You say that now, but what about five years from now when

you're paranoid to set foot outside the house in case you're followed? Or when you're mobbed by paps when you're trying to buy groceries? Or God forbid, when one of my crazy-ass fans physically *attacks* you because they're jealous of you being the woman I love? Will it be worth it, then?"

"So ... what are you saying? That you shouldn't have told me about you and Angel? That you think I'd be happier living the rest of my life believing *you didn't love me?*"

"No, I just—" He takes a step forward. "This is just the beginning. Now that it's out we're together, every news agency and tabloid will dig up any information they can on you. Where you live. Who your friends are. They might not have a lot of information yet, but they'll get it, and when they do, all manner of unholy shit is going to rain down on you and everyone you care about. And by the time you realize what the hell it is you've gotten yourself into by being with me, it will be too damn late to do anything about it. If you want to avoid that, you have to act now."

A chill runs up my spine. I don't like where this conversation is heading. "What are you talking about. Do what?"

He stares at me, conflicted and tense, as if he can't bring himself to say it.

"Liam?" I take a step toward him. "What do you expect me to do?"

The muscles in his jaw clench. "Walk away. Go live a normal life with a regular guy. It's not too late."

I have no idea what's going through his head right now, but surely he can't be serious. "You think it's not too late for me to walk away from you?" I let out a short laugh, and I'm surprised I only sound half as incredulous as I feel. "You have to be fucking kidding me. Of *course* it's too late! It was too late the night we met in Times Square, when you showed me your roof garden and told me about your brother and parents, and made me question everything I believed about true love." I walk toward him. "It was too late the first time you kissed me, tasting like cookies and cream while you ruined me for all other men." When I reach him, I put both hands on his chest. "And most of all, it was way too goddamn late the first time we made love, when my whole world tilted so far off its axis, I woke up to find it revolving around you."

I can tell by his expression he's trying to come up with arguments to convince me why I should go despite all that, but he won't find a single one that will stick.

"Liam, don't you understand? You can tell me to go and live my life all you want, but it's an impossible concept. My life is *with you*. Just like yours is with me. And no number of embarrassing pictures is going to change that."

He drops his head onto my shoulder and wraps his arms around me. "What happened to you today ... seeing you hurt and humiliated like that? It freaking killed me. I never wanted you to be dragged into this shit-show." He pulls back and looks into my eyes. "I'm so sorry."

"Don't be. Am I upset my naked body has now been seen by half the world? Yes. Do I give two shits about what people are saying about my body? No. Am I going to let this, or anything else short of death come between us? Absolutely fucking not."

I cup his face, and he looks deep into my eyes as I try to make him understand. "Don't you get it? Let the paps and the reporters and the rabid, maniacal fans throw whatever they like at me. It won't matter. I'd walk through fire to be with you, and I'd be grateful for the burns. Because you're it for me, forever, and if that means I have to endure a thousand naked pictures, or even a poorly shot sex tape titled ... oh, I don't know ... *Giant Geyser of Stickiness*, for example ... then that's what I'll do."

It takes a moment for my words to sink in, but when they do, he bursts out laughing and pulls me into his arms. "God, you're incredible. What the hell did I do to deserve you?"

"Well, for a start, you're really good looking. Then there's your body. And don't even get me started on your pretty dick."

He hugs me tighter. "Watch it, or I'll grab the video camera and make that porno a reality. We can get *Giant Geyser of Stickiness* filmed and edited before Alba and Luis get back in the morning. I dare you to get your porn face on."

"Oh, it's on," I say, rising on my toes so I can nuzzle his neck. "And when we're done we can upload it to the cloud, so hackers can find it."

He breathes heavily as I lay kisses from his clavicle down to his chest. "Brilliant. After all, any publicity is good publicity."

"Well, that's not exactly true," I say, teasing him with my tongue. "Sure, your enormous man member broke the internet, but the fallout could have been so much worse."

He pulls back so he can see my face. "How?"

"Well, you could have had a really small cock."

He gives me one of those smiles that takes my breath away. The kind I know he doesn't give to anyone else in the world. "God, I love you." He pulls me close and kisses me, slow and deep, and when he pulls back, I look into his eyes and see any lingering doubt has disappeared.

"We'll get through this," he says, determination hardening his features.

"Exactly. By next week, people will have forgotten all about it."

"I hope so. Still, I'm going to make the most of our time here. The longer I can pretend most people I meet haven't seen my dick, the better."

I stroke his chest. "I know how you feel. Not about the dick part, of course, but you know ... boobs. And sandy vag."

He smiles then kisses me again, a little harder than before. When he draws back, he grazes his hand up my ribcage to cup my breasts through my shirt. "I'm conflicted about people seeing you naked. On the one hand, I want to murder every single man who's seen those photos and reduced you to a sexual object. And on the other, I want to boast to the world I get to make love to that perfect body every day, so everyone else can go suck it."

"Huh," I say as I move away from him, so I can take off my shirt. "You mean you don't already brag about banging me? That's hurtful. I tell random chicks in lingerie shops all the time about banging you."

He watches as I finish unbuttoning my blouse and slip it off my shoulders. "Have I told you lately how much I love you?" He moves toward me slowly. "Have I told you that you're the greatest woman on the planet, and I'd be a shell of a man without you?"

"Well, no, but—"

He holds up his hand as he advances on me. "No need to

answer. These are rhetorical questions." Another step. "Have I told you that you're the wittiest, sweetest, sexiest woman who's ever existed? That you drive me insane simply by drawing breath? That I can't look at you without wanting to kiss you, and touch you, and make sweet, filthy love to you?"

He takes my hands and walks me backward toward the bench near the windows. "Because all of that is true. You're remarkable, Elissa Holt, and even though I don't deserve you, I fucking love you with all my heart."

When my back is against the window, he takes my face in his hands and lowers his head until our lips are almost touching. "And I'm sorry I ever suggested you should leave me. That was fucking stupid. I tried living without you once, and it was the worst six years of my life. If I ever suggest something like that again, feel free to hit me. Hard." He grazes his lips against mine, and the sudden rush of hormones makes me lightheaded. "You're my everything, Liss. You're my entire world. Nothing means anything without you."

When he kisses me, it's with a desperation I haven't felt before. It's part apology and part gratitude, and a whole lot of knowing we could be locked in a Turkish prison together and still count ourselves lucky.

As the kiss continues, our clothes become a casualty of our battle to be joined as quickly as possible, and when Liam sits on the bench next to the windows, I let out a long moan of relief as I sink down onto him.

He looks like a God sitting there, shrouded in sunlight in front of the sparkling ocean, gazing up at me as if I were a miracle come to life. When he's as deep as he can go, his mouth drops open, and I'll never tire of how his face morphs from relief, to wonder, to primal satisfaction every time he's inside of me.

"Just for the record," I say, as I stroke his beautiful face. "You're my everything, too. You always have been, and you always will be. No matter what."

When his eyes prickle with wetness, and he clenches his jaw, I know he finally believes it.

We end up making love for hours, and for the entire time, we forget about the future, and the tabloids, and the thousand issues that will be sent to try us in the coming years, because when we're together, nothing else matters except each other.

In a few months, the naked pictures will be old news, and the vultures in the media will stalk us to try and land a fresher scandal, but come what may, our relationship will only grow stronger. We've come to learn that we're each a precious gift to the other, and when you're blessed with a love as powerful and passionate as ours, no matter what life throws at us, every day feels like Christmas.

Part Three:

Happy Horny New Year

ONE

SUPER JOSH

December 31st, Present Day
The Kane Residence
New York City, New York

No one's perfect, and anyone who thinks they are is either a narcissist or a psychopath. But we all strive for perfection, which is why every New Year's Eve, the human race takes a long, hard look at itself and promises to be less of an asshole in the year to come.

We've all done it. Promised ourselves that *this time* "I'm going to eat healthy", or "I'll get off my ass and exercise more", or if you're me, "I'll go to the movies this year instead of sitting in my room watching movie spoof porn." (For the record, my favorite is *Edward Penishands*. It's a masterpiece.)

And it's this pathological need for annual self-evaluation that currently has me standing in front my mirror in my boxer briefs, wondering why the hell I'm freaking out about going to a New Year's Eve costume party.

To put things in context, when I was a kid, I wanted to be a superhero. Badly. I mean, sure, I also wanted to be Diego from *Dora the Explorer*, because who wouldn't want to hang with a cool talking backpack? But still . . .

My hero envy was *Serious Business*.

I was so obsessed with it, I begged Mom to take me to the X-ray lab at the hospital where she worked, so I could be exposed to Hulking levels of radiation. When that didn't pan out, I mixed up superhero serums from the fridge and pantry, certain that the worse they tasted, the more likely they were to work. In reality, the only power I developed was the ability to vomit violently until my poor abused stomach purged every ounce of the disgusting concoctions made from orange juice and barbecue sauce.

Despite my failure to achieve hero-dom, my room remained plastered with posters of Superman, Spiderman, The Avengers, X-Men, and the Justice League. I even had She-Hulk and Wonder Woman, and not just because those ladies were super-hot. I also respected them as kickass heroes who didn't take crap from anyone. Even back then, I appreciated powerful women.

My parents weren't at all surprised when I begged them for superhero outfits for every costume party and Halloween, and by the time I hit double digits, I had a stack of them. But even though wearing those costumes made me feel special and powerful, other kids thought the scrawny Jewish kid with glasses didn't fit the hero description, and I got teased every single time, even by my friends.

One Halloween when I was ten, I dressed as the Green Lantern. Unfortunately, Darren Pike, an asshole sixteen-year-old who lived in my building, had the same idea. He went berserk when he saw that we matched and punched me in the face so hard, he broke my glasses and my nose.

As he stood over me, ranting that I was a 'limp-dick imposter', it wasn't lost on me that even though he was a total douchebag who didn't think twice about assaulting a kid half his size, his buff physique made him look like a hero, and no matter how much I loved these characters, I never would.

That's when I realized why people always gave me such a hard time. Wearing those costumes while being a less-than-perfect physical specimen insulted the whole genre. Weaklings weren't heroes. At best, they were sidekicks. But let me ask you this: how far would Batman have gotten without Alfred? And would James Bond be anywhere near as kickass if it weren't for the geeks who made his gadgets? The short answer is 'no fucking way.' But do those backstage guys get any credit? No. Only the ripped dudes got to wear the fancy outfits and ride off with the beautiful women.

After I understood that, I stopped wearing the hero costumes altogether. I got interested in Star Wars and Star Trek, and discovered that in sci-fi you don't have to meet a particular physical standard in order to play make-believe. I was allowed to be an awkward, four-eyed Luke Skywalker, because Star Wars was for geeks and therefore not cool enough for most people to bother mocking.

So, I embraced my geekdom. Not that I had much choice in the matter. I was shortsighted, smart, hard-working, and the smallest kid in my class until I blossomed at the ripe old age of fifteen.

When I met Elissa for the first time, I was shorter than she was, and in the illustrious words of my warm and supportive father, I looked like 'a toothpick wrapped in spaghetti'. Elissa, on the other hand, had blossomed early and was not only gorgeous but had a good-looking boyfriend (who turned out to be a cheating dick), and a track star older brother (who was just a regular, garden-variety dick). So when we were paired together in drama club, my first thought was that she'd turn out to be a mean girl who'd destroy me in record time.

To my surprise, she was really nice. And funny. And *got* me. She was the first girl to look at me like I hadn't just pissed in her cornflakes. Against all odds, we became friends, and then to everyone's surprise, including my own, best friends.

Six months after we met, I finally got that mega-dose of pubescent testosterone I'd been dreaming of since the first grade, and I shot up to being six feet tall within a year. Not only that, but my spaghetti limbs filled out to such an extent, it took me a long time to get used to seeing a well-built man in the mirror every day.

For a while I pretended I was Peter Parker, and the sudden changes were due to a radioactive spider bite, but like Spiderman I was still a geek on the inside.

So, now I have a dilemma.

On Elissa's advice, I've been working out to try and relieve the feelings of inadequacy I've gained from living in Hollywood. I mean, come on. The dude who unclogs the drains at my L.A. pad is a supermodel with a six-pack. Not to mention my girlfriend's latest co-star is a freakishly handsome fitness model who makes me feel like Elmer Fudd. How the hell am I supposed to keep the love of a woman as spectacular as Angel Bell with that kind of competition?

For the past four weeks while Angel has been overseas, I've busted my ass in the gym every day doing sit ups, push ups, bicep curls, and bench presses ... I've done it all. I've even cut back on junk food and started drinking water instead of beer. If I were to brag to my dad about my new routine, I know exactly what he'd say: "So, what? You want a medal? Or a chest to pin in on?"

Well, Pops. I have a chest now, so yeah. Give me a damn medal.

Looking at myself in the mirror, I barely recognize my body. I've never had muscles like this in my life, and to be honest, they're taking some getting used to. None of my shirts fit anymore, and even though I can get away with my T-shirts being snug, my button-ups won't even ... well ... button up.

I do a few flexes and pose. Yep. Definitely weird.

My phone starts up with Elissa's ring tone, and I drop my pose to grab it, embarrassed I was behaving like a meathead, even in the privacy of my own room.

"Hey, you."

"Hey," she says. "Where are you?" I can hear chatter and the sound of glasses clinking in the background. "You realize this is a New Year's Eve party, right? That means you're supposed to get here before the new year."

"Yes, thank you, Captain Obvious. I'm still figuring out what to wear."

"What's to figure out? It's a costume party. You'll dress up as Captain Kirk, as usual."

I'm not embarrassed to admit that I paid three hundred dollars on EBay for an authentic Kirk uniform a few years ago, and it's become my go-to costume for any occasion. Even wore it to my cousin's Bar Mitzvah for shits and giggles. Aunt Bethany still isn't talking to me over that.

I'd like to say that I chose to hire an alternate costume for tonight because the other one's so tight now I look like a Star Trek strip-o-gram, but that's not it. It's because I've worked hard to look different, and goddammit, maybe just once in my life I want to feel what it's like to be the hero and not the geek. Angel deserves a leading man, not the comic relief. If I can pull this off, maybe I can stop being so goddamn insecure about the Adonises with which I seem to be surrounded.

"What did you and Quinn go as?" I ask.

"You'll see when you get here, which I hope is soon."

"Tell me it's not some nauseatingly hip couple's costumes."

She pauses. "Okay, I won't tell you that. But Josh, hurry uuuuup! Marco's asked me twice if you're coming, and I need my bestie hugs. I haven't seen you since Liam and I got back from the island. I miss you. Come drink with meeeee!"

I chuckle. I've been dying to see her, but my Gammy hasn't been well, so I moved out of Liam's pad and back to Mom and Dad's to help take care of her. Plus, Lissa and Liam have had their hands full dodging the media frenzy from their naked picture debacle. God, it's like most Americans have never seen naked bodies before. I don't see what all the fuss is about.

Ironically, when I said that to the girl who was filling Gammy's prescription at the drug store, she quipped that if I didn't understand it, I hadn't seen the size of Liam Quinn's man member. After judging her for using the term man member, I joked that the whole thing had been photoshopped, and I knew for a fact that Quinn was packing an acorn in his pants.

I've never seen someone look so disappointed in my life. I felt so bad, I tried to tell her I was joking, but the words wouldn't come out. I think it's an ingrained male response to pay out on other guys' dick size. Who am I to argue with nature?

"Josh? Helloooo?"

"Sorry. Just thinking about your boyfriend's dick."

"Me, too. Bestie mind meld!"

"Yeah, but most of the time when I ask what's on your mind you say Liam's dick, so I don't think it's much of an achievement."

"Yes, but knowing you're thinking about it too makes me feel special. Now, get your ass over here! There are a whole bunch of shots with our names on them. God knows I don't want you anywhere near sober when the countdown hits and you start lamenting about your woman being on the other side of the world."

"Way ahead of you. Had two beers with dinner. Mom did not approve."

"That's because you burp like a frat boy when you drink beer."

"I've told you before, Lissa, the bubbles have to go somewhere. Better out the top than out the bottom."

There's a knock on my door, and my Gammy calls out, "Joshua? Are you still there? Don't forget to show me your costume before you go."

I put my hand over the phone. "I'll be out in a sec." I go back to Elissa. "K, better go before she barges in on me in my underwear. Again. See you in twenty minutes."

"K. See you then."

I hang up and throw my phone on the bed.

All right, Kane. No more bullshit. No one's going to tease you tonight. Get your ass into that costume and go on your way.

I head into the bathroom and open the small plastic case on the sink. My eye doctor convinced me to try contacts last time I got new glasses, but I seriously couldn't be bothered poking myself in the eyeballs every day, so I've barely worn them. Tonight, however, I need to be spec free.

I take a deep breath and take off my glasses. It feels weird leaving them behind. They've become such an integral part of my identity, my face feels naked without them.

"Okay. Here we go."

I fight with the floppy plastic bastards for a good ten minutes before I successfully get them both in, and by then my eyes are streaming. I grab some toilet paper and dab my face. "Fuck me. Bet Clark Kent never had to go through this bullshit."

When I'm done, I check myself out.

Man, it's weird being able to see clearly without having anything on my face. Combine my lack of glasses with my slicked-back hairstyle and my new body, and I barely look like myself.

I take a deep breath.

Well, I guess that's the point, isn't it? Let's do this.

• • •

Five minutes later I stand in front of Gammy feeling weird and awesome all at once.

"Oh, Joshua," she says with reverence. "You look wonderful. So handsome."

"Thanks, Gammy."

"I thought you'd wear the other one I always see you in. Space Trek, or something."

"Star Trek. I thought I'd make a change tonight. Try something different."

"It's lovely. But you seemed more comfortable in the other one."

She's not wrong. This thing is so tight, it's like wearing full body Spanx. My internal organs are screaming.

"Yeah, well ..." I say, "I'm trying to get out of my comfort zone for a change."

She smiles and beckons me forward to where she's sitting on the couch. When I bend down, she kisses me on the cheek and holds my face. "Darling boy, I'm not sure why you want to change, but I thought you were perfect before all the workouts and protein shakes. And I'm certain your lovely lady did, too, so if this is for her, you may have wasted your time."

"I can't just be doing it to be healthy?"

"Of course. But is that why you're wearing that costume?" She gives me one of those looks that makes it feel like she's staring into my soul.

Busted.

"I gotta go, Gammy. Do you need anything? A drink? A pillow? *Grand Theft Auto* on the Xbox?"

She pats my hand. "I'm fine, bubbeleh. You go have a good night."

"I will." I kiss her on the cheek and slip on my overcoat. Can't risk being heckled on the subway.

"Oh, Joshua?" I turn to her. "Just remember that what you wear isn't who you are. It's what's on the inside that counts."

I smile at her. Trust Gammy to use my identity crisis as a teaching opportunity.

I give her one last kiss. "See you in the new year, Gammy. I love you."

"I love you, too, my sweet boy." She gives me a knowing smile before I head down the hall and out the door.

TWO

THE GANG'S ALL HERE

"Are you at the party yet?"

Angel sounds so close, I feel like I could reach through the phone and touch her.

If only.

"Just arrived, but I'm hanging outside so we can talk. To be honest, I'm not in a partying mood without you."

She still has another week of filming in Australia, and dammit, I never thought being apart from someone would be this tough. Sure, I missed Elissa when we were studying on opposite sides of the country, but it was nothing like this. Missing Angel is like having a slow-motion heart attack. My chest hurts like hell, and hearing her voice only makes me miss her more. Considering this is my first relationship that's lasted longer than me showering after sex, I have no idea if this is normal or not.

One thing I do know is that our separation is my own stupid fault, because I wanted to come back and help Elissa with the benefit concert. Even though I could tell Angel wasn't thrilled about me leaving, she supported me one-hundred percent. But what she didn't know is that I was also running from how it felt to watch her fall in love with another man every day on the film set, even if it was just an act.

I've never considered myself a jealous person, but watching Angel make out with someone else? I now have a deep, empathetic understanding of how it felt for Dr. Jekyll to transform into Mr. Hyde. Julian is an okay dude, and when it's just the two of us talking about comics or video games, I'm fine. But the second I see him talking to Angel, or worse, touching or kissing her … Yeah. Veins bulge, muscles tense, and I want to leave fun, affable Josh at the door so needlessly violent Josh can come out and play.

I know my reaction stems from my feelings of inadequacy, but that doesn't mean I'm wrong in thinking a guy like me doesn't have a snowball's chance in Hades of keeping a woman like Angel.

To her credit, Angel does a good job of making it seem like we could work, and despite my doubts, I really want to believe her.

"God, Josh, I miss you so much. Did you know it's been next year in Australia for ages now?"

"Yeah? Did you have a good time last night? Party with the cast and crew?" And of course, by cast and crew I mean hunka-beefcake leading man, Julian Dickface Norman. Let's not forget about that stupidly likeable asshole who's probably gearing up to replace me in her affections.

"It was nice," she says, stifling a yawn. "The producers put on a fancy spread at a venue right on Sydney Harbor. The fireworks were incredible. Julian said they were the best he's ever seen."

"I'll bet." I can just imagine him being all wide-eyed and enthusiastic. What a prick. "So, kiss anyone interesting at midnight?" I'm trying to sound casual, even though I'm gripping my phone so tightly, the plastic case creaks.

Angel laughs. "To be honest, I kissed a lot of people. There was a whole line of them. Men, women, waiters, dwarves, stilt walkers, a couple of Japanese tourists who wandered in by mistake. After the first dozen, I stopped counting. But don't worry, sweetie, there was strictly no tongue. I'm saving that for you."

I lean back against the wall and breathe. "You're trying to make my head explode with jealousy, aren't you?"

"Is it working?"

I let out a weak laugh. Normally, I enjoy her teasing, but right now I'm incapable of thinking about her kissing people without conjuring up an image of her and Julian. I've watched them go at it on set enough to know what their lip-locks look like. Julian kisses her like he never wants to stop, and even though I understand how the sweet heaven of Angel's mouth is responsible for that, he still has no right to feel that way about my woman.

"So what are you doing today?" I ask. "Taking it easy, I hope." If she tells me she's seeing Julian, there's no way I'm not losing my shit. I mean, how would she feel if I spent all my free time with a likable, attractive woman?

My phone vibrates, and when I check the screen, there's a text from Lissa. "HURRY UP, BITCH! Get your ass here NOW."

Okay, so, a likable, attractive woman other than Elissa.

"Actually," she says, "I have a cool day planned. The director's brother is taking me out for a cruise around the harbor on his yacht."

Okay, director's brother. Probably an old dude. Nothing to worry about. "That sounds sweet. Is it just going to be the two of you?"

"No, there are a few of us going."

A blood vessel behind my left eye starts to throb. "Oh, yeah? Like who?"

"Oh, you know," she says with a laugh. "The usual suspects."

I turn around and press my forehead into the wall. I know she doesn't mean to torture me, but being vague isn't fucking helping. "Right, so Megan, Kasey, Mark … Julian?"

My heart sinks when she says, "Yeah, I think so." But then she says, "Oh, wait, not Julian. He had a press thing to do."

I'm not sure, but I'm pretty certain I hear a whole fuckton of angels singing, "Hallelujah."

"Aw, shame. Oh, well, you guys will have a great time anyway, right?"

"I doubt it." She lets out a dramatic sigh. "I'll spend most of my time alone, pining for a man who should be whispering sweet nothings to my clitoris but instead is selfishly elsewhere."

Something seizes in my chest, and it's painful as hell. "Just for the record, that person is me, right? Because if someone else is whispering to your clitoris, we're going to have words."

She laughs like it's not a totally valid question. "Yes, babe. I'm talking about you. Geez, you're so needy tonight." She hums, and I can picture her lying back, smiling as I trail kisses down her neck.

"That's because I miss you. Tell me more about this fascinating man you're saving your tongue and clitoris for."

Another hum. "He's incredible. Warm, hilarious, handsome as hell, *and* amazing in bed."

"Wow, sounds like he's the whole package." Also sounds like she's describing Julian. Not that I know what he's like in bed, but my dented ego assumes he'd be a fucking genius.

"He really is, and I adore him."

Keep breathing, Josh. She's talking about you.

I try to calm my hammering pulse.

As great as it is being so in love with this woman I can't see straight, I know damn well that loving something precious goes hand-in-hand with the irrational fear of losing it. That's the wellspring for my jealousy. Up until now, my experiences with women have been fleeting and unimportant. Primitive urges mildly satisfied. But loving Angel is like being a caveman who's finally discovered fire, and I can't stand the thought of going back to living in the dark.

I hear movement, and when she speaks again, it's softer. "I hate waking up and realizing you're not there. Sometimes I'll turn around to tell you something and have half the sentence out before I realize I'm speaking to an empty apartment. Can we not be apart any more please? It vexes me."

I smile when I hear the pout in her voice. "Well, there's nothing more tragic than a vexed Angel." Damn, I want to hold her. Kiss her. Make long, passionate love to her. I want it more than I've ever wanted anything. Even that full-size Klingon warrior when I was twelve.

I pace to release some energy. "I promise I'll make it up to you when I see you."

"And if I can't wait that long?"

"I'll Skype-sex you when I get home tonight."

"Sold." She sighs again. "Okay, you'd better go. Elissa will tear you a new butthole if you don't get in there soon."

"Yeah, I suppose."

"Take heaps of pictures, okay? I want to see what everyone is wearing. And get some pics of you as sexy James Tiberius Kirk. I'm going to print those and keep them in my spank bank for when we're apart."

Just thinking about her masturbating to images of me makes my costume get super uncomfortable in certain areas. I open my mouth to correct her about what I'm wearing but then stop. I don't know why. Maybe because she'd suspect I'm wearing this thing to boost my self-esteem like a needy little bitch.

"I love you, Josh."

Chest pain. Lots of goddamn fucking chest pain.

"I love you, too, beautiful. Can't wait until you're home. I'll call you later."

After hanging up, I walk over to the coat check station. Tonight's shindig is in The Starlight Suites, which is a collection of super swanky function rooms that take up the whole top floor of the Braxton Building. As I slip off my overcoat, the girl behind the counter hands me a ticket.

"You got somewhere to keep that ticket in your costume, sir?" Her tone makes me look up, and I find her giving me an appreciative onceover.

Okay. Never got that reaction when I was Kirk.

"Sure," I say. "Right in my jockstrap along with my dignity. Thanks."

There was a time when I'd try to charm the pants off this girl within minutes. Now, she barely registers. Being in love is doing weird things to me in many ways. I guess not all of them are bad.

As I head through the double doors, I see Elissa wasn't exaggerating when she said Marco's New Year's Eve parties were epic. The huge ballroom is teeming with people. Buffet and drink tables are set up around the room, and waiters in black ties make sure everyone's glasses remain full. As I glance around, I see the who's who of the Broadway set, including a three-time Tony-Award-Winning actor dressed as Pikachu.

Dude. And I thought my costume took balls.

People have gone all out with their costumes. One girl is in full

Avatar mode, not wearing much more than top-to-toe blue body paint. She's laughing and flirting with a guy who's rocking a retro *Saturday Night Fever* vibe, white disco suit and all.

Yeah, that's a nightmare cleaning bill waiting to happen.

I nab a tall glass of beer from a passing waiter as I scan the crowd for Elissa. Not knowing who she's dressed as puts me at a disadvantage. It's like trying to find Waldo when he's not wearing his favorite striped T-shirt and hat.

"Well, happy New Year to me," a voice says from behind me. I turn to see a pretty blonde girl staring at me. She's not wearing a costume, just tight jeans with a T-shirt that reads, *I don't need a costume. People want to be me.*

She's assessing me over the top of her champagne flute, and her glassy expression tells me it's not her first drink of the night. "And what's your name, handsome? Or are you protecting your identity from the super villains?"

I give her a smile. "No, they all have the night off."

She leans in and puts a hand on my chest. "I'm Zoe. Stevens. Perhaps you've heard of me. Most people have."

"Yeah, I know you, Zoe. We met a few months ago at Cassie and Ethan's wedding."

She pulls back, confused. "I don't think so."

"Yes, you talked to me for half an hour about how Ethan used to have a huge crush on you in drama school and now that he and Cassie were married you wanted to keep your distance, so he didn't try to relive the past."

She shakes her head. "Yeah, I remember the conversation, but I had it with a geeky guy with glasses. Not..." She looks down at my body, " ... you." She gives me a wink like she's joking, but I'm finding it hard to get a read on this chick. "So, how do you know Ethan?"

"His sister is my best friend."

She frowns. "Oh, you're gay?"

"No."

"So, you and Elissa are both straight but don't fuck? That's weird."

"We're *friends*. She'd dating Liam Quinn. You know, the movie star?"

She gives me a condescending smile. "Sure, that's what the papers are saying, but I can't see it myself."

"They were together at the wedding."

She laughs. "Yeah, right. If Liam Quinn was at that wedding, I would have been the first person to know about it. Some people have Gaydar. I have Stardar. I can sniff out a famous person at thirty paces."

"Uh huh. So you would have seen that Angel Bell was at the wedding, too."

She thinks for a second. "Oh, yeah. She was dancing with her boyfriend. Some bookish, curly-headed dude."

"Yeah, that was also me."

She stares at me for a full three seconds before bursting into laughter. "Oh, right. Of course it was. And then you ran off into a phone booth and changed into this." She giggles and takes another sip of champagne before fixing me with a deadpan expression. "But seriously, all jokes aside, are you single or not? Because we could totally have some fun together. Do you have anyone to kiss at midnight?"

Before I can answer, a guy a bit shorter than I am appears beside us in a flesh-colored bodysuit.

"Really?" he says to Zoe. "You're trying to make me jealous by flirting with this guy? How dare you use my love of superheroes against me."

I take a closer look at him. Apart from cladding his entire body in pale pink lycra, he's also wearing a mushroom-shaped hat and large pinky-brown furry slippers. What the hell?

"Go away, Jack," Zoe says with a flip of her hair. "Josh and I are having a conversation, and he's *super* hot."

Jack turns to me and holds out his hand. "Hey, man. I'm Jack."

"Yeah," I say as I shake it. "Jack Avery, right?"

He gives me an impressed smile. "Have we met? Or have you just heard of the legend that is the man?"

"The second thing. You were at Cassie and Ethan's wedding. They told me all about the gang from The Grove, but I only got to meet Zoe. Nice to finally put a face to the name. I'm Elissa's best friend."

"Oh, cool," he says, shaking my hand. "I saw Elissa and Cassie out on the dance floor before." He leans in and whispers, "Just between you and me, did those two ever hook up? Because ... hot!"

The anger that floods my system must show on my face, because he quickly drops my hand and steps back. "Sorry, dude. Just kidding. Keep your cape on."

Zoe's disdain is clear. "What the hell are you even supposed to be, Jack? Apart from an insufferable jerk?"

He gestures to himself and smiles. "I'll give you a clue. I'm the most famous thing in the world right now."

Zoe stares at him, looking unimpressed. "You know I hate guessing. Just tell me."

"I'm Liam Quinn's cock." He grins at her.

Zoe's scowl falters. "Appropriate, considering you're such a huge dick."

They glare at each other for a second more before cracking up. Then, without missing a beat, Jack pulls Zoe into a searing kiss that makes me all kinds of uncomfortable.

"I hate you," Zoe whispers. "This is the absolute last time this is happening."

Jack proceeds to suck on her neck. "That's what you said the last twenty-eight times."

"You're keeping count?"

"One of us has to."

"You're disgusting."

"One of the many reasons you find me irresistible." He pushes her back into the wall and they keep going, getting more inappropriate by the second. I look around, but no one else seems to even notice.

"Okay, then," I say. "I'm just gonna go. See you guys around."

I take a deep drink of my beer as I move through the crowd. Let's hope this isn't an indication of how this night will go.

When I pass by a group and see Marco, I almost do a spit-take. He's usually dressed impeccably, but tonight he's rocking a full Elvis ensemble, complete with a constellation of tacky-as-hell rhinestones and pompadour wig. He throws up his arms when he sees me.

"Joshua, my lad! Glad you could make it! You look wonderful."

"Hey, Marco. You look ..." I'm so unused to seeing him with hair, I'm having trouble forming words. "Elvis-y."

He raises his eyebrows and his glass. "Why, thank you. I hope you're ready for a wonderful night. I'll see you later, yes?"

I give him a chin tip and continue on my way. Standing near a table overflowing with canapés is a guy dressed as Batman talking to a tall, lanky Riddler. As I pass, we all give each other knowing nods.

Finally, I hear a distinct laugh and spot Cassie on the far side of the room. It's only the height of the people she's with that gives them away as Elissa, Liam, and Ethan. I have to admit, they all look amazing.

Ethan is dressed as John Travolta in Pulp Fiction, and Cassie is almost unrecognizable in a black wig, white shirt, and black capris. It's uncanny how much she looks like Uma Thurman's character.

Liam and Elissa look even cooler. Elissa is turning more than just Liam's head in her Black Widow costume, complete with figure-hugging leather jumpsuit and bright red hair. And judging by Liam's sleeveless vest and the bow slung on his back, he's rocking the Hawkeye look.

As I approach, they all glance at me before going back to their conversation. It's Elissa who realizes who I am first and does a double take.

"Holy crap, Josh?!"

Then they all turn, and I've never felt so awkward. It's not bad enough I feel like an imposter in this costume in the first place, now I have two guys who could play this character in a second staring at me. I feel three feet tall.

"You look amazing!" Lissa says as she throws her arms around me. "I've been looking for Captain Kirk all night. Not Superman." She pulls back and looks at my body. "Goddamn, bestie, you got huge. What the hell?"

I shrug as the others smile at me. "You told me to work on my body."

"Yeah, but I didn't expect you to actually do it. Look at you!"

I admit I'm proud of myself. In high school, the most exercise I got was running to the cafeteria on Taco Tuesday, so hitting the gym every day and sticking with it is an achievement for me.

Liam claps a giant hand on my shoulder. "You must have put in some reps to get this big, dude. I feel slack in comparison. I haven't worked out at all while I was away."

Elissa elbows him. "Now, that's not true."

Quinn smirks like the cat who ate the canary. "Babe, bench pressing you hardly counts as a workout."

Cassie steps forward and cringes. "Ew, you two. If that's code for some new, weird sexual position, I don't even want to know." The look on Elissa's face suggests it is. Cassie ignores her and gives me a hug. "Hey, Super Josh. Kind of disappointed you didn't go with the old school Christopher Reeve costume. Those red undies on the outside were hella sexy."

I nod and look down at the dark blue textured suit. I might not be as buff as Henry Cavill, but I fill it out okay. "Yeah, well, couldn't run the risk of you being all up in my business in front of Vinnie there." I point to Ethan. "He might get jealous and shoot me in the face."

Ethan gives his best Vinnie Vega impression. "You shoot *one* guy in the face, and you never hear the end of it. Typical."

I breathe a sigh of relief that they didn't laugh me out of the party. Not that my friends would do that, but old wounds linger.

When a waiter arrives with a tray of shots, I grab them and pass them around. Then I raise my glass and say, "Okay, so, let's toast." They all hold up their glasses. "To good friends, good times, and an amazing year ahead."

Elissa puts her hand on my shoulder. "And to those loved ones who can't be here tonight."

"To Angel," Liam says with a sympathetic smile.

We all take a moment, and as grateful as I am to be surrounded by my friends, a celebration of any kind feels wrong without Angel. I decide right then that when I get home, I'm booking the first flight to Australia. She may be coming home in a week, but that's a week too long without her.

We all clink glasses. "Cheers."

After downing our shots, we hiss, and there's a little coughing from Cassie as the alcohol goes down.

"Happy New Year's Eve, you guys," she manages to say through gasps. "Now, let's party our asses off."

THREE

SUPER VILLAINS AND DRAMA QUEENS

It's obvious the person who designed this Superman costume didn't count on a dance off. Raising my arms is a challenge, but if I have to go through a little discomfort to wipe the floor with Ethan, then that's what I'm going to do.

"Give it up, Supes," he says, doing some sort of spinning thing that shouldn't be possible considering how much he's had to drink. "You're going down."

"Ha, don't you mean *getting* down?" I steal a few moves from John Travolta in *Saturday Night Fever*. The dude beside me in the full white suit tries to copy, but he's a freaking terrible dancer. Also, my prediction about him and *Avatar* girl was accurate, because there are bright blue marks all over his jacket and what look suspiciously like hand prints on his crotch. There's no way that guy's getting his security deposit back.

Just when I think I'm getting the better of Ethan, Liam shows up.

"Alright, ladies. Stand back and let me show you how it's done."

He goes into some cool hip-hop moves, and of course the bastard is a good dancer.

"Elissa, can you do something about this, please?"

She boogies on the sidelines. "I would, but I'm enjoying the view too much."

Cassie comes to the rescue. She stands in front of Quinn and pretends to send him off. "I'm sorry, sir. This is the Olympic dance off. Amateurs only. You're clearly in another league to these other yahoos."

Ethan and I stop and say, "Hey!" simultaneously.

Cassie shrugs. "Just calling it as I see it, gentlemen."

With a cheeky smile, she dances next to us, before Liam and Elissa join in. We may not be the best dancers in the world, but at least we're enthusiastic.

"Well, well, well, how fun," a condescending voice says behind us. "Superman and his little friends think they're dancing."

We turn to see a group of three guys watching us with supercilious expressions. One of them is dressed as Doctor Evil from Austin Powers, one is The Joker from *Suicide Squad*, and the one addressing us is wearing a super cool Loki costume that I'd compliment him on if I wasn't trying to stay in character.

"Loki," I say and cross my arms over my chest. "Just keep walking. You don't want to mess with us."

"Don't I?" he says with a sneer. He clicks his fingers, and the Joker goes and whispers something to the DJ. In seconds, the music changes, and the strains of "Uptown Funk" pour from the speakers. "Let's see you fend off these moves, Superman."

The three guys break into a fully choreographed routine, and there's no doubt these boys are trained dancers. They mix hip-hop with contemporary and jazz, and they're so damn good, I can only think of one way to beat them, and it's not pretty.

I turn to the others. "Stand back. I'll handle this."

Elissa grabs my arm. "No, Superman, you can't do this alone! It's suicide."

"I have to, Black Widow. I can at least buy you some time, so you can get to safety - the buffet table, maybe the bar."

"We won't leave you," Liam says, clamping his giant hand on my shoulder so hard, I bite my tongue to stop myself from making owie noises.

"Hawkeye, just go and keep the others safe. They're not even superheroes. Just hipsters with bad hair."

Ethan and Cassie flip me the bird then adjust their wigs.

As I turn to confront our enemies, Elissa takes my arm. "You're not going to do what I think you are, right?"

"Elissa, these assholes threw down the gauntlet. I'm just going to pick it up. Prepare to see them cry."

She tightens her hand. "Josh, no. You haven't done Le Dance Bomb since high school. You could die! Or, you know, get seriously out of breath."

"Then prepare to give me mouth to mouth, little lady, because I'm going in."

The super villains watch me warily as I stride over to them.

"Alright, gents," I say, feet wide and hands on hips. "You brought this into my classroom, so now, prepare to be schooled."

I start off slow, a step-touch here, a box-step there. They think they have me pegged and roll their eyes, but I'm just getting started. I move into what I call Disco of Doom: The Bus Stop, The Carwash, and something I made up called The Pogo Dandy. Confusion passes over their faces. They can't believe what they're seeing, and I don't have the heart to tell them they ain't seen nothing yet. Seamlessly, I morph into line dancing, complete with YIPs and YEEEHARs, and it's then I see the fear in their eyes.

That's right, boys. I'm going full dance spectacular, and there's not a damn thing you can do to stop me.

In quick succession, I hit them with The Nutbush, The Macarena, and a particularly ridiculous move Elissa dubbed Psycho Feta. When the villains get a load of that and start gazing on me in wonder, I know victory is within my grasp. Despite trying not to smile, their mouths curve, but it's not the undeniable victory I'm looking for. I need to break them.

My legs are cramping, and my lungs burn for air, but still I continue. My body is a blur as I give them The Electric Boogaloo, White-Hot Booty, and add some extra flair when I throw my cape over my shoulder so they can behold my twerking. Their smiles widen, but it's not enough. I throw in a demented version of the chicken dance, and one of them snorts but doesn't guffaw.

Goddammit. I'm so close to beating them, but I'm running out of steam. In a last desperate bid to break them, I throw myself into the moves from Thriller.

"Come on, Josh!" Elissa calls, and I screw up my moonwalk. "You've got this!"

My friends clap and cheer me on.

"Go, Kane, you magnificent weirdo," Ethan yells. "Bring it home!"

Despite their encouragement, my stamina is failing. The song is almost over, and I've run out of moves. If I don't think of something spectacular in in the next thirty seconds, this thing is all over, and Superman will be labeled a loser.

"Josh!" I turn to see Liam standing on the other side of the dance floor. "Let's do the lift."

I frown. He can't be serious. We tried it once in his apartment after we'd downed a bottle of tequila and watched *Dirty Dancing*, and he'd not only dropped me, he'd also pulled a muscle in his back.

"Liam, no. It's too dangerous."

He beckons to me. "We can do this. Come on!"

I shake my head. "Quinn, we can't ..."

"Goddammit, Kane, there's no time for debate! The song's about to end! Do the damn lift!"

I glance at the villains who are gazing at us smugly. I stop dancing and smile back. "You haven't won yet, bitches. Watch carefully, because I'm about to make you believe a man can fly."

Without waiting for their reaction, I run full pelt at Liam. Jesus Christ, I hope he was lying about not working out while he was on that stupid island, because I've put on about forty pounds of muscle, and I really don't want to die.

Everything seems to slow down as I reach him. He sets his mouth in a determined line before bending his knees and grabbing my hips, and when I jump into the air, he straightens his arms and pushes me above his head. For a gut-churning second, I think I have so much momentum I'm going to sail headfirst into the chocolate fountain, but at the last minute Liam corrects his position and I'm able to balance perfectly, one arm out in the classic Superman pose as my cape flutters behind me.

The sight is too much for the villains. They break into rapturous applause, as do the rest of the nearby partygoers. Even the DJ joins in by playing the Superman theme song.

The applause is still going when Quinn lowers me to the floor with a grunt.

"Fucking hell," he says as he stretches out his back. "How much do you weigh these days?"

"Rude, much? It's not polite to talk about a hero's weight."

Cassie and Elissa come over for hugs, and for the first time in all the years I've known him, Ethan looks impressed with me.

"You're insane," he says, clasping my hand and giving me a bro-hug. "But fuck, that was funny."

Even the super villains come over and congratulate me. It turns out, they're three of the hyena dancers in *The Lion King.* Appropriate.

Elissa orders another round of drinks, and I down my shot before heading over to a nearby couch to collapse. Damn, if I ever needed a reminder I'm not eighteen anymore, that dance off was it.

Elissa smiles as she comes and sits next to me. "That was freaking epic, my bestie."

"Yeah?" I say and rest my elbows on my knees. "I wish Angel were here to see it."

"Oh, she'll see it." She holds up her phone. "Don't you worry about that."

I lean back into the couch and sigh. "Cool. Wake me up when it's midnight, okay."

"Sure. Or, I could get us some food, so we can sit here and gossip about people."

She knows me too well. "Get the food."

• • •

"And that guy," whispers Elissa, "was caught backstage at *Seussical,* snorting cocaine off The Cat in the Hat's ass."

I laugh and wipe my mouth with a napkin. "I thought he went to rehab."

"He did. It didn't stick. Word is he's heading out to Hollywood. There's no way he can support his habit on theater wages."

I shake my head. It never fails to amaze me how much scandal there is on Broadway, and Elissa somehow knows it all.

While she devours a particularly large piece of brie, I study a girl a short distance away talking with Jack, Zoe, and a guy I haven't met.

"Lissa, don't be obvious, but do you know that whore over there talking to Jack and Zoe?"

A look of disappointment passes over Elissa's face. "I'm hoping it's the alcohol making you say that. Slut shaming girls isn't usually your thing."

"I'm not slut shaming. She's dressed as an ol' timey whore from the Wild West. Look."

She checks the girls out then shrugs. "She doesn't look familiar. Why?"

"She keeps glaring at Cassie."

"Seriously?" She indicates the guy next to glary-girl who's dressed like a Wild West villain, all in black with a ten-gallon hat. "See him?"

"Yeah."

"That's Connor Baine. You remember I told you about him being in love with Cassie, right?"

"Ohhhh, yeah. Another Grovian I didn't meet at the wedding. Cassie dated him for a while after Ethan dumped her, right?"

"Exactly. If the whore is staring daggers at Cassie, it's probably because she's the latest in Connor's rotating roster of girlfriends. He might have told her the story."

"Huh. Awkward."

"You got that right. Cassie and Connor used to be almost as close as you and I. But since they got all groiny with each other, they barely speak."

"See? This is why we were smart to never hit the sheets together."

"Also, because you're like my brother."

"That, too."

"And judging from the way Connor's been staring at Cassie, he's still holding a major flame. The boy needs to let it go."

I break into the opening strains of the Disney song, but Elissa gives me the stink-eye, so I shut up

"What about Zoe and Jack?" I ask. "What's their history?"

Elissa shrugs. "They were snarky friends in college. Doesn't look like that's changed."

"Then you missed their hot and heavy liplock earlier. And from what I overheard, they've been hooking up on the regular."

"Really?" She looks impressed I can contribute some juicy info for once. "Well, that's interesting. Zoe usually only dates guys who are rich or semi-famous. Even though Jack's doing well on the stand-up comedy circuit, he hardly gives her bragging rights."

She continues to talk, but I'm distracted by a flash of red on the other side of the room. When I turn to see what it is, I smile. There's a dark-headed girl talking with Marco, and she's wearing a replica of Lieutenant Uhura's costume from the original *Star Trek* series. A woman with excellent taste. She has her back to me, so I can't see her face, but she's flashing plenty of thigh. Dang, I'd almost forgotten how short that dress was. It barely covers her ass cheeks. Not that I'm complaining. She has incredible legs.

As I stare at her, I'm mildly horrified she's turning me on. This isn't supposed to happen now that I have Angel. Other women aren't allowed to have power over Magic Mike.

I avert my gaze and tell my dick to stand down. Well behaved penis that he is, he complies.

Maybe it wasn't the girl at all. Perhaps it was just the costume. Uhura was my first serious crush, and seeing her in those short skirts and long boots did new and unusual things to my twelve-year-old body. Coincidentally, that was when I discovered the wonders of masturbation. Ahhh, good times.

"Josh!" I'm brought back to earth when Elissa slaps me on the shoulder.

"Ow! What?"

"Stop staring off into space." Mentally, I whisper, *The final frontier.* "Angel's on the phone. Said you weren't answering yours."

I'm careful not to look in the direction of Sexy Uhura as I lean forward and take the phone. I don't think Angel would be impressed with me checking out another girl's legs. "Hey, sorry about not answering. I left my phone in my coat."

"It's fine. That's what I figured when I couldn't get you."

The music and crowd noise makes it hard to hear, so I block my other ear with my hand. "So what's up. Are you okay?"

"Yeah. Just wanted to hear your voice."

"Aw. I'm not sure how much you can hear, but it's the thought that counts. Are you on your yacht adventure yet?"

She laughs. "Yes, and it's amazing. We've cruised past the Opera House and the Harbor Bridge, and now they've laid out a full seafood and champagne spread. I could get used to this."

"Take photos. I want to see everything."

"I will. I'll text them to Elissa soon. It a beautiful day here."

I look out the giant picture windows next to us. "Yeah, well, it's snowing here. Not much, but all the people in Times Square will be freezing their balls off."

"Or boobs, as the case may be."

"Exactly." The music seems to be getting louder, and I have to raise my voice. "Sorry about the noise. I'll call you back when I get somewhere quieter."

"Okay, babe. I love you."

"I love you, too, beautiful." Elissa makes ridiculous kissing sounds, so I shove her off the couch. She lands on the floor with a tight squeal. "I'll talk to you soon."

As soon as I hang up, I want to call her back. Why is that everything's better when I'm with her, even if only by phone?

I'm still contemplating that when Elissa tackles me and throws me onto the floor.

• • •

For a small woman, Elissa is as strong as an ox, and she keeps a firm grip on my hand as she leads me through the crowd.

"Where are we going?"

"Over to the bar."

"I was going to head outside so I could call Angel back."

"You can in a minute. There's someone I want you to meet first. You're going to love her."

She leads me over to where Ethan and Cassie are talking to an attractive woman dressed like a flapper. She's older than we are, but she's wearing the hell out of a short slip dress made of fringe. Her slick black bob is topped with a headband and a feather. As we stop beside her, Zoe, Jack, and Connor join us.

"Erika!" Elissa hugs the woman, and the others follow. It seems I've stumbled into a mutual love fest. Of course, I've heard about Erika. Even though Elissa didn't have a lot to do with her at The Grove, she was Cassie and Ethan's mentor, and from what I understand she had a hand in getting them together. Seems like a pretty cool lady all around.

When everyone has finished fawning over her, Elissa brings me forward.

"Erika, I'd like you to meet my best friend, Joshua Kane. "

I hold out my hand, and Erika shakes it. "Nice to meet you, Josh. Super outfit."

I laugh. "You, too. Both the outfit and the meeting." She's intimidating but warm. In that respect, she reminds me a lot of Elissa. Attractive, too. It makes me wonder why she's here alone.

She chats with everyone about what they've been up to since graduating, and it's interesting stuff. Zoe spent some time organizing performances with underprivileged youth, which didn't gel at all with my image of her, and Connor did a Taiwanese movie in which he had to speak his entire role in Chinese.

When Ethan and Erika strike up a conversation about a Shakespeare festival he's about to appear in as Hamlet, I move over and hold out my hand to Connor.

"Hey, man, we haven't met. I'm Josh."

He takes my hand and smiles, and I get the feeling he's had more than his fair share of liquor tonight. "Connor. I saw you briefly at the wedding but didn't get a chance to say hello. Those were some pretty sweet moves you made on the dance floor."

"What can I say? I have a gift."

Cassie comes to stand beside me, and Connor's smile falters for a second before he says, "Good to see you, Cassie."

Cassie smiles. "You, too."

His girlfriend sidles up to him and hands him a beer before gripping his arm possessively.

"Josh, Cassie," Connor says. "This is Ava."

She smiles at us, but it's as fake as Marco's Elvis wig.

"Nice to meet you, Ava," Cassie says. "Great costume."

There's a slight twitch to Ava's eye when she says, "Thanks. You, too."

If Cassie notices Ava doesn't like her, she doesn't let on. There are a couple of seconds of awkward silence when we're all just staring at each other, before I break the ice by saying, "So, are you an actor too, Ava?"

"No," she says in a curt tone. "I'm a bartender. Before Connor and I got together, he was one of my best customers. Used to come into the bar every night." She gives him an affectionate glance, and Connor smiles down at his beer before taking a mouthful. Then he sways a little.

Yep. If the boy doesn't want a major hangover tomorrow, he's going to need to stop drinking now.

When he looks over at Cassie, I almost feel sorry for him. It's clear he has it bad.

"So, Erika," Jack says. "Do you miss us? Be honest. We were your favorite class ever, right? I mean, just look at the amount of awesome in this group. It's off the charts."

Erika smiles. "You were certainly one of my most challenging classes, Mr. Avery, that's for sure. However, between the bickering, Ethan and Cassie's relationship dramas, Zoe's constant requests for bigger roles, and your propensity to leave whoopee cushions on random chairs every second day, I admit that the lack of hijinks in subsequent classes has been ... nice."

Connor pushes his cowboy hat farther back on his head. "Yeah, but nice boring, though, right? It's safe and forgettable. Like me. But you'll sure as hell remember Ethan Holt, because he was a giant pain in your ass."

We all laugh, but I don't miss Cassie's confused expression.

"It's true," Erika says. "I've yet to meet a student quite as volatile and opinionated as Mr. Holt, but lucky for him, being a pain in the ass can sometimes be endearing."

Ethan gives a shrug. "Lovable asshole. That's me."

"Well, you've got the asshole part right," Connor mumbles under his breath.

Damn, son ...

Thank God Ethan's too busy bantering with Erika to hear it. I can't imagine he'd need much of an excuse to start pounding on the dude who spent a significant amount of time between his beloved wife's legs. Or maybe that's just me. I've yet to meet one of Angel's ex-lovers, but I can't imagine it would be a pleasant experience.

"Holy shit." Ava stares open mouthed as Liam joins the group. He greets Erika then puts his arm around Elissa and kisses her cheek.

"Is that Liam Quinn?" Ava says, star struck. "No way."

"Yes, way," I say. "The Stallion, in the flesh. But with clothes on."

She's not the only one who does a double take. Jack goes as white as a sheet, and Zoe looks like she's about three seconds away from a full-on head explosion.

Man, did they really not see him at the wedding? Maybe my dad's right. Our generation does need to look up from our cell phones every now and then.

Elissa introduces Liam to everyone, and it could be my imagination, but I swear he winces a little as he shakes their hands. The big lug probably pulled something lifting me. I did warn him.

"So, Jack," I say, never one to miss an opportunity to stir the pot. "Why don't you tell everyone who you've come as tonight?"

Jack glances at Liam and gives a nervous chuckle. "'Come as'. I see what you did there. But, nah, I'm good. Thanks."

"Oh, come on," Elissa says, looking him up and down. "I was wondering what you were. Ooh, I've got it. You're a Fun Guy!" Everyone looks confused. She points to his hat. "Mushroom? Fungi? Get it?" When everyone groans, she gestures to the waiter for more drinks. "Man, you guys are lame. Shots, please."

"Actually," I say, "he's a giant dick. See, the mushroom hat is the head, his body's the shaft, and the fuzzy slippers are the balls. Clever, right?" I nudge Elissa. "Out of everyone, you should recognize exactly what he is. God knows, you see it enough."

Jack swallows as Elissa stares at him with dawning horror. "Oh, no, Jack Avery, you did *not* come as Liam's dick."

Jack giggles. "Well, not yet, but play your cards right—"

"Jack!" She slaps his arm. Hard.

I cover my smile with my hand. Lissa's kind of adorable when she's tipsy and pissed. I think Liam's of the same opinion, because he doesn't seem the least bit upset. Instead, he's watching enthralled as his woman fixes Jack with her most withering gaze.

"Now, Elissa, calm down ..." Jack says, trying to laugh it off. "No need to get testes."

Connor snorts and takes another swig of beer. "Testes. Good one."

Liam clears his throat and attempts to look angry. "She has every right to be pissed, dude. That costume's not cool with me, either. You're way too small to play my dick."

Zoe snorts. "At least he didn't come dressed as your girlfriend's boobs. God knows he's gawked at those pictures enough to draw them from memory."

Now Liam does look angry. He scowls at Jack. "Dude!"

Jack throws up his hands. "It's not true! I've told Zoe a million times, I was reading the *articles*." He whispers to Zoe, "And even if I was looking at her boobs, you have no reason to be jealous. You have great tits, too."

"Ha!" Zoe says. "As if I'd ever be jealous over you, Jack."

Ethan steps away from Erika and holds up his hands. "Hey, guys. Let's just cool it, okay?"

"That's right, Holt," Jack says. "If you tell her to calm down, she'll listen. After all, she thinks you're God's freaking gift, even though you've shown *zero* interest in her since day one."

"Not true," Zoe says. "Holt's kissed me seven times."

Cassie's face turns read. "Only in acting class. Or in shows. Never because he chose to."

Jack crosses his arms. "I rest my case."

Zoe slaps his arm. "Shut up, Jack!"

"You're lucky he never showed interest in you," Connor mutters. "It's worse when you get to have them, only to find they don't want you back."

All of a sudden, all eyes are on Cassie. She throws up her hands. "Connor, what the hell?"

"Don't you dare speak to him like that," Ava says. "He loved you, and you destroyed him to go back to a guy who'd dumped you, *twice*. That's insane."

"Ava, that's enough." Connor looks horrified, but he started it.

I have no goddamn clue what happening right now.

Jack looks between Cassie and Ava and rubs his hands together. "Ladies, if you want to settle this, I can get a kiddy pool filled with jello here within the hour."

"Shhh," Zoe hisses. "Let Ava talk. Cassie's finally getting roasted for hogging the two hottest guys in our class."

Jack's face turns serious. "That's bullshit, Zoe, and you know it. After me, Holt and Baine are second and third hottest, at best."

Cassie's about to say something when she notices Erika watching them with tears in her eyes.

"Erika?" Cassie goes over to her, but Erika waves her off. "Hey, what's wrong?"

In a second, all the petty squabbles are forgotten, and everyone is united in checking to see if Erika's okay. When she notices the attention, she laughs. "I'm sorry. This is silly."

"What is it?" Jack asks, sincerely concerned. "Did we say something to offend you?"

"I'm fine. I've just ..." She looks at her ex-students and smiles. "I've just missed you all so damn much. It's fantastic to see you bunch of drama queens again."

• • •

As the group around Erika continues to reminisce about their time at The Grove, I tune out and wonder if I can sneak away to call my girl. I feel like an outsider listening to their shared experiences, and I'd rather find a quiet corner and talk to Angel. Of course, finding a quiet corner around here might be a challenge.

As I glance around the huge room, my gaze involuntarily lands on the girl in the Star Trek uniform again.

Seriously, Kane? You mentally freak out over your girlfriend spending time with her co-star, and then you have the balls to lust after a stranger because she's wearing a short skirt?

Lame.

When I see who's standing next to Sexy Uhura, I stop dead in my tracks.

I nudge Elissa. "Hey, look." I point to the guy wearing a slick dinner suit. "Isn't that Daniel Eastman?"

Elissa follows my gaze. "Holy shit! What's he doing here? I didn't realize Marco knew him."

Before Liam Quinn claimed the title of King of the Hollywood hunks, Daniel Eastman held the crown. He became a huge star playing an international spy in the *Edward Stiles* movies when he was younger, and even now he's still a major box office draw. Sure, he has a few more wrinkles these days and is sporting some grey around his temples, but even I can objectively say he's an attractive dude.

Elissa grabs my arm. "Marco's bringing him over. God, Liam is going to lose his shit. Eastman is his idol."

"Everyone," Marco says, as he arrives at our little group. "I have a special guest for you all to meet, and I'm sure I don't need to introduce him."

When they see who he's talking about, their jaws hit the floor. Daniel stands next to Erika and smiles at us. "Evening, all. Sorry about the formal wear. Just came from a stuffy dinner. Having a good time?"

"My God," Jack whispers. "It's actually him. A bonafide living legend in our midst."

Daniel holds out his hand, and we all just stare, too intimidated to move. "I won't bite, you know."

That breaks the ice, and we all nearly fall over ourselves trying to say hello. Liam is extra enthusiastic.

"It's an honor," he says as Daniel shakes his hand. "You're the reason I wanted to become an actor. I've watched all your movies dozens of times. You're the master."

"Ditto to that," Ethan says. "My favorite is *Twice Dead*. Total classic."

As everyone breaks into excited chatter about their favorite Eastman movies, Marco turns to Erika, who seems shocked into silence.

"Darling," Marco says. "You remember Daniel, don't you?"

She flashes Marco a look before holding her hand out to Daniel. "Of course. How are you?"

Daniel brings her hand up to his mouth and kisses it. Wow, this dude is smooth.

"Better for seeing you," he says, standing close to her. "You look ... breathtaking."

They stare at each other for a few seconds, and it's clear there's a truckload of sexual tension parked between them.

Interesting.

Erika's the first to break eye contact, and after she pulls her hand back, she takes in a shaky breath. "If you'll excuse me, I see someone I must speak with."

Daniel seems to deflate as she leaves.

Okay, this is intriguing. Why am I the only one taking notice?

A few months ago, Daniel was involved in a messy divorce from his wife of twenty years. It was all over the papers. Insiders said his wife took him to the cleaners, and Daniel just rolled over and took it. There were whispers of infidelity with some of his younger co-stars, but judging from this exchange, I wonder if his mistress might have been someone closer to his age.

"Danny," Marco says. "You don't seem to have a drink. Let me remedy that. What will you have?"

Daniel keeps his eyes on Erika until she disappears into the long hallway on the other side of the room. "I don't care what you give me, but make it a double."

FOUR

GREEN-EYED MONSTER

As the clock ticks closer to midnight, the party buzzes with excited energy. People are laughing, drinks are flowing, and even though no one is sloppy drunk, we're all at the stage where our inhibitions are fading, and our verbal filters have gone home for the night.

"I mean, you've seen the guy, right?" I say to Elissa as we sit side by side on a long, leather couch. "Do you think I'm crazy being paranoid about him?"

She nods. "Yes."

"Like, is it crazy to think they might be rehearsing a sex scene in her apartment one night, and OOPS, all of their clothes fall off, and they accidentally fuck?"

"Yes, it's crazy," she says emphatically. "That would never happen."

"How do you know?"

"Because I know Angel. And she's so nutso in love with you, she'd never even look at another guy." Her phone dings, and she checks the screen. "Well, speak of the devil. Here." She passes me the phone. "She's sent you pics."

I smile as I see her stunning face on the screen. Her smile is so dazzling, it could light up Manhattan.

She's taken a selfie with the Sydney Opera House in the

background, and she wasn't lying when she said it was a gorgeous day down under. The sky is clear blue, and from what I can see of the yacht, it's one of those luxury jobs with all the bells and whistles.

I scroll to the next photo, and what I see makes my smile drop. "No." I scroll to the next picture, and the next, and that vein behind my eye starts throbbing again. "No, no, no."

"Josh?"

"He wasn't supposed to be there," I mutter to myself as I stand and flick back through the frames. "He had a press thing to do." Why the ever loving *fuck* are there pictures of Angel hugging Julian, and sitting on his lap, and staring at him adoringly as he throws his head back and laughs. "Fuck!"

"Bestie, you're not making sense," Elissa says as she pulls Liam to sit next to her. "But on the upside, that costume makes your package look freaking huge."

"Babe," Liam says. "I know you've had a few shots, but it's still not cool to talk about another guy's package in front of me."

I'm fixated on a photo of Julian and Angel on the deck of the boat, arms around each other as everyone else looks on. They look like a goddamn ad campaign for overpriced perfume.

"But, babe, it's *right there*," Elissa says. "Like, boom! In my face." She looks up at me. "Did you stuff a sock down there tonight, or what?"

I glare at her. "You said she wouldn't even look at another man. Then how do you explain this?"

I show her the pictures, and her face drops. "Josh, don't panic, okay? This doesn't prove anything except she's having a good time."

Liam squints at the screen. "These look like press shots. She's just playing it up with Julian for the cameras. I should know. I've done that with her a million times. It's good publicity for the film."

Elissa takes my hand. "See? It doesn't mean anything. It's just a bunch of friends on a boat."

"Yeah," I say, trying to stay ahead of my rising anger. "But they're the only two friends who look like a couple."

"Josh —"

I've had enough platitudes. I pull my hand away and stride toward the long hallway on the other side of the room. On the way, I angrily jab Angel's number.

• • •

"Come on," I say through gritted teeth as Angel's phone rings out for the fourth time. "What the fuck are you doing that you can't answer the damn phone?"

My brain automatically throws up a whole bunch of scenarios that would explain her absence, and I pace the length of the men's bathroom to try and get them out of my head. It might not be the most glamorous location to confront my girlfriend about her behavior with another guy, but at least it's a little quieter in here, and right now my rage needs space.

"Come on, Angel. Pick up, for fuck's sake."

It goes to voicemail again, and I smack the phone down on the bench in frustration.

"Shit!"

I take a deep breath and let it out.

Okay, Mr. Hyde, just calm your goddamn farm. Flying off the handle isn't going to help anything.

I put my palms flat on the bench as I take slow, measured breaths. I know Angel. I love Angel. There's no way she'd betray me. Even if those pics suggest she'd like to.

I've managed to dial my crazy down from *shit fit* to *moderately unreasonable* when Connor walks through the door. He stops when he sees me.

"Hey, man. You okay? You look a little murderous."

I stand up straight and pick up the phone. "Yeah, man. Thanks. Just ... woman issues. I'll be fine."

He nods. "I know how that is. If I thought I could make money off my ability to fuck things up with women, I'd write a book. You're dating Angel Bell, right?" When I nod, he grimaces. "Yeah, tough gig, dating a star. You have to jump over so many more hurdles than with regular people, but I guess you're learning that the hard way."

"You could say that." I put down the phone and pull off my

cape, thinking that I should probably pee while I'm here. Those six beers in my system sure aren't making my bladder any less full. But when I reach over my shoulder to grab my zipper, I realize this isn't a one-man job.

I turn to Connor. "Hey, man. Give me a hand here? I feel like one of those magicians in a straight jacket, except the only magic you're likely to see here is me peeing without opening my pants."

He laughs. "Well, this is a scenario you don't think about when you watch a superhero movie. Does Superman need an assistant every time he takes a piss?"

"Yes. But they're called a *pissistant*. Important support job."

Connor chuckles and yanks down the zipper before heading over to the urinal. As quickly as I can, I pull the top half of my costume down and join him.

Ahhhh, that's better. My bladder no longer hates me.

I should switch to water when I get back out there. I'm buzzed but not drunk, and that's how I'd like to stay. Keeping a cool head about the thing with Julian is hard enough without more booze egging me on.

Connor and I finish up at the same time and stand side-by-side at the sinks as we wash our hands.

"So, enjoying the party?" I say.

Connor rinses off and looks at me in the mirror. "Yeah, but I think I'm doing it wrong. I'm in the doghouse with Ava for spending too much time with my friends."

I turn off the faucet and grab some paper towels. Connor follows suit.

"In Ava's defense," I say, "I don't think it's your friends she's pissed about. It's Cassie."

He throws towels into the trashcan and turns to me. "You know the history between me and Cassie?"

"Yeah, but even if I didn't, I would have been able to figure it out by seeing you together. You're awkward around each other while trying to be friendly. And then there's the way you look at her."

He leans against the bench. "What does that mean?"

I laugh. "Dude, it's so clear you're still in love with her, Stevie

Wonder could spot it a mile away. I'd take bets that's why Ava wants you to stay away from our little group. Hanging around with the chick her boyfriend's still pining for is no one's idea of fun." Or seeing pics of a guy who wants to steal your girlfriend.

Connor takes his hat off and runs his fingers through his hair. "Shit. I thought I was ready to face Cassie tonight. I really did. But every time I see her, I ..." He looks at me. "Sorry, man. This isn't your problem."

"No, but this seems to be the *Bathroom of Manly Bonding*, so ..." I lean against the bench. "As far as Cassie goes, I get it. She's cool, and funny, and beautiful, and you think that no one will ever compare. But believe me, you'll find someone else. It just might take some time."

"It's been four years."

"I thought my best friend was the most incredible woman on the planet for ten years before I met my girlfriend, so don't beat yourself up. And for God's sake, don't become like old-school Ethan, either. That dude went through hell to deal with his bad boy issues. You seem like a decent guy. Don't let one bad experience get you down."

He nods. "Thanks, man. You a therapist or something?"

I pull my suit back up. "Kind of. Assistant stage manager."

He laughs and gestures for me to turn around so he can zip me up. "So you're used to dealing with moody actors, then?"

"It's what I live for." I clip my cape back into place and turn to him. "And just in case you need further help in dealing with your feelings for Cassie, she can recommend a great therapist. Don't be ashamed to ask."

He holds out his hand, and I shake it. "Thanks, Josh. You're all right. Now, what about your girl troubles? Is there anything I can do to help you out?"

"No, but if you see me on the news up on charges for murdering a handsome asshole named Julian Norman, you were with me all night, okay?"

He nods and smiles. "Definitely."

After he leaves, I check my reflection in the mirror. Okay, so at least I don't look like a crazy-jealous freak anymore. Now, if I could just stop behaving like one, that would be great.

FIVE

OVERDUE REUNION

When I come out of the bathroom, I press Angel's number and try to stay calm as it rings. I wander toward the end of the hallway, hoping the noise will stay back in the ballroom. On the fourth ring, Angel picks up.

"Josh?"

"Hey." *Okay, good start. Now, make some small talk.* "So, I got the pictures. Seems Julian ended up coming after all, huh? What's that all about?" *Or, just dive straight into the issue. Whatever. Idiot.*

"Yeah. His press thing finished early, so he made it just in time."

"I'm so glad." I'm trying to keep the sarcasm out of my voice, but I know I'm not succeeding. "It's great that you two are so comfortable around each other. You know, with the touching, and hugging, and sitting on his lap."

There's a moment's silence, then Angel says, "Josh ... please tell me you're not freaking out over Julian."

I clench my fist. "Of course not. Why would I? Just because he's always around and looks at you like you're an incandescent Goddess. Why would that worry me?"

"Oh, come on. We're friends. That's it."

I lean back against the wall and clench my jaw. "His hands are all over you in those pictures. I don't think he sees you as just a *friend*, Angel."

"So? He could have his bedroom wallpapered with my photos of my ass for all I care. I don't like him that way. I like *you*."

I push off the wall and walk to the end of the hallway, trying to keep my voice steady. "So you're admitting he likes as more than a friend?"

"God, I don't know. Maybe. He's said a few things that were … flirty, I guess.

I stop in the doorway to what looks like a library and exhale. "Are you fucking serious?"

"It was harmless." She's speaking to me like I'm a child. It's not helping.

"What did he say?"

"Josh —"

"Angel, tell me." I grip the doorjamb as I wait for her reply.

"Jeez, I can't even remember. I said something about looking like a three-day-old corpse first thing in the morning, and he made a crack that if I'm the standard for corpses these days, he'd have to rethink his stance on necrophilia. It was stupid. A joke."

She's right, it was stupid. And gross. Doesn't make me want to punch him any less. "What else?"

She sighs. "He says flirty stuff all the time, but that's just how he is. He tells all the women how beautiful they are. Barb in makeup got a bunch of flowers just like the ones he sent me, so you can't read too much into that. Barb's a hundred and sixty, for God's sake."

I stand up straight and curl my hand into a fist. "He sent you—" I look at the ceiling and pray for calm. "He sent you *flowers?*"

"Josh —"

"When?"

"A few days ago. I was down and missing you. He tried to cheer me up."

"I'll bet." I have this guy's number. He wants to cheer her up by rubbing his cock all over her vagina. Sneaky, duplicitous bastard. "Did all of this happen after I left?"

She pauses. "Uh … yeah, I guess. I wasn't really paying attention."

I shake my head, and I'm clenching my jaw so hard the muscles ache. I thought he was a decent guy, but it seems he was just saving his Master Plan of Epic Douchery for when I wasn't around. "Fucking bastard."

"Josh, it's no big deal. Really."

"Yes, it goddamn is, and I want you to stay the fuck away from him."

"What?" She takes a breath, and so do I. When she speaks again, it's clear she's pissed. "What did you just say to me?"

"You heard me." I'm pissed, too. If I were standing on the outside looking in, I'd say I was being an overbearing prick. But in the eye of this storm of insecurity and jealousy, my demands seem perfectly reasonable. "I don't want you spending time with a guy who clearly wants to fuck you."

"Josh, he's my co-star. I get paid to spend time with him."

"Not off set, you don't."

Her tone turns steely when she says, "He's a friend."

I walk into the library and pace near the window. "No, he's not, Angel. He's a douchebag who thinks you're batting below your average and is dying to swoop in to save you from your inferior boyfriend. How can you not see that?"

"He can't steal me, Joshua," she says, her voice getting harder. "I'm not a fucking *object*."

"I know that, but —"

"No, you don't, otherwise you wouldn't be saying this crap."

"Well, how would it be if the shoe were on the other foot, huh? Would you care if I was hanging around with a woman who wanted to get me in the sack?"

"I wouldn't be thrilled about it, no, but I'd trust that you loved me and wouldn't do anything to betray me."

"I do trust you."

"No ... you don't. You're getting hung up on some petty manufactured rivalry with Julian, and it has to stop. Julian isn't the anti-Christ. He's a nice guy, and if you can't accept that I'm not going to screw him just because you're not around, then I don't even know what to say to you right now."

"For fuck's sake, Angel, that's not what I —"

"No, Josh. This conversation is over. Go back to your party. I don't feel like talking to you anymore."

"Angel, wait –"

When the line goes dead, I slam my hand down on a console table next to me. "Goddammit!" I shake my head in frustration. "You fucking idiot, Kane. What the hell are doing?"

"I agree. You could have handled that better."

I spin around to see Erika sitting in a large leather armchair and sipping a drink. She looks like a Bond villain.

"Hello, Mr. Kane. Welcome to my library of solitude."

"Oh, hey." Great. Now someone other than Angel knows I'm an out-of-control asshole. "Sorry, I didn't know anyone was in here."

"Clearly. Trouble in paradise?"

I rub my eyes and sigh. "Please tell me relationships get easier over time."

"Can't do that. The best ones are the hardest, but they're also the most worthwhile." She gives me a sympathetic smile. "Would you like to join me for a drink? You look like you could use one."

I walk over and sit on the couch next to her chair. "Well, I shouldn't really drink and fly, but what the hell. Hit me."

She gets up and goes to a well-stocked drinks cart in the corner. "What can I get you?"

"What are you having?"

"A mid-life crisis. Plus, whiskey."

"Okay, I'll have a whiskey, hold the crisis. Already have one of those, and it's a doozy."

"Want to talk about it?" She pours us both generous servings then sits back down and hands me a glass. "I'm guessing Angel didn't take kindly to being told what to do."

"You heard that, huh?"

"You weren't exactly whispering."

I slump back into the couch and look down at the phone. "She's working with this guy who makes me crazy. I'm usually pretty chill, but this dude ..." I take a mouthful of whiskey and relish the burn. "I want to pummel him. A lot."

She nods in understanding. "O, beware, my lord, of jealousy. It is the green-eyed monster, which doth mock the meat it feeds on."

I look over at her. "Shakespeare, right? Othello?"

"Yes, and if you know the play, then you know jealousy leads to nothing good."

"I'm starting to see that, but I don't know how to stop it."

"Is this an ongoing issue for you? Something that's happened in other relationships?"

I laugh. "Yeah, haven't really had one before. This would be my first."

She looks surprised. "Ahh, I see. Then maybe you should take a step back from the situation? Look at it from a distance."

"How do I do that?"

She crosses her legs and leans forward. "Imagine Elissa started hanging out with a guy who was crazy for her. He flirted and bought her gifts ... made it clear he wanted more. What would you say to Liam if he asked her to stay away from him?"

"I'd say, 'Damn straight. Get that asshole out of her life as quickly as possible.'"

"But that doesn't demonstrate a lot of faith in Elissa, does it? Are you saying that if Elissa doesn't stay away from the guy, she'd inevitably cheat on Liam?"

"Of course not. Lissa loves that giant oaf more than life. She wouldn't have sex with someone else if you paid her."

"So then what difference does it make if there are people around her who want to take her bed?"

I look at her as I try to grasp the concept and apply it to my own situation. Erika tilts her head and smiles. "Do you see now why Angel was so mad? By voicing your jealousy about Julian, she thinks you're doubting her love for you."

"But I'm not. I just –"

"That's how it seems. You don't think she loves you enough to resist temptation."

"But you haven't seen this guy. You don't know how attractive he is."

"It doesn't matter. That's like saying she'd buy something from a shop because the storefront was pretty. Window dressing may be nice to look at, but it's meaningless unless she loves what's inside.

"Okay ... you may have a point."

"I'm glad you think so." She gives me a smile. "You and Angel will work through this. Give her a few minutes to cool off, then call her back."

"What if she can't forgive me?"

"Why wouldn't she?"

"Because I've been a dick to her. Up until this point in our relationship, I've managed to hide my dickish tendencies."

"You know the saying, 'Love is blind'? Well that's completely ass-backwards. Love lets you see people in perfect, crystal clarity. It doesn't make flaws invisible. It paints them in 3-D high-definition and demands you to love them anyway. Angel will forgive your dickishness, I have no doubt."

"I appreciate the vote of confidence."

She sips her drink, and up until now it hasn't occurred to me to ask why she's sitting in an empty room, drinking by herself, but there's nothing right or natural about this picture.

"So," I say. "You know all about my crisis. Want to tell me about yours?"

She leans back in the chair and crosses her legs. "That's kind of you, but I'm sure you have better things to do than listen to my troubles."

"Not really. I have a few minutes spare while I wait for my girlfriend to stop cursing my name." I take a sip of my drink. "To be honest, I'm surprised to see you're not here with anyone tonight."

"Why does that surprise you?"

"Because according to Cassie and Ethan, you're an amazing acting coach and an even more amazing person. Also, you're smoking hot. I predict you had a truckload of men offer to be your date, but instead you chose to come alone. Am I right?"

She looks down into her glass and smiles. "I'd rather be alone than with the wrong person."

"Uh huh. So why do I get the impression that the right person is here, and yet you're still by your lonesome?" When she looks at me in confusion, I say, "I might be stating the obvious here, but it's pretty clear you and Daniel Eastman want to jump each other's bones."

Her expression turns to shock. "How on earth did you ...?" She takes a mouthful of whiskey. "And I thought I was hiding my feelings so well."

"If by *well*, you mean *not at all*, then yeah. Good job."

I look at her expectantly, but she shakes her head. "Josh, I don't think you want to hear this story. It's ... complicated."

I lean forward and look her in the eye. "Erika, my best friend went through six years of hell before she got to be with the love of her life, and now because of who he is, her boobs are more famous than all the Kardashians put together. Her brother has gotten on and off the relationship rollercoaster with Cassie so many times, they both have season passes, and despite all of that, they're now the most sickeningly in-love newlyweds you've ever seen. I myself had to sleep with a metric shitton of neurotic actresses until I found the woman of my dreams, and yet I still have to endure my lady love getting paid to mack on guys who make me want to beat them with a large stick. I'm more than qualified to handle *complicated*."

She gives me a resigned look. "Okay, fine. But first you need to know some backstory. I've spent a lot of my adult life alone, and for the most part I've been okay with that. I have a fantastic house, a nice car, a job I love ... and every year I get to mentor wonderful actors who've become like family to me. Students like Cassie and Ethan. Hell, even Zoe and Jack." She runs her finger around the rim of her glass. "And I know some people think the reason I'm single is because I'm a heartless bitch who couldn't keep a man if she tried, but the truth is the only man I've ever wanted I couldn't have, so I didn't feel the need to settle."

"And that man was Daniel Eastman?"

She nods. "Back when I was in drama school, my roommate was from L.A. We quickly became best friends, and she kept raving about her boyfriend on the west coast who was trying to break into movies."

"Okay, I see where this is going."

"After a few months, Daniel came out to visit, and I'd heard so much about him from Ellie, I felt I already knew him. But even with all of her glowing descriptions, she hadn't done him justice."

She takes a sip of her drink. "From the moment we met, there was this ... spark. I tried to tell myself it was just a silly crush, but I'd had crushes before, and what I felt for Daniel was in a different universe."

"Did he feel the same way?"

"At first I didn't think so, but then I noticed how often he stared at me. How he'd steal long glances, even when Ellie was talking to him. Whenever he was close, I could feel he was resisting the urge to touch me. Ellie seemed oblivious, but every time Daniel and I were in a room together, the tension between us was unbearable."

I lean back and put my arm along the back of the couch. "So, what did you do?"

"The only thing I could. I avoided him as much as possible. I loved Ellie like a sister, and she was head-over-heels for him. There was no way I was going to allow myself to lust after her man. But the feelings I had for Daniel went so much deeper than just physical attraction. We connected intellectually, spiritually, and emotionally, and each time I thought I couldn't be more attracted to him, he'd say or do something to prove me wrong." From her expression, it seems even talking about this makes her feel guilty.

"Did anything happen between you?" I ask.

She swirls the whiskey around in the glass. "Daniel and I spent nearly three years dancing around our attraction, and every time he came to visit, staying away from him became more impossible. Then, the New Year's Eve before we graduated, Ellie had tickets to attend a huge Broadway gala. On the day of the party, she had a stomach bug, so she insisted Daniel take me instead."

"Oh, jeez. Bad idea."

"The worst. The whole night was a test of our loyalty to Ellie and our self-control. Even sitting next to him at dinner was torture. I've never wanted a man so much in my life."

"I'm sure the midnight countdown was interesting, then."

She nods. "It took everything we had to not kiss each other. That was when Daniel told me he was in love with me, and he couldn't go on pretending he wasn't. After I told him I felt the same, he asked me to give him a week to end things with Ellie."

"What did you say?"

She takes a deep breath. "If I'd said yes, I would have betrayed a girl I loved like family. If I'd declined, I would have sacrificed my happiness, as well as Daniel's. So ... I told him I'd think about it." She laughs bitterly. "As it turns out, fate made the decision for us. Three days later, Ellie announced she was pregnant with his child."

"Ohhhhhh, shit."

She exhales a shaky breath. Even after all this time, it's clear the memories still cause her pain. "Daniel did the only thing he could. He asked her to marry him. A few weeks later, Ellie dropped out of drama school and moved back to L.A. to be with him. And the rest, as they say, is history."

Man, I feel so sorry for her, I take a drink on her behalf. "So you didn't keep in contact with them over the years?"

"For a while Ellie and I exchanged letters and phone calls, but it was too hard. Every time I spoke to her, all she talked about was building a life with Daniel, and even though I was happy for her, I couldn't help feeling resentful. Daniel called me just before the baby was due. He was drunk ... told me he was sorry and that he wanted things to be different." She looks down at the fringing on her dress and tries to straighten it. "After that, we saw each other on occasion, usually at events or parties, but we never spoke."

"Damn, that's cold. How could he cut you off like that?"

"It was for the best. I understood that. Daniel was a good man, dedicated to his wife and family. Neither of us wanted to ruin it."

"But now he's divorced. There's nothing keeping you apart."

She laughs. "It doesn't matter. It's too late."

I lean forward. "Bullshit. I saw how he looked at you out there. If you said the word, you could have the life you wanted with him all those years ago. A husband. Children of your own."

"Josh, I'm forty-two. I've given up on all of that."

"Women everywhere are having kids well into their forties. Why shouldn't you?"

She rubs her forehead. "It's not that easy. Daniel was with Ellie for *twenty years*. They have grown children together. Even if I could get around both of those concepts, which I can't, how would it look if Daniel came straight out of his divorce and started something with me? Ellie used to be my best friend. We may not speak anymore, but it's still a betrayal." She shakes her head, eyes downcast. "Whatever chance we had to be together is dead and gone."

We're both startled when a voice says, "Don't you think I should get a say in that?"

We look up to find Daniel standing in the doorway, and judging from his expression, he's not thrilled about what he just heard.

I move forward on the couch and prepare to stand. "Ahhh, so, that's my cue to leave."

Erika puts out her hands to stop me. "No, Josh, it's fine. Stay where you are."

I'm not sure if she wants me to stick around for moral support or because she doesn't trust herself to be alone with him, but either way, her expression doesn't inspire me to argue. Instead, I lean back and try to be as unobtrusive as possible.

When Eastman stops in front of her, Erika stands to face him. "Daniel, I'm sorry Marco dragged you here. If he'd bothered to ask me—"

He takes her glass and drains the contents before placing it on the table. "It wasn't his idea for me to come here tonight. It was mine."

"Why?"

He glances at me for a second before going back to her with a determined expression. "You know why, Erika. I've been in love with you for nearly half my life, and there hasn't been a single day during that time when I haven't thought of you. The only reason I wasn't here sooner is because Ellie signed the final papers on our divorce tonight at dinner. The second she was done, I came to you. Please don't tell me I'm too late."

He moves closer, and judging from how they both lean toward each other, there's some major league chemistry going on. When he puts his arms around her, she puts her hands on his chest. I'm not sure if she's trying to push him away or draw him closer.

"Daniel, we can't—"

"Yes, we can. I'm done living without you. It's finally our turn, and I'll be damned if I let you talk yourself out of it." He cups her cheek, and she closes her eyes as she leans into his touch. "Please, Erika ..."

She looks up into his face, her resolve fading. "According to the media, you're sleeping with your latest costar."

"Untrue," he says and gazes at her like she's a work of art. "I've never been unfaithful to Ellie. We're getting a divorce because Ellie's in love with her goddamn therapist."

"Oh, Daniel ..."

"I'm okay with it. I'm glad she finally has a man who loves her in ways I never could. In reality, our marriage died years ago, and I was too busy feeling guilty over loving you to end it." He moves his hands up to her shoulders and back down to her waist. "When I told Ellie about my feelings for you, she gave us her blessing. She's found happiness, and she couldn't begrudge me doing the same. So, Miss Eden, if you have no other objections, I'm going to kiss you now."

"Daniel, I—"

He cuts her off with a kiss so passionate, I wonder if they've forgotten I'm sitting here.

"Ah, okay, then," I say, as I put my glass down. "I should leave you two alone. I'm sure you have a lot to ... discuss."

Daniel spins Erika around and pins her against one of the bookcases. "God, you taste even better than I'd imagined."

In response, Erika moans and grips the back of his shoulders. "Don't stop."

They kiss again, getting steamier every second, and when she pushes his dinner jacket off and starts unbuttoning his shirt, I hightail it to the exit.

"I'm just going to close these," I say, grabbing the double doors. "You kids look like you need your privacy."

As soon as the doors click shut, unrestrained moaning comes from the other side.

• • •

I stand guarding the doors for a few minutes, concerned someone might barge in on them. I'm contemplating making up a *Do not disturb* sign when I hear a sniffle, and when I turn, the girl dressed as Uhura is coming out of the ladies' room and heading toward the ballroom. She sniffles again.

Shit, is she crying?

"Hey!" I don't know why the hell I call out to her, but it doesn't matter. She doesn't turn around.

I hurry down the hallway after her. If there's one thing I hate to see, it's a woman in tears. I doubt she'd tell a random stranger what's wrong, but I have to try. Mind you, with the way things have been going tonight, it seems like confiding in me is the thing to do, so you never know. Maybe I could cheer her up by talking about Trek stuff for a while. God knows, my hero suit is starting to chafe. I'd love to go back to being a geek for a while.

She stops at the edge of the ballroom and looks around.

"Excuse me, miss?" I know the likelihood of her hearing me over the music is slim, but I try anyway.

When she moves into the crowd, I pick up my pace.

I'm nearly to the end of the hallway, when I see Zoe striding toward me.

"Josh, I need your help." She looks anxious, but at least she's not crying.

"Maybe later, Zoe, okay?" I try to keep an eye on Uhura, but when Zoe blocks my path, I lose her in the crowd.

Dammit.

I guess she'll just have to survive without me.

"Josh —"

I hold up my hand. "Zoe, is this urgent? I have an important call to make."

I can tell by her expression that Zoe isn't someone who enjoys waiting. "Fine. I'll be here when you're done."

I walk back up the hallway a few yards and dial Angel, hoping she's calmed down enough to accept my apology. I'm disappointed but not surprised when it goes to voicemail.

"Hey, this is Angel. When you hear the tone, imagine it's me swearing because I missed your call. Byeeee."

I take a calming breath as the tone sounds. I'm not sure if I can find the right words to make her understand how much I regret our fight, but I'm sure as hell going to try.

"Hey, beautiful girl. It's me - the stupidest man on earth. I'm guessing you don't want to talk to me right now, and I can't say I blame you. I behaved like an ass. I let my insecurities get the better of me, and I took it out on you. I can't tell you how sorry I am." I lean against the wall and drop my head back. "I hate that I made you think I don't trust you, because that's not how it is at all. Of course, I trust you. The only person I don't trust in this relationship is myself, and that has nothing to do with you, or even Julian." When I close my eyes, I get an image of her in my mind. It makes me smile, but it also makes my chest ache with how much I love her.

I hear someone clear their throat, and when I look down the hallway, I find Zoe there, tapping her wrist. I wave her off.

"Anyway, sorry you're hearing all of this in a message, but I needed you to know that I love you more than anything, and I hate that I upset you. Give me a call back when you get a chance."

I hang up and walk back to the impatient blonde.

"So you've finished your call?" she asks as I stop in front of her.

"Do you see a phone up to my ear?"

She crosses her arms. "That seemed like a lot of groveling. What did you do?"

"Nothing that bears repeating. What's up?"

She looks over her shoulder to the ballroom, then back to me. "I need a favor."

"Okay. What is it?"

She chews her lip for a second then says, "I need you to kiss me."

Just when I thought this night couldn't get more bizarre.

"Zoe, I appreciate that you're helpless in the face of my overwhelming sexual appeal, but as I've already told you, I have a girlfriend."

She looks at me like I'm speaking Swahili. "And?"

"And even though she'd probably like to smack me in the face right now, she's placed a long-standing reservation on my lips, so I can't help you."

I try to go around her, but she sidesteps to stop me. "Wait. Just listen a second, okay?"

"Come on, Zoe. It's almost time for the countdown."

"I know, that's why I'm here." She has this pleading, desperate look in her eyes that ruins my resolve to not get involved in any more drama tonight.

"Okay, what's this all about?"

She moves closer. "Look, I don't want to marry you, Josh. I just want you to kiss me at midnight."

"Why?"

"To make Jack jealous."

I cross my arms over my chest. "Why aren't you kissing Jack instead? You guys seem close."

She laughs. "That the problem. We've been hooking up for months, but once he's done with his booty call, that's it. He leaves, and I don't hear from him again for weeks." Her confidence falters when she says, "I'm sick of being treated like a fuck buddy. I want ... more."

Man, I feel like Dr. Phil tonight. I've spent more time dealing with other people's dramas than concentrating on my own.

"Have you told Jack you're not happy with the way things are?"

She looks at me with incredulity. "What, and risk him laughing in my face? No thanks."

God, this girl has so many walls, she could rent herself out as a paintball arena.

"Zoe, don't you guys ever drop the bullshit and just be real with each other?"

She looks at the ground. "That's not how we are."

"Then how the fuck do you expect to have any kind of relationship? You don't even know who you are underneath all your insults and banter."

She leans back against the wall and drops her head. "Being mean to him is easier than showing him how much I crave his attention." Her voice has gotten so quiet, it's hard to hear her. "It's ... safer."

She seems so terrified of vulnerability, I feel sorry for her. "I understand opening up is scary, but only being intimate with Jack when you're having sex is like going through life eating breakfast cereal for every meal. It might be satisfying in the short term, but eventually, you're going to need some real food."

She looks up at me in confusion. "I don't eat cereal. Too many carbs."

I roll my eyes. "I'm not talking about food, Zoe. It's a metaphor for your inability to truly connect with Jack because of your intimacy issues."

"I don't have intimacy issues." Her defenses flare for a second, but then she goes limp, and she says in the smallest voice, "It's just ... when I think about opening up to him ... telling him how I feel ..." She looks up at me. "I get so nervous, I want to hurl. I'm not used to caring about anyone the way I care about him."

"Do you love him?"

She stares at me, brows drawn down. "That's the scariest part of all. I think I do."

I put my hand on her shoulder and smile. "Well, admitting it to yourself is a good place to start. Now you just have to say it to him."

Just then, Jack appears at the end of the hallway and squints at us. "Zoe? Is that you?"

I squeeze Zoe's arm. "Okay, showtime."

Zoe's expression fills with panic. "What, now? No, Josh! I'm not ready."

"Yes, you are."

"No! I can't do this."

"Yes, you can."

"Shit!"

When Jack moves toward us, I push Zoe up against the wall and kiss the hell out of her. For a second she freezes in surprise, but then she pushes her hands into my hair and kisses me back.

Goddammit, my hair's going to be completely ruined after this. The things I do for people.

To make a good show, I moan and run my hands over her body. She does the same to me. Our kiss seems to go on forever, and for a horrible second I fear Jack has stormed off, but then a hand clamps over my shoulder and wrenches me backward.

"What the fuck, man?!" Jack's face is bright red. Okay, maybe this was a bad idea. He looks like he's ready to kill me. "Get the fuck away from her!"

I wipe my mouth. Jesus, that's a lot of lip gloss. "Sorry, man. I thought you guys were just friends. Didn't realize there was something more between you."

Jack looks at Zoe, then back at me. "Yeah, well ... there is."

"Oh. So, you're dating?"

It's clear Jack is nowhere near ready to make these kinds of admissions, but what the hell. These two need to stop dancing around each other and start the new year with a bang. Literally.

"Yes, we're dating," Jack finally admits. "Among other things."

"Zoe," I say, acting confused. "What the hell's going on? You told me he didn't have real feelings for you."

Zoe glances at Jack. "I ... ah ... I didn't think he did."

"That's bullshit," Jack says, moving over to her. "I might not have come out and said it, but, Jesus, Zo ... you have to know that ... well, I ..."

For the first time since I met her, I see Zoe let down her guard. She's so desperate for an admission from him, she's on the verge of tears.

"You, what, Jack?" I press. "Like her? Big deal. I like my dental hygienist, but that doesn't mean I have a say in who she makes out with."

He snaps around to face me. "I more than like her, asshole, so I do get a say."

"More-than-like. Wow." I act impressed. "Well, that's different. Zoe, do you *more-than-like* Jack, too?"

For a moment, I worry she'll chicken out, but then she squares her shoulders and puts her arms around Jack's neck. "Yes, I more-that-like him. In fact ..." She takes a deep breath. "I'm ... in love with him."

Jack freezes for a second, shock and disbelief on his face. Then, he breaks into a blinding grin. "Seriously? You love me?"

Zoe gives him a wary look. "Yes, and if you dare make a joke out of this, Jackson Avery, I'm going to rip off your balls, and I'm not talking about those hideous slippers."

"Oh, sweetheart." Jack leans down and kisses her tenderly. "I couldn't make a joke right now if you paid me. I've been in love with you for years, you beautiful idiot. I was just waiting for you to realize you loved me back."

He kisses her again, and for the third time tonight, I feel like the epitome of a third wheel. I have no idea why people feel comfortable enough to make out in front of me, but I wish like hell they'd stop. It's bad enough I'm here without Angel. Having to witness everyone else having mouth sex is goddamn torture.

"So I guess that means you're not kissing me at midnight, then, Zoe?" She moans and grabs Jack's ass. "No? Okay, then."

I leave them behind, and when I get back out into the ballroom, Marco is on the dance floor making a speech. There's only a couple of minutes left before the countdown, and I'd like to find my friends before then.

The phone buzzes in my hand, and I breathe a sigh of relief to see Angel's name.

"Hey, beautiful," I say. "I'm so glad you called me back."

"I got your message." She doesn't sound angry anymore which I'll take as a good sign.

"Good. I'm so sorry about earlier. I was a total dick. I had no right to say those things to you."

"It's okay. I shouldn't have defended Julian so much. He is too flirty considering I have a boyfriend. And after our fight I got to thinking you were right. If a girl was all over you like that and sent you flowers, I'd want to rip her tits off."

"Yeah?"

I can hear the smile in her voice when she says, "Yeah. You're mine, and I'll fight anyone who tries to take you away from me."

"Ladies and gentlemen," Marco says, "the magic hour is upon us, so grab your loved ones, and let's count down to the new year! Ten! Nine! Eight!"

Shit.

The whole crowd joins in, and I hold the phone close to my mouth and yell so Angel can hear me. "They're doing the countdown! Hold the line, okay?"

I push past people as I try to find my friends. It would suck if I didn't get to them in time.

"Seven ... six ... five ... four ..."

At last, I see Elissa, Liam, Cassie, and Ethan over by the windows. I do my best to hurry, but people keep getting in my way, and by the time I make it to them, the countdown is done.

"HAPPY NEW YEEEEEEAR!"

People clap and cheer and scream so loudly, the noise is deafening, and even though I'm only a few feet away from Elissa, she can't hear me call her name. When I get close enough to tap her on the shoulder and wish her a happy new year, she's already macking on Liam like there's no tomorrow. Cassie and Ethan are no better.

I sigh and look around. "Happy new year to me, I guess." All around me, mobsters are kissing policewomen, Harley Quinn is kissing Batman, even Sonny and Cher are having a passionate reunion. Everyone seems to be getting their new year's liplock except for me.

I put the phone back up to my ear. "Angel? You still there?"

"Yes," she says. "I'm deaf, but I'm here. What's going on?"

"Oh, nothing. Just standing in the middle of a huge tongue orgy. Not feeling left out at all."

She makes a sympathetic sound. "Aw, honey. I'm sorry."

"You should be. I'm the only miserable asshole who doesn't get to kiss someone tonight."

"Now, that's not true. You kissed Zoe a few minutes ago. Surely that counts."

My whole body tenses. "What did you just say?"

"I said, you kissed Zoe. Looked like a good one, too. If you love me, you'd better make sure mine is better." Goosebumps crawl over my entire body when she adds, "Now come find me, and bring your sweet, talented mouth."

Everything seems to go into slow motion as I turn and search the crowd. My heart pounds double time when I see Sexy Uhura standing a dozen yards away in the middle of the dancefloor. She smiles and pulls off a dark wig to reveal bright auburn hair, and I'm so goddamn happy to see her, I get a lump in my throat.

She beckons to me with one finger, and that's all I need to unfreeze my limbs. I stride over to her, cape fluttering behind me, and when I reach her, I cup her face with both hands and kiss her like I've never kissed her before. It's the perfect image of the hero finally getting the girl.

I grunt as she sets my whole body aflame with a single touch, and when our mouths open and tongues slide, the fireworks inside me put Times Square to shame. Unlike when I was kissing Zoe, this one I feel in every single molecule.

"What the hell are you doing here?" I ask as I cup her fucking gorgeous face. "You don't finish for another week."

"There was a fire on the set. Production is delayed until they can rebuild it. I got in this afternoon."

"So, you've been lying to me on the phone all night?"

"It wasn't lying so much as misdirecting you. I didn't want to ruin the surprise."

"So, the boat trip –?"

"Happened a few days ago."

"And our fight?"

"Totally real."

"The crying in the bathroom?" My brain is spinning that she's been faking me out this whole time.

"Good acting. I was pissed at you for what you said, but not hurt. The crying just added a touch of theater to make it fun. By the way, your atonement for being a jealous fool will be in the form of giving me many orgasms when we get home."

I lower my mouth to hers. "Yes, ma'am."

I kiss her again, and dear God, she tastes incredible. I put my arms around her, desperate to get closer, and I don't mean to cup her ass with both hands, but it somehow happens. When I pull her tight against me, she moans when she registers how hard I am.

She pulls back, all swollen lips and uneven breathing, and I swear if we weren't surrounded by hundreds of people, I'd rip off that microscopic dress and take her on the spot.

"Did you suspect I was here?" she asks.

I tilt her head up and kiss her neck. "Not at all. But I did feel guilty as hell for lusting after Sexy Uhura, so thanks for that."

"Really? Even when you didn't know it was me you wanted to fuck me?"

I graze my teeth along her skin. "God, yes. So very much."

She tangles her fingers in my hair then pulls back. "Ew. What the hell am I touching here?"

"Dunno. Some overpriced crap. I needed the strong stuff to get rid of my curls."

She pushes my hair back into place and strokes my face. "But, I like your curls. And even though it's nice to see your eyeballs all uncovered, I like your glasses, too. In fact, I like all your parts. This one in particular." She reaches between us and palms my erection, and holy sweet mother of a sensual god, it feels so good my eyes roll back in my head.

"Fuck," I say, my voice rough and low. "I need to be inside you immediately."

"You read my mind."

She kisses me again, and it's so full of need, it screws up my breathing. When I pull back, I'm hit with the dawning horror that there are zero places for my boner to hide in this outfit.

"Let's get out of here," I say, pulling my cape around me.

"But shouldn't I say hi to the guys?" She gestures to our friends who are still tongue deep in each other's mouths.

"Nope," I say, grabbing her hand and pulling her through the crowd. "They can have you tomorrow. Tonight, you're all mine."

On our way to the exit, I pass Erika and Daniel. They both look disheveled but happy, and when they see me they give me a knowing smile.

"I see your girlfriend made it after all," Erika says.

Angel waves at her. "Are you kidding? Look at him. How could I possibly stay away?"

Just before we reach the door, I notice Zoe and Jack standing in the corner with their arms around each other. They're gazing at each other adoringly, and when Zoe sees me, she mouthes *Thank you* and gives me a warm smile.

I wave back and continue on my way. My work here is done.

"What's that look for?" Angel asks as I grab our coats.

"Nothing," I say and drag her to the elevator. "I'm just glad that tonight had a happy ending for more than just me."

SIX

TRUE HERO

Snow flutters around us as I hail a cab, and once we're inside, things get frantic in a hurry. The weather makes the trip longer than usual, but we don't care. Thank God the cabbie seems happy to turn a blind eye as we make out like fiends.

After being apart for so long, our bodies are needy and demanding, and by the time we pull up at Angel's building, she's practically straddling me.

The cabbie clears his throat. "That'll be fifteen dollars."

I toss a wad of cash at him and throw open the door. "Keep the change."

When we get into the lobby, the reception clerk smiles at us as we stride past.

"Nice to see you again, Miss Bell. Mr. Kane."

"You, too."

The doors to the elevator have barely closed before I press Angel against the wall and plunder her mouth again. I'm aware we're on the security camera, but right now nothing matters except satisfying my insatiable need for her. My hand is hidden behind my coat when I push it under her dress and into her panties.

"I need this," I say, teasing her with my fingers.

She closes her eyes and moans. "God, yes, Josh. It's yours."

When the elevator opens, we practically run down the hallway. Once we're inside the apartment, we tear at each other's clothes. First, our coats slump onto the floor in messy heaps. Then I bend her over the couch, so I can get to her zipper before yanking it down so hard, the fabric tears.

"Don't worry about it," she says as she pulls it off. "I'll get another one."

I get rid of my cape, so she can undo my suit. As soon as I pull it down to my waist, she stops dead and stares.

She rakes her gaze all over my body. "I thought you were wearing one of those costumes with the foam muscles built into it. What the hell is this?"

I look down at myself. "It's my body. I worked out."

"*You* worked out?" she says, her voice rising in pitch. She moves forward and gingerly runs her hand over my pecs and abs. "You *worked out*?! Holy crap, Josh. Are you kidding me? How the hell did you do this in just four weeks?"

For a terrible second I think she hates my new bulges, but then she shoves me against the wall and presses hot kisses all over my torso. "You're ridiculously hot, with or without muscles. You know that, right?"

I press my head back into the wall as she pulls my suit down my legs and off before kneeling in front of me. "Yeah, I know."

I clench my fists and moan when she takes me in her mouth. I can't process a single coherent thought as she drives me insane with her lips and tongue. What she's capable of making me feel is beyond staggering. When I look down and watch, it's even worse. Damn, she's beautiful, and Erika was right when she said window dressing didn't matter. As stunning as Angel is physically, it's the parts you can't see that are the most beautiful. Everything about her turns me on.

She works me with her mouth and hand, and when my abdomen is burning from the effort of not coming, and my dick feels like it's going to explode, I carry her to the couch, pull her panties to the side, and repay her in kind.

"God, Josh ... yes." She anchors her hands in my hair as I suck in the way I know drives her crazy. Fuck, I've missed this. It's not just about having my mouth on her, even though that's one of my all-time favorite things. It's also about bringing her so much pleasure, she moans my name, over and over again.

No other woman has ever reacted to me the way Angel does.

Being away from her for the past few weeks may have been difficult, but seeing how I affect her makes it all worthwhile. I'm barely getting started on making her beg for release when she pulls me up to sit on the couch. She doesn't take her eyes off me as she slides off her underwear and unclasps her bra. But when she bends over to unzip her boots, I grab her wrist.

"Leave them on."

She raises an eyebrow. "Really?"

"Fuck, yes."

I pull her forward to straddle me, and it's only when she slides down and I'm buried as deep as I can go that the tension that's been with me all night melts away. Being joined with her makes me feel like a god, and what's more, she looks at me as if she believes that's the case.

"I've missed you," she murmurs into my skin. "You feel ... ohhh ... incredible."

I don't even have the words to tell her how amazing she feels. I ache to please her. To try and show her everything I'm unable to express any other way.

We take turns at leading the pace. She circles her hips as I thrust slow and deep, and we're both so worked up, it doesn't take long before we're both holding on for dear life. She comes first, head thrown back, nails scraping my shoulders. Seeing her like that is enough to have me following seconds later, moaning and gripping her as tight as I can.

As the last shudders fade, we wrap around each other, sweaty and panting. We may be unable to move, but we're also happier than any two people have the right to be.

• • •

Later, when we've both showered, and I've washed my hair and packed away the contacts, Angel pulls me into bed and snuggles into my chest.

"There's the Josh I remember. Except for these of course."

232

She pokes my pecs and abs. "These are going to take some getting used to, you know."

"Yeah? But you approve?"

She pushes up onto her elbow. "Josh, if you want to keep working out and being healthy, you know I'll support you, but please say you didn't do this because of Julian."

I turn on my side to face her and cradle my head in my hand. Her eyes widen when she spots my bicep, and she proceeds to caress it while I talk.

"Regardless whether Dickface Norman inspired me, I've worked my ass off to achieve these results. Are you telling me it makes zero difference to how attractive you find me?"

She laughs. "Don't be an idiot. I couldn't be more attracted to you if I tried. You can ruin my panties simply by saying hello, and that's not because of how many muscles you have. It's because you're an amazing, intelligent, *sexy* man with a fascinating mind and the best heart I've ever known. It has nothing to do with your body."

"Uh huh. Is that why you've been stroking my bicep like a pet?"

She looks at her hand as if it has a mind of its own. "Uh, yes. I just wanted to make your new bicep feel at home, because he's lovely and plump, and ... kind of hot." She leans over and gives it an incredibly sexy open-mouthed kiss. "Welcome, giant bicep. Maybe I wouldn't hate it if you stayed a while."

I narrow my eyes. "You're weird."

"Never said I wasn't." She snuggles into me and traces her fingers over my chest. "So, I get why you tried to bulk up, but why didn't you go as Kirk tonight? Are you too buff to be a Trekker now?"

"Of course not. It's just ..." And here's the part that's hard to explain. "I don't know. I guess I felt like for the first time in my life, I have the body to play a hero, so I wanted to see what it felt like."

"Josh ..." She looks up at me and strokes my cheek. "I hate to break it to you, but pulling on a neoprene body suit doesn't make you a hero. Jumping on a plane to help your best friend run one of the biggest shows of her career does. And helping Connor address his women issues does. And caring enough to urge Erika to follow her heart does. And don't even get me started on the sacrifices you made to help Zoe and Jack through their bullshit tonight. I thought you were going to choke on her lipgloss."

I cringe as I blush for the first time in years. "You saw all of that stuff?"

"Eh. Saw, stalked, eavesdropped. Even caught some of it on my phone. I was like a stealthy ninja, if ninjas had amazing legs and an ass that just won't quit." I slap her ass, and she squeals.

"And you don't mind that I kissed another woman?"

"If you hadn't looked more uncomfortable than a pastor at a porn convention, maybe. But as it was, seeing you do all that stuff tonight just made me love you more. You could have moped around like a self-centered asshole because you were forced to go stag, but you didn't. You chose to make a difference instead."

Okay, this blushing thing is getting worse. I don't like it. My face feels like it's being barbecued. "I don't know that I *chose* to make a difference. That's just the way things went."

"No, it's not. You help people every day, and you're just so used to doing it, you don't even notice anymore." She grazes her fingers down to my belly button before coming back up to my chest. Then she repeats the pattern. "Want to know when I first realized I was falling for you?"

"Okay." The way she's stroking my happy trail is making it difficult for me to concentrate, but whatever.

"Do you remember when we were rehearsing Shrew, and the first episode of our horrible *Angeliam* reality show went to air?"

"Yeah. Back when I lusted after you from afar, because I thought you and Quinn were engaged."

"Well, that night Liam's fangirls came out in droves on social media to abuse me. I was mostly used to being called an ugly whore who should go kill herself, but still. It was particularly vicious while it was being aired. I was here by myself, feeling pretty down, when out of the blue, you called me. You told me to get off the internet and stop reading the ramblings of the intellectually deranged, and then you offered to bring me the ice cream flavor of my choice to cheer me up."

I stroke her arm and smile. "I remember. You turned down the ice cream, but we ended up talking on the phone for hours."

"We did. You were a hero to me that night. And it doesn't matter if you look like a hot geek or a total beefcake, you'll always be my hero. Have no doubt about that."

She pushes up and kisses me, and it's so full of gratitude and adoration, I kick myself for ever doubting her devotion to me. Every man should be as lucky as I am.

She pulls back and gazes into my eyes. "I love you, Joshua Eli Kane. Happy New Year."

I smile and stroke her cheek. "Every year is happy as long as I'm with you, Angela Constance Bell." I kiss her slowly and deeply, and it's so steamy that when we pull apart, my glasses have fogged up.

"Now," I say, as I take off my glasses and place them on the nightstand. "How about you go put your Uhura costume back on, and I'll dress up as Kirk so I can explore your final frontier."

She smiles and cringes at the same time. "You better not be talking about anal, young man."

I raise a brow. "It says a lot about you that your mind went straight there. Filthy woman."

"Oh, so you weren't thinking about butt stuff?"

"No, but since you keep bringing it up, maybe I should run out and buy some lube."

She giggles as I climb on top of her and push between her legs, and I'm so damn happy I feel high.

I may have spent most of tonight dressed as one, but superheroes be damned. This magnificent, beautiful, incredible woman loves me totally and unconditionally, and even without special powers, that's enough to make me feel like I could fly.

"Any new year's resolutions you want to share?" I ask as I kiss a spot behind her ear that makes her squirm.

"Yes. Spend less time away from you."

"Good choice."

She slides her fingers into my hair and grips my head as I suck on the juncture between her neck and shoulder. Her squirming increases. "What about ... oh, God ... your resolutions?"

I cup her breasts and tease her nipples with my tongue. "I have three items on my list. Eat healthy, get in shape, and spend way more time making my woman scream my name."

I kiss a path from her clavicle down to her stomach, and she digs her fingers into my shoulders as I nibble her hips.

"Is that right?" she asks, her voice tight and breathy.

"Uh huh. And considering I've already nailed the first two, I guess I should get started on the third.

She gasps in anticipation when I push her legs apart and grip her hips, and when I put my mouth on her and whisper sweet nothings to her clitoris, she does indeed scream my name.

Happy New Year to me.

ACKNOWLEDGEMENTS

As is the case with any book, this one wouldn't have been possible without some amazing friends and supporters.

Firstly, to my amazing agent Christina Hogrebe (and the whole gang from the Jane Rotrosen Agency,) - thank you so much for your unwavering support and unrelenting wisdom. You always know what to say and do to get the best out of me.

To my darling husband Jason for being my personal cheerleader and wonderfully insightful pre-reader. I'll never get tired of you telling me how proud you are whenever I finish a book. And don't even get me started on your reactions *while* you're reading. You're hilarious.

To my long-time friend and grammatical mentor/editor, Caryn Stevens - how cool is it that we're together again, Catty-Wan? (<-- Note the appropriately placed question mark. Hah!) Thank you for whipping my writing into shape, and for doing it in record time on this project. You saved my head from exploding from the pressure of my deadlines.

To my beautiful best friend whose relentless enthusiasm and love for my characters always warms the cockles of my cold, dead heart - I love you so much, Andrea. You are like a permanent ray of sunshine in my life.

To the wonderful girls who support me, kick my ass, and keep the wheels of Team Rayven oiled and rolling - Chloe, Cecile, and Chanpreet - you girls rock my world. Thank you so much for your time and energy. You're all stars.

Thanks to the amazing Nina Bocci for her epic pimpage, as well as all the incredible bloggers and readers who help thrust my words into people's eyeballs. Without you, I'd be throwing a whole bunch of books into the void where they'd stagnate, unread and unloved.

To all the Pams and Chignons - thank you so much for your support and wisdom. If it weren't for you, I'd spend my days banging my head against the keyboard muttering, "I don't get it. I don't understand," over and over again. Thanks also to Nina Levine for holding my hand while I navigated the great unknown.

To Regina Wamba for her gorgeous cover - girl, you're the bomb. And the diggity. *All* the diggity.

And finally, an enormous thanks to you, my wonderful, passionate readers. I adore every single one of you, whether you're one of the bodacious Babes from Romeo's Dressing Room, or just a quiet, consistent supporter. You guys are the reason I write. In particular, you're the reason this book came about. You all touched me so much with your heartfelt pleas for more from our Starcrossed crew, I couldn't help but revisit these crazy couples, and I'm so glad I did. Thank you for giving me an excuse to climb back into their world for a little while. I thoroughly enjoyed myself.

Don't forget, if you ever want to reach out and say 'hi', I'm all over social media, and you can subscribe to my newsletter with this link: http://eepurl.com/bRdvrH

Alternatively, you can join my private reader group on Facebook (simply search for Romeo's Dressing Room,) or contact me through my website: WWW.LEISARAYVEN.COM

Once again, thank you all for your support and generosity, and I wish you all love, light, and lots of laughter in the year ahead.
Love and hugs, Leisa x

WANT MORE LEISA RAYVEN? YOU GOT IT!

COMING SOON!

Mister Romance

Max Riley is the man of your dreams. At least, he will be, for a price.

As his alter-ego Mr. Romance, Max is an escort-with-a-difference. No sex, just a swoon-worthy dates to die for, and the cream of New York's socialites can't get enough. His specialty is bringing women's greatest romantic fantasies to life, whatever they might be. Want a dominating billionaire, a bad boy with a heart of gold, a hot geek, sexy biker, or best friend who's secretly loved you from afar? Max can make it all happen, and even though women fall in love with him on a daily basis, he's careful to keep his real identity a secret.

Enter investigative journalist and professional cynic, Eden Tate. Having caught wind of the urban legend of Mr. Romance, Eden is like a dog with a bone, determined to publish a scathing expose on Max and his ability to swindle lonely society women out of their money.

Desperate to protect his anonymity, Max challenges Eden to give him three dates. If she doesn't fall totally in love with him, she can run her story with his blessing. However, if she succumbs to his charms, the story dies.

Eden is confident she can resist Max's tacky, make-believe personas, but when a traumatic night leads them back to his apartment and she gets to know the man beneath the facade, her story takes on a whole other twist; one in which her heart will have the final say as to whether she chooses a career-making tell-all, or the fascinating man with the mysterious past.

Read an Excerpt

The first time I hear the term 'Mr. Romance', I'm convinced my sweet-but-naive baby sister has been duped into believing yet another urban legend.

I stop filling the coffee maker and turn to Asha, who's sitting at the breakfast bar in our cozy apartment, looking way too put together for six a.m. on a Monday morning.

"You're telling me that you can hire a man to make your wildest romantic fantasies come to life, Ash? Come on. There's no way that's a thing."

"It's true!" she insists. "Joanna was dishing the dirt in the break room at work. She overheard a whole bunch of women talking about him at some thousand-dollar-a-ticket charity event on the weekend."

"What the hell was Joanna the secretary doing at that kind of event?"

"Her cousin is related to some obscure Latvian royalty or something. The crown prince's limo broke down on the way in from the airport, so Joanna was invited at the last minute to take his ticket."

I give my sister a deadpan look. "Latvian royalty. Of course. Makes perfect sense."

My sister works at a publishing house, and even though I haven't met all of her co-workers, the ones I have met are definitely on the strange side of quirky.

"Isn't Joanna the compulsive liar?" I ask.

"Well, yeah, but that doesn't mean she doesn't know stuff. She overheard a handful of women talking about this God-like uber-stud. One of them claimed one date with him cured her depression. Another said he saved her marriage, because until he unlocked her libido, she'd forgotten how much she enjoyed sex. This whole gaggle of women thinks he's their romantic savior. Jill-off Jesus, or whatever."

I shake my head and watch as coffee dribbles through the filter. Always the more imaginative out of the two of us, Asha has inherited all of my mother's blind optimism, but zero common sense.

"So what you're telling me," I say as I pour two cups of fresh Joe. "Is that this mythical man-beast about whom Pants-On-Fire-Joanna was raving, is some kind of … what? Superhero gigolo?"

"He's an *escort*," Asha clarifies.

"Isn't that just a dressed up label for man-whore?"

"No. He doesn't have sex with his clients."

"You just told me he did."

"No, I said he makes their *romantic* fantasies come to life."

"And that doesn't include sex?"

"No."

I screw up my face. "Doesn't sound very romantic to me. A guy who doesn't want to sleep with me? I can get that for free."

COMING IN APRIL, 2017!

For more information and to keep with all the latest Leisa Rayven news, go to WWW.LEISARAYVEN.COM

Made in the USA
San Bernardino, CA
15 May 2017